FAITH THROUGH FALLING SNOW

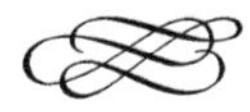

SANDY SINNETT

5 Prince Publishing

Published by 5 PRINCE PUBLISHING

PO Box 865, Arvada, CO 80001

www.5PrinceBooks.com

ISBN digital: 978-1-63112-240-8

ISBN print: 978-1-63112-241-5

Cover Credit: Marianne Nowicki

Author Photo: Emily Sinnett Photography

In memory of all those who fought and suffered from Alzheimer's; and in honor of their families, many of whom I call my friends, for your courage and strength as you stood by their side through every moment, good and bad.

ACKNOWLEDGMENTS

To Jesse, Wyatt, Emily & Ethan; I love you with all my heart! I'm honored, grateful, and blessed beyond measure to be your mother. Always remember that God is the only One to follow in this life, even when it's hard.

To Mom; These past three years have been the toughest of my life, and I couldn't have made it without you and your support. I love you with all my heart! Thanks for sticking with me through the good times and even the not so good.

To my Dad, in heaven; I miss you so much! I tried so hard to finish before you left, but I know you're still proud of me. Thank you for being my biggest fan. We shall see each other again someday. I love you!

To Ralyn; my sweet cousin and truly one of my best friends in this crazy life. I'm not sure what I would have done without your friendship, love and laughter these past four years. Oh girl… the stories and laughter we've shared makes me so happy inside. I'm truly grateful for you and love you to pieces!

Laura; my soul sister and best friend! You are a joy in my life, and I adore you! You are my constant positive. Thank you for your unwavering support and friendship for the last 23 years. Love you girl! I'll never forget our fun road trip to Fargo, the coffee crawl or Bruno! #2MarsNback

To my Coffee Group & Bookstore Peeps; To Randy, Rex, Ryan, David, Sarah Lou, Sarah, Faron, Kendra, Pam, Russell and Amy. Thank you for welcoming me into your group, I've enjoyed the countless mornings of interesting chat topics and fun banter, but mostly for your relentless encouragement to keep writing. I am grateful to be your friend. Randy. See? I didn't kill you off!

To Monty; this journey hasn't been one we ever expected to travel, but I am grateful for your continual support and friendship, and for being a wonderful father to our beautiful kids every day. I wish you all the happiness in this life, you deserve it!

To Rose; thank you for your support and for all you do in the community, I hope you enjoy reading about 'Jeannette Rose'.

To my readers, friends and fans; without you I wouldn't have finished this book, especially you, Dan. Your messages and texts of encouragement kept me writing in what were probably the darkest years of my life. Thank you for being the flicker of light that kept me reaching for my dreams and kept my passion for writing alive. I hope you enjoy it!

OTHER TITLES BY

SANDY SINNETT

Hope in the Rain

Grace After the Storm

FAITH THROUGH FALLING SNOW

Sandy Sinnett

PROLOGUE

SUMMER'S END

Caleb walked into the coffee shop sporting his neatly pressed khaki shorts and polo shirt, anxiously awaiting the end of Jenny's shift. He sat down at a table in the back and played on his phone to kill time. In the corner behind him sat a table full of what looked to be 'regulars', laughing and carrying on with one another. One gentleman kept poking fun at a younger lady typing on her laptop, asking her if he was 'still alive'. Caleb rolled his eyes, not fully understanding their conversation, but it was amusing all the same while he waited. A few minutes later, Jenny came out and sat down at his table and forced a little smile. *Such the snappy dresser he is,* she thought. Caleb always dressed nice. Even his dark brown hair was neatly combed; never a hair out of place. The ultimate perfectionist. *Too perfect.*

Jenny's dark brown hair was pulled back in a ponytail with a few loose bangs hanging down, wearing black capri pants and a plain white t-shirt under her little green apron. Her face turned solemn, knowing she was about to ruin his evening with her news. Caleb looked up and wrinkled his nose; she knew immediately he didn't like that she hadn't changed clothes for their date. He had a certain way he liked her to dress—behave even. Jenny noticed it off and on when they first started dating, but lately it had become more evident. His *preferences* were... particular to say the least.

"Well hey, cutie! You ready to get out of here? I'm sure you'll need to change and freshen up," Caleb stated in his matter-of-fact tone.

Jenny was a tad offended by his comment, but simply smiled and brushed it off. "Well, hey there to you, too. I'm afraid I won't be changing clothes, though. I have to pull another shift tonight, Caleb. I'm so sorry! Rain check?" She poked out her bottom lip and batted her eyelashes playfully.

Although disappointed by her news, Caleb was unable to resist her sweet charms. "This is the second time this week. Maybe they should hire more people," he whined.

"It's almost the end of summer, everyone is taking vacations," she explained.

"I get it. Probably good they're taking them before you and the other students go back to school. Can you believe we'll be going off to college next week? I can't wait!" Caleb's excitement was evident.

"Yeah, crazy," she replied, void of emotion.

"You don't sound too enthused. You're not actually going to miss this place, are you?"

"No, I'm good. I'll miss my friends, that's all. Well, I'd better get back to work."

"Well, what about dinner Friday night? It will be our last date in town before we leave." He asked.

"Sure. Sounds good. I work that day, so just pick me up here at 5:30?"

"I'll be here." Caleb stood up and kissed her on the cheek.

Jenny waved as he walked out the door, but an odd sense of

relief fell over her. She was actually happy she had to work tonight. Caleb had a sweet spirit and kind heart which made it hard to feel the way she did. Unsatisfied. She was very fond of him and they had grown close over the last few months, but somewhere deep inside her heart there was still something missing. She had also been doubting her decision to go off to school for the past month but gave herself more time to think things over first. Over the past couple of weeks however, she could see her mom still needed her a great deal having just lost her dad earlier in the year. Her waning feelings for Caleb seemed to have made her decision even easier and it was now time to admit she didn't want to go back to school in the fall. She couldn't. Leaving her mother alone wouldn't feel right, and although she knew Caleb wouldn't fully understand, it would only get harder the longer she put off telling him. Her closing shift lingered on for what seemed an eternity; her thoughts teetering back and forth about Caleb and her feelings for him, or lack thereof. She knew their relationship needed to end, and since her decision about college was also confirmed, it was time to break the news about both.

Her extra shift was finally about done, so she went to the back and began the closing duties while the lobby was empty, hopeful she might even get out a little early. That was wishful thinking, as it turned out, when she heard the doorbell chime to announce a customer. She threw heard head back and sighed, then chucked her rag at an empty bucket on the floor.

"Ugh, alright Mr. Customer, you'd better be *really* nice and order something quick and easy. Why you had to walk in fiiii-iive minutes before closin' is beyond me!" Jenny ranted to herself quietly. Her southern drawl was always stronger when she got flustered or mad. '*Southern spunk*', her mom called it. Jenny casually walked out front, but when she saw the young man standing at the counter, her jaw dropped open. If she had to guess, he was probably close to her age, and although a little worse for wear, she was quite taken with his gorgeous tan, scruffy face and stormy blue eyes that nearly swallowed her whole. His dishwater blonde hair stuck up all over his head, and the faded jean shorts and stained NYU t-shirt added a particular charm to the whole 'vagrant' look, right down to the frayed brown flip-flops that had once been white. Honestly, he was a hot mess, but the corner of her mouth turned up as she admired him, and a tingling sensation ran through her body, a reaction she didn't expect. *Kudos, Lord! When I asked for the customer to be easy, I never imagined you'd send me a college man that was also easy on the eyes! Wait a minute. What am I doing? I can't flirt; I have a great guy. Get your head on straight, Jeannette Rose. He's a customer like any other. A cute one though. I mean I'm not dead, right?* She could barely focus at first, but finally snapped out of it and asked for his order.

"Hey, there! What can I get ya, NYU?" she asked, her tone somewhat curt.

IT HAD BEEN a long day's drive for Evan, and he was grateful to find the café still open, more than ready for a cold mocha. He began to look over the drink menu, but no sooner had Jenny walked up behind the counter than his gaze was on her. Immediately he noticed her huge, brown eyes and there was a sweet, yet cheesy smile plastered on her face, which he found oddly charming. Her ponytail swung side to side as she walked up, and Evan's heart jumped inside his chest. He was speechless, caught off guard by her sweet southern accent.

"Umm," he mumbled.

Jenny waited patiently for his order, but she was tired and ready to go home. Although she enjoyed the view, she needed to move him along. She snapped her fingers in front of his face.

"Hey slick. You gonna order something *tonight* or do you want me to come back after your nap?"

Evan found her sassy attitude rather cute and replied in kind. "Slowdown, Sassy-pants — I'll order when I'm good and ready." He stared up at the menu, intently studying it to agitate her. "Okay, I think I'll have a large iced mocha, with an extra shot."

"Yes, *sir.* Can I get a name for the order?" A completely legitimate way of learning his name, of course.

"I'm the only one in the store, why do you need my name?" His voice squeaked, tired from the long day.

She took a breath and let it out. "Fine. What kind of milk would you like?"

"I really don't care," he replied, growing more frustrated with her by the second, in his tired state.

"Any milk. Got it."

Evan paid for his drink then sat down at a table with a clear view so he could watch her make his drink. He enjoyed messing with her, no doubt, but was feeling somewhat guilty for giving her such a hard time. He rubbed his eyes and sighed, exhausted from the day.

Jenny finished his drink but instead of announcing his name and making him come get it, she delivered it to his table and set it down with force. "Your drink... *sir.*" She scoffed.

He smiled, amused by her spunk. *She's even cuter when she's mad.* "Look, I've had a long drive today and I'm pretty wiped. Sorry if I was being a jerk."

Immediately, she relaxed and even managed a smile in return. "Thanks, and you were actually," she winked. "But so was I. Sorry. I'm just ready to get home, this is my second shift today. You go to NYU?" She asked, showing off her rosy pink cheeks.

"I was, but it was time to leave. School isn't really my thing."

He took a sip of his mocha and she watched his face cringe. "Ugh, yuck! Did you use skim milk or something?"

Jenny snickered. "Umm… soy actually. You said you didn't care, *remember*? I didn't know if you were lactose intolerant, so I thought I'd play it safe, this late at night." A mischievous grin spread across her face.

He laughed quietly. "Touché, and on that note, I think I'll be on my way with this *most* delicious drink." He stood up to leave and Jenny couldn't help but notice the nice, tan biceps under the sleeves of his t-shirt. "What are you staring at?" He asked coyly.

She turned her head quickly and ignored his question. "You know what, I still have a lot of cleaning to do and it's closing time. I think it would be best for you to head on out, if you don't mind."

"Seriously? You're kicking me out?"

"No. I'm *asking* you to leave. Besides, you said you were about to leave anyway, so technically it was your idea first."

"Guess I'll be sure and come in earlier next time, so I don't get kicked out."

"Your choice. It's a public place and my shift ends at 1:30 tomorrow, so hopefully I won't even be here." She replied, a subtle mention to the end of her next shift.

"Not exactly a 'customer focused' attitude there, Sassy-pants. That must be your middle name. I'll have to remember that."

"No, it's *Rose,* but only my friends call me that and you don't fall in that category." She purposely shared her middle name to throw him off, not wanting him to know that everyone called her 'Jenny'.

"Sassy-pants it is, then." He smirked, then reached over and grabbed his cup off the table. When he picked it up though, he squeezed it a little too tight and the lid popped off. Coffee and ice went flying all over Jenny and the floor.

"Ugh! Really? I just mopped these floors for crying out loud!" Jenny threw her hands up in frustration.

"Hey that wasn't my fault. You're the one who obviously didn't put the lid on correctly."

She stomped over to the counter and grabbed a towel, then started cleaning up the mess.

Evan sighed with guilt. "I'm sorry. Here, let me help." He knelt beside her and started to pick up ice, and accidently brushed up against her shoulder. She smelled like honeysuckle wafting through the air on a warm summer night, overwhelming his senses. He breathed her in and smiled.

"You think this is funny, big boy? I don't need your help, so unless you want me to remake your beverage, I suggest you leave. Now." Jenny's voice cracked, on the verge of tears.

He saw her bottom lip quiver and knew he'd pushed too far. "I'm sorry, Rose. I'll go." He stood to leave, sad at the way things were about to end.

"Please tell me you're only passing through?" She expected to hear a 'yes', but secretly hoped for a 'no'.

"Well, sorry to disappoint, *Rose.* I'm not only sticking around, but I'll be back tomorrow." He winked and walked out.

Jenny watched the door close, then broke down crying, releasing her frustration from the entire day, everything from Caleb, to work, to the mess on the floor. It felt good to get it out. Finally, her closing duties were done and the tall, tan, annoyingly handsome customer was now a distant memory. She went to lock the front door and turn off the sign however and as she peered out the glass, she noticed a bright orange, beat-up Jeep idling in the parking lot with only its parking lights on. Inside sat someone who looked like the young man who had made the last 30 minutes of her life completely miserable. Sort of…

Her heart rate sped up again at the sight of him, until she

gave it a bit more thought. *Maybe he's waiting to rob me, or worse! Or maybe he's being nice and wants to make sure I get out safely? Or maybe he's a barista-kidnapper waiting to throw me in his Jeep and sell me into a life of espresso-making slavery! Nah.*

She sighed in exasperation from the evening and trusted that his intentions were good. "Okay, Lord. I take back everything I said earlier. That man *wasn't* nice at all, and this is NOT going to be easy if he is sticking around!" She said out loud. "And why do I get the distinct feeling that this summer's end may be unseasonably warm and exceptionally complicated?" She turned off the lights and the neon 'Open' sign, locked up, then walked to her car as fast as she could.

Once she was safe in her car, she held her breath as he slowly drove his Jeep in front of her car.

He smiled a big smile, then waved and sped off.

Ugh. Good riddance!

CHAPTER 1

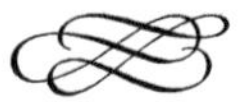

She is not afraid of the snow, for all her household are clothed with scarlet. -Prov 31:21

Whiteout. That moment when a beautiful, gentle snowfall becomes a storm so unbearable that the snow turns to a thick, white sheet, nearly impossible to see through and you can't see your hand in front of your face. The wind blows so hard that the once-soft flakes are now tiny ice needles, sharp and painful as they prick the surface of your skin, reminding you that you are in control of *nothing*.

The fall season hadn't fully made its way to North Carolina yet, but Laci was already looking forward to the thought of winter and the hope of falling snow. Her love of the rain, even in frozen form, hadn't wavered. She loved the snow; watching it fall to the ground with grace and elegance and marveled at the thick blanket of white; so quiet that it absorbed even the smallest of sounds or the loudest of thoughts. After her breast cancer, a miscarriage, and almost losing Hannah, her new sister-in-law, Laci's faith had been tested over, and over again. Through it all, she and Mitch had weathered every storm together. It made them stronger in many ways, and although hard to imagine, even more in love than the day they married. Laci couldn't imagine her life without him by her side. He was the love of her life and her best friend, the one that carried her when she couldn't carry herself. He reminded her, daily, that God brought them together, and together they would face life head-on, loving and laughing all the way; even through the blizzard that was headed directly toward them. The coming winter would bring a special gift as well though—the newest member of the Young family—and for the first time, Laci was finally excited, especially after Hannah shared her dream. The dream that took away Laci's fear and gave her hope that everything was going to be okay. The dream that showed her having a healthy baby boy!

The trip back home from Oregon was over and they were back to everyday life. Summer's end was near, and school would soon begin. Laci shuddered at the thought of the holidays that would follow right behind, 'they would be here before you could say spit', as Mitch would say. *This will be the best Christmas ever. Right, Lord?* Her internal words of affirmation lifted her spirits as she stood in front of the mirror, washing her face before bed. *Our baby will be here soon, and I need a white Christmas to greet him, got it?* The self-talk was also an indirect prayer in disguise, and saying it kept her sane. It was her thing.

* * *

THE LONG ASPHALT driveway was lined with tall oak trees on each side, decorative landscaping lights, and neatly trimmed hedges. *Kind of posh for the country, but oh well,* Evan thought.

Growing up, his family always had a nice home, but never an abundance of anything to speak of—not to this extent. They had plenty though, and that was enough for him.

Although it was still a tad weird at times to think about his mom being married to someone other than his dad, he was glad she had found love again and was happy. At first, Evan wasn't thrilled that Mitch had stolen his mom away, but it only took a couple times being around him to realize he was a great guy and was obviously crazy about her. It was evident how much they loved each other. Evan chuckled at the thought of how much his mom had changed in the short time they'd been together, for the better. Specifically, the fact that she was actually living in the country, which she swore she would never do again. Laci had always been more of a 'city girl', but by some miraculous turn of events, Mitch had managed to uncover the 'country girl' that was buried deep inside. This new life was the second chance she'd deserved. Even when they spoke over the phone, Evan could hear the happiness in her voice loud and clear. The real shocker though, came the day she called and told him that Mitch had taught her how to fish. Evan about fell over laughing, doubting her somewhat, but the proof came later when she texted pictures of herself holding a little fish, proud as a peacock and smiling ear to ear. That's all he needed—a visual confirmation that her new life with Mitch, albeit in the country, suited her in every way.

Evan still missed his dad every day though. Some days it was hard to breathe when the memories came rushing back. Those same memories were comforting and brought a smile to his face, but it was soon followed by the heartache of missing him and almost made it worse knowing he would never see or talk to him again. *Will it ever get any easier,* he thought to himself. Mitch would never replace his dad, but he hoped that moving here—getting to know him better and learning the business—

would help them grow closer over time. And that's something Evan needed more now than ever before.

He turned his headlights off as he approached the 3,000 plus square foot log cabin but parked farther back so he could surprise them. The aged front porch steps creaked as his heavy feet pressed down, so he crept up slowly. Laci often mentioned they rarely locked their doors out where they lived, so he turned the knob. *Sweet! Rather creepy if you ask me, but at least I'm not a robber, so, works for me.* Once inside, he closed the door behind him then stood motionless. He immediately closed his eyes, then inhaled to take in the sweet aroma. *Ahhhhh,* he exhaled in a whisper. The smell of his mom's two favorite things still lingered in the air—coffee and maple syrup. Evan smiled, and his mind flooded with memories of eating breakfast for dinner; a family tradition. Those are the days he missed most, all of them gathered around a big kitchen table, laughing and cutting up together. He wandered around a bit. *Where is everyone?*

"Mom? Em?" He shouted up the stairs, then heard a door slam.

Within seconds, Travis and Emma came barreling down the stairs, jumping in his arms and hugging his waist.

"Whoa! Slow down there, buddy!" Evan rocked backwards, nearly falling to the floor as Travis tackled him. The sound of their laughter rang through the house like a bell tolling on Sunday morning.

Laci's head popped up at the sound of her son's deep voice and she immediately headed downstairs—a tad faster than snail speed.

"Evan, sweetie! You're home! You're finally home!" She exclaimed, tears already pouring down her cheeks, which didn't take much these days.

Evan opened his arms and carefully embraced his mom given her fragile, pregnant state.

"You're not going to hurt me with a hug, silly boy." She snickered.

"Well, I'm scared it might pop or something. I can't be responsible for that." Evan laughed. "Everyone else in bed already?"

"Are you kidding? I wish! Then I could get some work done around here," she chuckled. "Mitch and Caleb are still out in the winery and—" Laci sniffed his clothes. "Are you serious? You've already been to the coffee shop in town?" She laughed, recognizing the scent from her favorite local café. Evan, too, shared her addiction for the finer coffees in life.

"I had to! You would have stopped too, mom, and you know it! Plus, it had been hours since my last one and I felt like the 'driving dead'. I was *dying* for some caffeine, ha ha!" He joked, trying to be funny. "Get it? Driving dead? Dying for caffeine?"

"I got it, dude. Let's take a walk outside and tell the guys you're here, okay? This way you won't hurt yourself at the unsuccessful comedian routine." She grinned, then licked her finger and marked a virtual point in the air for herself. "Mom one. Evan half."

"I see how it is. Alright then, Madre, it's on! I'll zing you later when you least expect it."

As they were about to leave, the front door opened, and Mitch and Caleb walked in. "Perfect timing, guys! Look who is finally home!" Laci squealed.

Mitch smiled. "Well, hey there, Evan! Welcome to Crystal Creek." He walked over and shook Evan's hand.

"Hey, Mitch! How are you?"

Mitch laughed, then pulled Evan into a hearty hug, slapping his back in the traditional caveman way. "Get in here, bud! Good to see you. Glad you made it in safe," he added.

Evan was somewhat shocked at Mitch's high-spirited greeting, but it made him feel good. At ease. "It was a long drive, but it's nice to be home. And thanks again for letting me—well, you know." Evan struggled to express the words he felt.

Mitch stood back, his hand still resting atop Evan's shoulder. "No thanks needed, Evan. You're my stepson and I love you. I'm glad you're here. Plus, I must admit," he chuckled under his breath. "I wasn't too sure what I was going to do about finding help at the winery after ole Caleb here announced he was going off to school, and with Brad gone too, you're kind of an answer to a prayer for me."

"Yeah, heaven forbid your son go off and get an education," Caleb said sarcastically, then punched his dad in the arm for fun.

"You know what I mean." Mitch replied.

Evan was amused by their banter. "How are ya, Caleb? Good to see you, man. Sorry for all that flack you're suffering here, dude." Evan joked and shook Caleb's hand.

"All good man; it's a daily ritual around here. Trust me, your time is coming." Caleb laughed.

"Alright you three. Break up the love fest, it's getting late. The kids need to go to bed, and Evan still needs to get his bags and get settled in his room," Laci said, then took Mitch's hand and pulled him closer to her side. "Then you and I need some *quality* time together my sweet, yet still Creepy Stalker Crawdad-fan." She winked at him.

Evan rolled his eyes, "TMI, Mom!"

"Get your head out of the gutter, Evan Kramer. Quality time doesn't automatically translate to—*you know*," she giggled.

"Aww, really? That's too bad." Mitch said sarcastically, then pouted playfully.

"Well, now that you mention it, I suppose it *could* translate that way." Purposely messing with Evan a little.

"Okay. On *that* note, I need some ear plugs then I'm off to bed. Where is my bed, by the way?" Evan asked.

"You're such a prude, Ev. I'm just having a little fun at your expense." She hugged Evan's waist. "I'm so glad you're home, bud. I love you." She gave him another squeeze for good measure.

"I love you too, Mom. Goodnight," he replied and hugged her tight.

"You're sleeping downstairs, Evan, but let's go out and get your bags then I'll show you around." Mitch opened the front door and they walked outside. "Hey, sorry if we made you feel uncomfortable back there. That's kind of our thing—the whole playful banter stuff."

Evan chuckled quietly. "It's all good, Mitch. I won't lie; it's still a little weird for me to see you together, but I know it won't always be that way. Honestly, I can't remember a time when she was ever like that with my dad, and a there were moments I even wondered if she was really in love with him. That probably sounds strange. I like seeing her happy with you though. It's good."

"I've been head over heels in love with your mom ever since she opened her mouth sitting next to me on that plane. Now I can't even imagine my life without her in it." Mitch smiled. They pulled Evan's bags out of the Jeep and headed back inside.

"You two are lucky to have each other. I hope I find that someday," Evan replied.

"You will. Have faith and remember it's all in God's timing, not ours. And for Pete's-sake, enjoy being young while you can! You only get that once, so don't waste it." Mitch and Caleb guided him to the basement. "Your room is down there. You first."

When he reached the bottom of the stairs, Evan's mouth fell open as he looked around and surveyed his surroundings. It was a fully furnished apartment, complete with a full kitchen, snack bar, nice black appliances, and a living room—the ultimate bachelor's pad! They didn't skimp on the amenities either. The 52" wall-mounted LED curved screen TV and Bose speakers were definitely an attention-getter. He even had his own Keurig coffee pot.

"This is sick!" Evan's enthusiasm overflowed at first, but then it hit him. "Wait a minute. Whose room was this?" He inquired.

"It was my room, man. I won't be needing it anymore though, so I moved back upstairs after they told me you were moving here."

"Wow. Caleb. I don't know what to say. This is too much, man. I never meant for you to give up your space. Trust me, I can sleep anywhere, and perfectly happy on the couch or a cot in the barn." Evan's chest was heavy with guilt.

"Ev, I wanted to do this, trust me. We're brothers, right? I wanted you to have a space to call your own; a place that felt like home." Caleb replied.

Mitch laid his hand on Evan's shoulder. "Welcome home, Evan. We'll let you get settled in and get to bed. Early morning tomorrow, remember?" He smiled.

"Yeah… I mean, yes sir. You got it!" Evan smiled and offered his hand in thanks. "Thanks again, both of you. You don't know what this means to me."

"You're welcome, son. But you might want to save that thanks until *after* your first day on the job," Mitch laughed.

"All good, Ev. I'm glad you're here to give my old man a hard time while I'm gone, trust me. He's right about the early start though." Caleb added, then chuckled under his breath.

"Soooo, exactly how early do we start?" Evan asked in a high-pitched voice, already anticipating an answer he probably wouldn't like.

"Five a.m."

Evan's eyes popped open. "Umm, that's… wow. That's early,"

he stuttered. "But I'll be up and ready. You can count on me." Evan's confidence made Mitch smile.

"Okay then. See you bright and early, slick." He turned and started to walk up the stairs.

"Hey, Mitch?"

"Yeah?"

"Just so we're clear, was that waking up at five, or starting work at five?" Evan asked, to be somewhat funny.

Mitch never replied. He and Caleb simply laughed all the way back upstairs.

"Sweet dreams, Evan." Caleb shouted back down.

MITCH WALKED BACK to his room and found Laci sitting on the edge of their bed going through her nightly ritual of applying lotion to her tummy. She swore it would prevent new stretch marks, so he let her believe the dream.

She looked up at him and smiled. "Everything okay down there? Thought I was going to have to come down and drag you boys back up here."

"You've got a great kid there, Lace. He's a hoot, and humble too—more than most kids his age."

"Yeah," she smiled. "I kind of like him. We've had our moments from time to time, but I'm sure proud of the young man he's becoming... even if he did drop out of college." She shook her head and giggled.

Mitch stood motionless by the bed, admiring his beautiful bride. "You get prettier every time I look at you, darlin'." He walked over and knelt beside her on the floor, then took the lotion and assumed the job of pampering her skin.

Laci giggled. "I'm getting fatter and fatter by the second, Mitch Young. I think you need your vision checked."

He didn't reply, simply continued to massage the lotion into her soft skin; her feet, legs, thighs, then gently laid her back on the bed and slid her oversized t-shirt up to expose her baby belly. The room overflowed with the sweet scent of coconut, and Laci smiled as she enjoyed his touch. He kissed every inch of her pregnant tummy from top to bottom, and side to side. The next kiss, however, was met by the sudden jolt from inside her stomach. Their baby's kick. It was so hard that Laci's entire belly shook. Mitch quickly sat straight up and laughed out loud.

"Why, hello there, peanut! You must like it when Mommy gets tummy rubs too, huh?" He spoke to her belly. The baby's boisterous activity didn't deter him, however, and he continued to pamper Laci's body from head to toe.

"You're getting me all worked up, Mitch Young, now stop it!" Laci smiled.

"Well as it so happens, I kind of like you 'worked up', darlin'." He set the bottle down.

"I guess you'd better do something about it then." She smiled, then pulled his handsome face to hers and sank into his warm lips. Their deep kiss gave her chills as Mitch's hands explored her body, pleasuring her in every way.

"Momma's happy," he whispered, feeling her heart pound inside her chest.

"Very happy indeed," she replied wistfully, a smile on her face.

Despite a few logistical challenges, they made love for what seemed like hours then Laci curled up in his arms and faced him, her face still flush from pleasure.

"Promise me this will always be this good," she whispered.

"Well that's a little difficult, darlin', since you won't always be pregnant."

Laci dug her fancy nails into his thick arm muscles and growled playfully. "I'm serious, Mitch. I don't mean *this,* as in the current moment of time, I mean THIS—our life together."

"I can't promise that, Lace." Mitch's face somber.

Laci tightened her lips, rather miffed at his reply. "Wow. Don't fluff it up for me or anything." Her brow furrowed in confusion.

"Calm down there, Momma. I can't promise it will always be *this* good, because tomorrow will be better than today," he said softly, then brushed her bangs away from her eyes already welling with alligator tears, "...and the day after that, still better. Every day I spend with you will always be better than the one before. So, you see? What you ask me to promise is impossible, darlin'." He leaned down and kissed her warm, tear-stained cheeks.

"Do you have *any* idea how many brownie points you scored with that overture, Mitch Young?" Her voice cracked.

"And I hope to earn many, many more, my love."

CHAPTER 2

The five-a.m. start time was an entirely new concept for Evan, but he managed to wake up by 4:45 and drag himself to the kitchen to fix some coffee to kickstart his day. Mitch and Caleb spent the first half of the day showing him around and explaining all about the art of wine, and some basics about the business.

Evan looked at his phone to check the time, then raised his hand.

Mitch looked at him and chuckled. "Ev, buddy, you're not in college anymore, remember? You don't have to raise your hand."

"Yeah. Sorry, some habits die hard."

"What's up?"

"Umm… I was wondering when we would break for lunch. I sort of have an errand to run." Evan's mind drifted to Rose, anxious to see her again.

Mitch looked at his watch. "I guess it is pretty late. Sorry about that. I can get a little carried away at times. Go, take as long as you need. I need to check on your mom anyway and get some 'honey-do' chores done around the house. Text me when you get back and we will wrap up a few things here."

"Sweet! Thanks." Evan hopped up and ran out of the winery like a chicken fleeing the coop.

Mitch and Caleb both laughed out loud.

"That kid hasn't even lived here twenty-four hours. Where on earth could he be going?" Mitch asked.

"I don't have a clue, but it must be important."

* * *

EVAN RAN BACK to the house and put on a clean shirt, added a few squirts of his favorite cologne, then took off in the Jeep. Minutes later, he pulled into the coffee shop parking lot and hurried inside. He got in line, relieved to see her still working. Evan simply stared, admiring her radiant smile and noticed the little ringlets of hair that hung down on each side of her dimpled cheeks. He couldn't move, nor was he paying attention.

Jenny shot him a quick glance as he walked up to the counter and her cheeks instantly flipped on a pink glow. She smiled and cleared her throat to get his attention.

"Hey, Jeep-man, your turn." She giggled.

Evan shook off his stupor and moved in front of the cash register. "Sorry. Yeah, I'll have a black and white mocha, extra shot." He stated, somewhat embarrassed. *Way to go, Ev! Great impression!*

"One tuxedo mocha coming right up." She made his coffee, passed it across the counter, and then disappeared into the back room. Evan found a table and sat down to collect himself as best he could, then waited for her to come out. Two minutes. Five. Seven. Ten. *Where is she?* He wondered, figuring she had fled out the back to avoid him. He was about to leave when she reappeared in the lobby, walked up to his table and sat down. Then, to his utmost shock, she reached across the table and squeezed his nose!

Evan's brow raised with curiosity. "What was that for?" A little smirk now on his face.

"*That* was for holding up the line," she said in a chipper voice.

"Well... *Rose,* maybe if you weren't so pretty, I wouldn't have lost my train of thought!" He blurted out. Evan's eyes grew wide – surprised by his own words.

Jenny snickered and had nearly forgotten he only knew her middle name. "My, my... Jeep-man thinks I'm pretty. I'm very flattered, and glad you came back for our date."

"So, this is a date, huh?" Evan grinned. "Well, you sat with me first, so if you say it's a date, then it's a date. Seems kind of soon, don't ya think? I mean we only met yesterday. I thought this was just two people having coffee."

For once, Jenny was at a loss for words, and it actually surprised her. Even as frustrated as he made her, she liked how it felt. All she could do was smile.

"Don't worry, I know I'm hard to resist," he added, puffing out his chest as he sat back in his chair.

"Ugh!" Jenny groaned. "That's not what I meant."

"I see. So, what does 'date' mean around here then? Is it different down south?" Evan enjoyed their playful banter, and he couldn't help thinking how much Jenny reminded him of his mom and how she would easily get flustered.

Jenny scowled and crossed her arms. "I can drink my coffee at another table just as easy you know."

"True, but you wouldn't have near as much fun." He winked at her.

"Maybe. But if I stay, then we play twenty questions."

Evan's mouth dropped open and his smile quickly disappeared. "Twenty? Are you being serious?"

"You're such a wimp! Fine. I'll cut it down to ten. Two parts each." She laughed.

"That's bett—wait, that's still twenty."

"Well aren't you sharp! Nothing gets past you, does it, Jeep-man?"

Rose's sarcastic wit amused Evan. She wasn't like the other girls he'd dated at school. They always seemed to say what he 'wanted' to hear; like they were unable to form their own opinions or individual tastes. Rose was the opposite. She was bold and feisty—her own person.

"Are you going to formulate a real question or keep razzing me?" He asked.

"Yes, yes, fine. I will *formulate*. First one; what is your name, dude?"

Evan laughed. "Evan Kramer."

"Okay, Evan Kramer, why did you leave school?"

Evan brushed his hair back with his fingers, causing it to flop down in his eyes and made it even more out of place and disheveled. "Gee, don't start with an easy one or anything." He took a sip of his coffee. "School was fine at first, but after a while I couldn't remember why I was going—the purpose of it. I don't like schoolwork. Never did. So much of it is wasted on things I'll never need. Don't get me wrong, I love to learn, just in different ways. Academic classes are great, and necessary to some degree, but I get lost in them. So, with only a year to go, I quit school, worked the last couple of months at a job I had in New York, then headed here. Sounds stupid, huh?"

"It's not stupid at all. I get it, but you were so close to finishing your degree. Will you ever finish?"

"I'd like to someday. Maybe online or something. But I finally realized it wasn't about getting a degree anymore or the status of having the quote-unquote, degree. I wanted to start living life and learn as I go. Is that bad?"

"Not at all. Maybe you found the one thing that we all want... happiness. Most people search for years and never find it. Some find it too late and don't get enough time to enjoy it."

"Maybe. I know getting a degree is good, and depending on what I do, it could be hard to grow without one."

"I don't agree. I think the world is changing on that level, and more places are being understanding of people, both kids and adults, who can't sit in a classroom all day and take notes. Those same people can walk into a warehouse and revolutionize a storage system, build beautiful furniture, paint masterpieces for others to enjoy for years to come, or whatever their skill might be. It's about what the individual can bring, not solely based on an official piece of paper. Trust me. I've had a few friends get an online degree and cheated their way through. It's scary to think how they will be considered for jobs over others who have years of actual hands-on experience."

Evan laughed. "Wow. I had no idea how passionate you were on the subject."

"Sorry," she said, blushing. "I get a little carried away."

"Don't be sorry! You're even more beautiful when you get all fired up."

"I—wow." Jenny was speechless and her cheeks lit up a bright shade of pink.

"Did I say something wrong? I'm sorry if I did; it accidently, on purpose, came out. But you are beautiful, you know that?"

"No, you didn't say anything wrong, it's just—well, I haven't heard anyone tell me I'm beautiful before. Not quite like that, anyway."

"That's a shame. I think you deserve to be told every day."

Jenny could feel the heat rising in her cheeks. "Thank you," she replied, then lowered her head. Her heart and mind were racing, but soon consumed with thoughts of guilt. *I can't feel this way! I have a boyfriend, or I did. Maybe it's time to admit the truth.* She brushed off the thought, enjoying the moment a little longer. "Okay, question two: you obviously live around here. Do you have a job yet?"

"That's easier, at least." He laughed. "Yeah, I live with my mom and her new husband. Well, they've been married almost two years now, and she's pregnant. My stepdad runs a winery outside of town, so I'll be learning the business and working for him. His son didn't want to take over the business and decided to go to college. His name is Caleb Young. You know him?" Evan asked, figuring they were around the same age, and given the town was so small she probably knew most everyone.

Jenny took a sip of her drink, and right as Caleb's name was dropped, she choked. She coughed several times, pounding her chest. *Really Lord? Caleb's brother? Is this your idea of humor, because I'm not laughin'. I'm choking actually, if you hadn't noticed!*

"You okay? Do I need to perform CPR?" He asked in jest.

Jenny shook her head as she continued to cough. "Wrong pipe," she squeaked, and took another drink. "I'm okay. Umm, yes. I know Caleb. We went to school together, but can you do me a big favor and not mention to him that we met? I know it's an odd request. It's a long story and I promise to tell you more the next time we meet, okay?" Jenny didn't know what else to do. She wasn't ready to tell him her life story, or that she was about to break up with his stepbrother.

Evan raised a brow. "Sure, I guess," he said with some hesitance. "I'm going to hold you to that explanation though. I'm sure there is more to the story, which means I'll get to see you again, correct? Besides, we didn't make much of a dent in those ten, two-part questions."

Jenny was relieved she hadn't upset him by her request. "I should probably go. This was really nice though."

"Not so fast, Sassy-pants. Will I see you again? Maybe have dinner or catch a movie some time? There is a movie theater in this town, right?" Evan's knee bounced up and down under the table, his nerves getting the best of him.

Jenny stood up and smiled, the corner of her mouth curled up. "Yes, I would like that. It might have to wait until next week, though. I've got a busy work schedule coming up—mostly nights—and I help my mom on my time off with things around the house."

"You promise you're not brushing me off?"

Jenny's eyes popped open wide. "No, I swear! I'm really not," she stressed in her southern drawl. She walked over to the counter and grabbed a pen and paper. "Here, I'll prove it." She scribbled her cell number down and slid it over to him. "Text me, then I'll have your number, too." She winked.

Seeing her number on that card made his day. "Thanks, Rose."

"One more thing. You can call me Jenny. That's how my friends know me, not by Rose. My full name is Jeannette Rose, but I gave you my middle name on purpose. Sorry, I don't like sharing too much personal info until I get to know someone." She giggled.

"Ah, I see. Anonymity does have its benefits," he smiled. "So, does this mean we're friends now... *Jenny?*"

She laughed out loud. "We'll see. You're on the right track, Jeep-man," she replied in a playful tone.

Evan stood up to leave. "Well, on that note, I'll say goodbye and look forward to seeing you again soon." He winked as he walked away. At the door, he turned to her once more. "Would you mind if I text you sometime before we meet again?"

"I'd enjoy that," she replied, unable to stop smiling.

"Alright. I will text you soon. *Jenny,*" he said, messing with her. He stood there a minute longer looking at her, then walked out the door. *Unbelievable. Who would have thought that leaving school would lead me to this beautiful, quirky, spirited girl! Is this for real?*

* * *

BACK AT THE WINERY, Evan bounced into the office and found Mitch at his desk reading the paper.

"Hey Mitch, I'm back. Sorry I'm a little late." Evan said, partially out of breath.

Mitch laughed. "That's one of the many perks of being a family-owned business, Ev; flexible hours. Don't sweat it. The only time it gets to be a problem is during crush season. The fall is our busiest season, after the grapes arrive, and I'll need you to stick pretty close then."

"Absolutely. I won't let you down, Mitch."

"Evan?" Mitch asked, amused by Evan's eagerness.

"Yeah?"

"Chill out, dude. It's okay to have a little fun too."

Evan chuckled in reply, "That's good."

"Where did you eat lunch? Your mom thought you'd be coming back inside."

"Yeah, I didn't actually eat. I grabbed coffee at the coffee shop in town with a new friend."

"You've been here less than twenty-four hours and you already have a friend? That's great! Laci wasn't kidding about you being a social guy."

"Ah well, I like people, I guess. I probably get that from her. My dad was a fun guy, but probably not as outgoing in that way."

"I'm glad you're taking after her. She's definitely the queen of social butterflies, one of many reasons I love her. So, what do you say we get back to work?"

"Let's do it!"

As they walked over to join Caleb, Mitch's heart was filled with pride, having not one, but two, sons working by his side in his winery, even if it was short-lived. Brad would always be missed, but this was by far the best work crew he'd ever had.

* * *

THE FOLLOWING DAY, Laci sat at her writing desk and stared out the window. It was a late August morning and a record high heat as the rain poured down. She smiled, then jumped as she felt the baby kick. "Oh!" She blurted out. "A little feisty today, aren't you? If you keep that up, then these next few months are going to be *really* long," she said, rubbing her big belly.

"Mom! Where's Mitch?" Evan shouted down the hall.

Evan had only been home a day, but he dove right in to help Mitch at the winery, eager to learn the business. Since his arrival, the house had become extra lively with his deep, boisterous voice and him running in and out. Laci was grateful for every second of it, too. A lively house made her happy and she had definitely missed his crazy antics over the last year with him away at school.

He popped his head through the open door. "Mom, have you seen Mitch?" he asked, clearly out of breath from running.

"He's right there, you goof, standing at the office door. I think he's looking for you." She replied, pointing out the window.

"Ugh! I was just there, and he wasn't anywhere around! Okay, see ya later. We are all headed to town."

"Tell him he'd better come up and say goodbye to me."

Evan rolled his eyes. "Mom, seriously? We are just running to the store."

"Evan, yes, *seriously*. I happen to like saying goodbye and giving him a kiss, so sue me," she replied sarcastically.

"Thanks. Could have gone *all* day without hearing that one."

"Give me a break, Ev! You're a big boy. I could elaborate if you'd like, tell you all about," she paused for a second then sang, "...the birds and the bees and the flowers and the trees." She rocked back and forth to the familiar tune. "It's what two people do when they love each other, ya know." She laughed.

"I know, *Mother*! And on that *note,* I'm leaving. Fa la la la fa la la la," Evan chanted with his fingers stuck in his ears to make sure he wouldn't hear any other weird comments she might make. "Goodbye, Mom!" He yelled.

Laci laughed so hard her belly shook as if she were Santa herself. She loved messing with Evan like she used to. A few minutes later, Mitch tiptoed into her room and wrapped his arms around her from behind, his scruffy, unshaven face tickling the nape of her neck as he kissed it softly.

"You *summoned* me, my love?" He whispered in her ear.

"Well, I wouldn't exactly say 'summoned'. That sounds a bit demanding, don't you think?"

"I kinda like demanding on some things," he laughed, then walked around and lifted her out of the chair. He noticed her tummy had grown quite a bit larger, creating some distance between them now. Mitch laid his hand on her belly, rubbing it gently and saying hello to their little one inside.

"He almost kicked his way out earlier; even made me jump!"

"He is anxious to see his daddy, of course, and I for one, can't wait to see him." Mitch bent down and kissed her belly. "Only a few more months little guy, then we are going to play football and play catch and do all kinds of fun things!"

"Let's hold off on playing catch for a bit, shall we? The little guy should probably learn to walk first," Laci laughed. "So, what are y'all going to do in town?" She asked.

"Oh, that old bookshelf broke on me; need a new one. Brad isn't around to make me one, so looks like I've gotta buy it.

There were definitely perks to my brother being a carpenter as well as my partner," he said, his tone somewhat melancholy.

"I know you miss him babe, but we both knew he wouldn't be around here forever."

"I know, guess I didn't expect him to leave so soon. I wish they would move down here someday."

"Hannah's family estate means everything to her, and she fought hard to keep it. She'll never give it up and I don't blame her."

"That's true. I wouldn't give mine up either, I suppose. Things are different now."

"Change isn't always a bad thing, babe. Evan is here now, and really wants to learn the business so just be patient and teach him what you know. He'll get there eventually. The nice thing is you still have another day with Caleb, so enjoy your time with him," she said in a soft, soothing voice.

"You always know what to say to make things better. How do you do that?" He smiled, pulling her close.

"One of my many talents," she replied.

"You are definitely talented, Mrs. Young, I'll give ya that," he smiled and kissed her on the forehead. "I'd better get out of here though before Evan throws a fit. We'll be back in time for lunch though. You *are* cooking up a big spread for us, right?" Mitch winked at her.

"Gosh love, I hadn't planned on it, but I could for a price," she replied, batting her eyelashes.

"Really? And what would your price be I wonder?"

"Hmm... I doubt you could afford me, Mr. Young," Laci replied in a strong, fake southern drawl.

"Don't worry your pretty little head about that, darlin'. I'll pay your price, whatever the cost. Always." Mitch leaned down and pressed his lips to hers, giving her a sweet goodbye kiss. "I'll text you when we're on our way home, and then you and I will pick back up where we left off, after dinner, okay?

Goosebumps sprang up all over Laci's arms, not wanting to let go of him. "Promise?" She asked.

"I promise, darlin'." He kissed her one more time, then walked out.

Laci finished up her blog post, then headed downstairs to the kitchen. There was a note stuck to the fridge from Emma, 'Mom, Travis and I are playing down at Sissy and Jake's. Be back later.'

Her second oldest son, Todd, was at work and Laci suddenly realized that, for the first time in weeks, she had the house to herself. *I'm alone and I don't even know what to do with myself! I think I'll just start making lunch. Mitch will be shocked if I actually pull it off this time, seeing as I normally cave and have it delivered.* She cranked up her favorite country music and began to dance around the kitchen, perusing the pantry as she tried to decide what to make. The doorbell rang. *Figures. I knew it was too good to be true!*

Maggie stood at the door; a basket full of goodies in hand. Most likely for the kids.

"Hey, Maggie. What brings you by?" Laci asked, surprised to see her.

She smiled and stepped through the door without hesitation. "Should you really be dancing around like that, Laci?" She asked, then walked directly to the kitchen.

"How did you see—,"

"Well sweetie, I walked past your window and saw you spinning around in here. You should be taking it easy, Laci. That probably isn't good for the baby." Maggie set her basket down on the snack bar. "I brought all the fixings for lunch. I stopped the boys on their way out and figured you might not be up to cooking for lunch. I hope that's okay," Maggie said, flashing Laci her big southern smile.

Laci took a deep breath. *Lord, give me strength!*

As much as Maggie and Laci's relationship had improved since the miscarriage, there were still moments that Laci had to bite her tongue and simply ask God to restrain her from taking Maggie's life into her own hands.

"You know, your timing is perfect, Maggie," *Be nice, Laci. Be nice!* "I was getting ready to whip up some lunch for the guys, but I'm sure what you have will be much better. What did you bring?"

"Wonderful! Honestly, it's nothing special, just a few roast beef sandwiches and some of my special sweet potato French fries. Mitch has loved them since he was little."

"Thanks, Maggie. I appreciate you thinking of us. Here, let me help you get things set out."

They visited with one another while unpacking the basket, talking about the baby, the weather, and other nonessential topics. Mostly a vanilla conversation… until it wasn't.

"So, Laci. I was hoping you could give me some advice, dear." Maggie's tone changed a bit, sounding somewhat shy and nervous.

Laci raised an eyebrow, puzzled by her request. "Sure, Maggie, I'm happy to help if I can. What is it?" *Please don't let this be about your Ladies Auxiliary drama. It literally hurts my head,* she thought to herself.

"You see dear, I kind of, well," she stammered. "…you see, I have a date later tonight. I was wondering if you might look at these pictures and help me pick out an outfit. It's been some time since I've had a gentleman caller," she explained. "Mitch doesn't exactly know yet. I'm a bit hesitant to tell him, so I would like this to stay between us ladies, if that's ok. For now, at least. Please don't think badly of me."

Laci's expression was obviously one of shock, her mouth now agape and she found herself oddly unable to reply. *My heavens, what has she done? She's putting me right in the middle and I cannot be in the middle of her and Mitch on this! What do I do, Lord? Who on earth would date her? Shame on me. How could I even think that? Of course, someone would want to date her. She's so nice and... polite. Ugh!!*

"Wow, Maggie. I must admit, that is *not* what I expected you to ask advice about. I'm not sure I'm really qualified though. Who is this gentleman that will be taking you on a date?" Laci shook her head. "Wait, I'm sorry I shouldn't have asked that. It's none of my business. Would you like some tea while we wait on the boys?" Laci stammered, trying to process the whole request with her pregnant, adult ADD state of mind.

Maggie laughed. "I don't mind you asking, Laci and figured you'd be a bit surprised. At first, I wasn't going to ask, but honestly, you're the only one I trusted enough to share about this. My lady friends up at the club are polite and friendly of course, but they are all still married and none of them are 'looking for love'. His name is Richard Westmore. He's an attorney in town, and we've known each other for years. He even knew my husband when he was alive, and they were quite good friends. We worked together on a few charity fundraisers for the Ladies Auxiliary and, well I guess you could say we enjoy one another's company. I like him quite a lot, Laci. I don't feel comfortable telling the other ladies. I hope you don't mind."

Suddenly, Laci realized that God had given her a most unexpected blessing. This moment. A real 'mother-in-law/daughter-in-law moment' to share and build upon. *You knew this whole lunch thing would turn out this way didn't you, Lord? Oh, how I love your sense of humor!*

Laci walked over and took Maggie's hand in hers. "First, let me say that Mr. Westmore is a lucky, lucky man. Second, I'm honored that you chose to share this with me, Maggie, and flattered you would ask my advice. I don't think you need it though. I'm always in awe of your outfits and how 'put-together' you are. I have been since the very first time I met you. I remember you walking into the kitchen that weekend Mitch brought me here to visit, so stylish and beautiful, even at nine in the morning, which was insane! It's I who should be asking YOU for advice." Laci smiled.

"I remember that weekend well! You were so nervous, and such a cutie. Your smile was the first thing I noticed. I knew then, as much as I didn't want to admit it, that you two were already madly in love with each other." Maggie looked down, seeming embarrassed.

"You never told me that." Laci was shocked by her honesty. "I was, and still am, head over heels in love with your son. He took me by surprise, that's for sure, and I have never been happier, Maggie. He's the love of my life."

"I know that now, dear, and I'm sorry. I realize I can be a bit of a fuss-bucket. All I ever wanted was for us to be friends. I try too hard and always seem to mess things up. I do love you, darling. I hope you know that by now," she replied, a tear escaped her eye.

"Uh, uh. No, you don't, Margaret Young. No tears! If you start, then I'll start." It was too late. Maggie's words touched her heart like never before, and it seemed they had finally bonded as mother and daughter. "Now, let's have a look at those outfits, shall we?"

The two of them sat at the table looking at outfit selections on Maggie's phone, then Laci picked her favorites. They talked nonstop, rambling on about dating, their men, being moms, and all the while laughing and giggling like a couple of silly schoolgirls. The wall had finally come down.

"Laci, I can't thank you enough for letting me talk with you about all this. It's such a relief to tell someone! Please don't tell Mitch yet. I will tell him in my own time, I promise. I want to go on this first date and see what happens. I'm not sure he would understand. I haven't dated anyone since his father died years ago," she added.

"It will be our secret for now, but please don't wait too long to tell him, Maggie. I don't like keeping things from him, and he needs to know." *Great. Mitch will take one look at my face and know I'm hiding something. How am I going to keep this a secret?*

Maggie leaned across the table and gave Laci a hug. It took a little longer than she wanted it to, but that day, she finally felt like part of Maggie's family, like her daughter.

"What's all this, ladies?" Mitch asked as he entered the kitchen, just in time to see them exchange a hug. Mitch's expression was a mixture of surprise, confusion and a smidge of apprehension.

Laci jumped at the sound of his voice. Neither she nor Maggie had heard them come in. "Mitch! You're home! Hi sweetheart," she replied nervously, and got up to greet him with a kiss. *Good heavens! I gave him a 'Judas' kiss! I'm surely going to meet the devil down in Georgia now.*

"What's going on, Lace?" He whispered in her ear.

"A little girl-bonding while we fixed your lunch, that's all. Your mom brought over quite the spread for you boys," she replied with a cagey little grin. "Come in and sit down, everything is ready."

"Uh-huh. That sounds ominous." He turned to his mom. "Hello, Mama," Mitch said and gave her a kiss on the cheek.

"Hello, darlin'. Did you find your shelf?" She asked, trying to throw off any suspicion.

"We did. It's unloaded and ready to go."

"Yeah, it's about a hundred degrees in that warehouse too.

Where is the sweet tea, mom?" Evan asked, plowing his way through the kitchen.

"Wow, you finished up in no time. We didn't even see y'all drive up." Laci said, her voice still nervous and shaky.

"I can tell. You ladies certainly looked like you were enjoying yourselves though. Almost seems like you're up to no good, if I had to guess," he added, still suspicious.

Maggie laughed, then winked at Laci. "A little mother-daughter bonding, Mitch. Now both of you sit down and eat." Maggie kissed Mitch on the cheek. "Boys, why don't fill your plates and go outside on the porch. There is silverware on the table."

"Yes ma'am," Evan and Caleb replied, almost in unison.

THEY SAT DOWN TO EAT, and an awkward silence settled over them, both still feeling a little uncomfortable not having spent much time around each other in over a year.

Evan broke the ice. "What's gotten into your Grams, dude?" He asked.

Caleb laughed. "She did seem kind of odd, huh?"

"Something's up that's for sure. They acted like... well almost as if they *liked* each other."

"Is that a bad thing? I thought your mom liked my grandma." Caleb was digging.

"She does, at least, I think. My mom never thought that Maggie liked her all that much. She doesn't say much about it anymore though. I know it's been hard for her to be the 'new wife'," he paused. "Do you like her?" Evan asked.

"Your mom?"

"No dude, the dog. Yes, my mom. Who else?" Evan's sarcastic comment made Caleb laugh.

"Chill, bro. Just checking. Yeah, your mom is great. After

they lost the baby, it was pretty hard, but that's all better now. I know my dad is sure loopy over her, which is cool."

"Same with my mom. She's crazy about him. I don't know if I'll ever be that way about a girl," Evan replied, then immediately thought about Jenny and smiled. *I think I could be loopy about her, eventually.*

"Yeah, crazy." Caleb's thoughts turned to Jenny as well, and he realized he had never felt 'loopy' about her since they started dating. Was he supposed to be? He brushed it off.

"So, do you have a girlfriend?" Evan asked.

"Yeah, sort of. We've been dating a few months now."

Evan laughed. "It's kind of like being pregnant, dude. You either are or you aren't."

Caleb chuckled. "I know; and I am, but I think it's about to end. We are both about to leave for college, the *same* college, but it's just..." Caleb sighed.

"You don't want to be tied down." Evan stated in a matter-of-fact tone.

"Exactly!"

"Nothing to be ashamed of dude. I've been there and I know how much fun being a single college guy can be. It's totally normal to want that."

"I'm picking her up after her shift ends at the coffee shop tonight to tell her. I'm not sure she will be too understanding."

Evan heard the words 'coffee shop' and froze, wondering who he might be talking about. *There are a lot of girls who work there. Surely, it's not Jenny,* he thought.

"No, probably not." Evan laughed.

"Thanks for the pep talk, brother."

"Hey man, just tellin' it like it is. Breakups suck, especially when she likes you more than you like her."

"Jenny's an awesome person though. She might take it better than I think, right?"

Evan coughed, choking on his last bite. "Jenny? That's—that's her name?" He stuttered, making sure he heard right.

"Yeah, why?"

"Ah, no reason, and you're right. She might take it better than you think." Evan's heart sank at the realization that *his* Jenny and Caleb's were one and the same. *Now I understand why she asked me not to mention her name. But why? Why wouldn't she tell me they were dating? Unless something has changed.* Evan remained quiet and never divulged that they'd met, as promised.

"Well, good luck Caleb, really. I know it's not fun."

"Thanks, man."

"So, after you break up can I get her number?" Evan said, jokingly as he slugged Caleb's shoulder in fun.

"You're an ass, Evan." Caleb chortled as if to tease, but he wasn't at all amused by Evan's comment.

"What? It was a joke, dude. Lighten up! It will be fine. Seriously."

They picked up their plates and walked back to the kitchen. Evan's head was still spinning as he tried to make sense of everything. *I'm not sure what's going on, but I'm gonna give her the benefit of the doubt and play this out for now, I guess.*

"Caleb, wait," Evan said. Caleb stopped and turned around with a solemn look on his face. "Hey man, I'm really sorry. I was trying to lighten the mood. I know it won't be easy, but if you tell her your true feelings, she'll be okay, trust me. Be honest." Evan needed to give his stepbrother a little encouragement, despite the fact that he already had a crush on his soon-to-be 'ex' girlfriend.

"Thanks, Ev." Caleb smiled.

* * *

THE BOYS RETURNED to the winery, and Maggie got up to clean the lunch mess.

"Maggie, you don't have to do that. You cooked. I can clean," Laci said, grabbing her tummy as the baby kicked.

"Ah hah! See? Even he is telling you to rest. Besides, this is the least I can do after barging in and begging you for fashion advice. Now go sit and rest okay? I'll be done in no time."

"Thank you, and I was happy to help you, but I'm not sure I know what the word 'rest' means anymore." Laci laughed softly. "This Christmas event is going to be a lot of work. I'm glad it's being held right after Thanksgiving. Hopefully this little guy will stay inside 'til after it's over."

"Why don't you hire a part-time intern to help you out? You could use a break, and that would allow you some breathing room. Have that person do all the shopping and lifting and you won't be tempted to do it," Maggie suggested.

"That's actually a really good idea, Maggie."

"I still have one or two now and then. Better write it down so I will remember it later," she laughed. "Speaking of remembering, I'd better stop and take my medicine before I forget," she said, looking for her purse.

Laci looked at her, puzzled by her comment. "Maggie, you took your medicine right before we ate. I brought it over to you."

"My goodness, yes, that's right! I remember now. So silly that I forgot that. I got so wrapped up in preparing lunch and visiting, it slipped my mind."

"I do it all the time too, don't worry. Some days I don't even remember my kids' names," Laci replied jokingly, then left to go rest."

Maggie smiled as she watched Laci waddle out of the kitchen, then finished cleaning up. Ready to leave, she walked to the family room and found Laci curled up in her chair reading a book. "Laci, darling, I'm going to head on home. Can I get you anything before I go?" She asked.

"No, no I'm fine. Thank you for all your help today, Maggie. I'm going to stay right here and rest a bit longer before I go out to the office." She stood up to say goodbye. "And Maggie... have a wonderful time tonight okay?"

"Alright dear, I'll try. I must admit, I'm as nervous as a hooker in church on Sunday!"

Laci busted out laughing as that was, by far, one of Maggie's best southern sayings yet. She hugged Maggie's neck. "It will be great. I have no doubts."

"Thank you, Laci," she paused, then took a deep breath. "... and Laci, if you ever feel comfortable, I'd really like for you to call me 'Mom'. But it's okay if you don't." Maggie exhaled. She had been wanting to ask for a while but today felt like the right time.

An emotional basket-case as it was, Laci was overwhelmed with emotions and squeezed her tight as tears streamed down her cheeks. "Oh, Maggie! I mean, Mom. Thank you for asking. I'd be honored to call you Mom." She pulled away to see Maggie wipe a few tears away herself.

"I'm so glad to hear that," she replied. "I'll call you tomorrow and let you know all the juicy details."

Laci giggled. "Not *too* juicy I hope."

Maggie opened the front door. "Goodness gracious Karen, stop. You're gonna make me blush! See ya later, sweetie." She turned and walked out.

Laci closed the door, then tilted her head, suddenly it occurred to her that Maggie had called her 'Karen'. *How odd. Maybe she just slipped, it happened so fast. She's never done that before.* Normally, it would have upset her that Maggie mistakenly called her by Mitch's late wife's name, but not after what they had experienced today.

She sat back in her chair and pulled out her journal, still amazed by all that had transpired between them and decided to write about it. God had finally made a way for her to become a daughter in Maggie's eyes.

Maggie closed the door behind her then sighed heavily. *Please don't let that sweet girl suspect anything. Not yet. She has enough to deal with right now!* She thought, then walked to her car and drove home.

CHAPTER 3

Caleb finished sealing up the last of the bottles for the day, but his technique seemed a bit aggressive, which wasn't his norm.

"You okay over there?" Mitch asked. He'd noticed that Caleb seemed to be a bit out of sorts that afternoon. "Caleb!" Mitch shouted.

"Yeah, what?" Caleb perked up at Mitch's loud voice.

"What's up with you this afternoon? You've been awful quiet since lunch."

"A lot on my mind, that's all. Hard to believe I'm leaving and Evan will be taking my spot here at the winery. Jenny and I will finally be in college. The same college," Caleb's voice was heavy, tainted with indifference.

"Is that a bad thing? I thought this is what you wanted? College, culinary program, own your own restaurant..."

"Are you kidding me? I can hardly wait to get started!" His voice suddenly exuberant and full of energy.

"Hmmm, that certainly changed your tune. So, why so glum?"

"I don't know, Dad. Jenny and I going away to the same school, and we're dating. Which means I won't be dating anyone else."

"That's kind of the point of having a girlfriend, Caleb. Are you two having problems?"

"No, we're great. She's great. It's just—" Caleb hem-hawed around his true feelings.

"Spit it out son, you can tell me."

"What if I want to date other girls, Dad? Am I stuck in this relationship now because I talked her into going to school with me?"

"Whoa, slow down son. Let's back this train up a bit, okay?" Mitch and Caleb walked over and sat down at the tasting bar. "First of all, you and Jenny have only been dating, what, three months, maybe four?"

"Yeah, so?"

"Are you in love with her?"

Caleb looked at his dad. "I don't know. How do I know if I'm in love?"

"Well for starters, you wouldn't have to ask. You'll *know.* You care about her, yes?"

"Yeah! Jenny is a great girl! She's happy all the time, always positive, and loves her job, and she's always helping others too. She's great." Caleb's reply was like a pre-recorded commercial for Jennyisgreat.com.

"Caleb don't forget that you and Jenny are only dating. You're not engaged or married. If this is how you feel, however, then you need to tell her now, so she knows exactly where things stand between you two. That's only fair."

"I feel like a heel, but part of me is really excited about dating other people. I don't think we have very much in common, you know? She's a great gal, though."

"I think we've established that Jenny is great, without a

doubt, and I know exactly what you mean. I did my share of dating years ago and I remember how much fun it was. It was also disappointing at times. Mostly, it taught me a lot about girls; what to do, and definitely what *not* to do." Mitch chuckled at the thought. "Remember this though... never settle for something that you feel, deep-down, isn't right for you. If you have doubts or questions, then always trust your gut. You'll thank yourself later and be happier for it."

"What am I going to do without you, Dad?"

Mitch raised his eyebrow. "Am I going somewhere?"

"You know what I mean, the part where you're not close by to talk with anymore. It's going to be hard, that's all."

"Caleb, this is the digital age, son. I am only a text or phone call away, day or night, you hear? I will always be here for you, and if I need to hop in my car and drive to you, I will." He put his arm around Caleb's shoulder.

"Thanks, Dad," Caleb choked in reply.

"Now get out of here, our day is over, and I think you have someone to talk to."

"I do."

LACI WAS FOLDING clothes in the living room when she heard the front door open. Caleb walked in; his sad face was too obvious to overlook.

"Hey Caleb. What's up? You look deep in thought," Laci asked as he walked past.

Caleb took a few steps backwards to meet her gaze. "I'm meeting Jenny at the coffee shop. I'm gonna break things off."

"Wow. I didn't see that one coming."

"It's been coming for a little while now, for me anyway. I don't think we are right for each other and honestly, I'm kind of excited about going to college and—"

Laci interrupted. 'You want to check out all the fish in the sea?" She smiled.

Her comment made him laugh. "Yeah, pretty much. I don't want to hurt her, though."

"Caleb, you need to be honest with her and don't feel bad about it. You're both so young, and you have every right to explore that big world out there! That's something I wish I had done more of, when I was your age."

"You think she'll hate me?"

"I think it will sting a bit, especially if she cared anything for you. And it might sting for you, too, honestly. But no. If she cares about you and your happiness, she will understand in the long run."

Caleb walked over and hugged her neck. "Thanks, Mom. Gotta go," he said.

Laci's eyes grew wide at his comment, but she didn't make a big deal of it. Inside however, she was jumping for joy! "Caleb, wait a sec, I almost forgot. Do you have any friends that might be looking for a part-time job? I'm going to hire an assistant to help me at the winery with the fall events."

"Cool! I don't know of anyone off the top of my head, but I'll text a few people and let you know," he replied and ran off to his room.

AFTER HE WAS out of sight, Laci took a breath and her eyes welled with tears. *He called me Mom!* It was the first time she'd heard it and nearly took her breath away. She had all but given up that he would ever say it. The joy in her heart was overflowing and she could barely contain herself.

Mitch walked in the door. As he looked over at Laci, he saw the tears in her eyes.

"Lace? What's wrong?" He asked in a worried tone, making his way over to her.

"Your son... he—" Laci could barely speak, still in shock.

"What? Did Caleb say something mean to you?" His voice raised.

She giggled. "No, no, just the opposite! Mitch, he called me 'Mom' and gave me a hug!"

Mitch smiled and sighed in relief that there was nothing wrong, then wrapped his arms around her and squeezed her gently. He knew how much she had wanted him to call her 'Mom', and never thought it would happen. She had only asked him to call her 'Mom' one time, and never again, and she never expected it. She knew it was something that would have to be earned, in his eyes. Caleb had given her a precious gift that evening.

"You're a basket case, aren't you?" He asked with a chuckle.

"Yes," she replied, blubbering.

* * *

CALEB WALKED into the coffee shop and felt a queasy, nervous sensation in the pit of his stomach, not sure how to start the conversation with Jenny. She had meant so much to him these last several months. *Am I doing the right thing here? What if I never find anyone else?*

He had more than a few reasons to stay with her, but deep inside, he knew it was the right thing to do. He needed this.

Jenny walked into the lobby, noticing Caleb was fashionable as usual in his designer jean shorts and pin-striped polo. He always could turn her head with his clean-cut look, but oddly enough, that was also part of what didn't appeal to her; he was almost too 'put together'. She snuck up behind him and tapped him on the shoulder. "Hey there. You ready to go?"

Startled a bit, Caleb turned around and smiled. "Hey Jen! Yeah, let's go. You hungry?"

"Umm, sure I'm kind of hungry, I guess. Whatever you want though, I'm not picky." Jenny's reply was a little less than enthusiastic.

"You okay?" He asked.

"Yeah, just tired." She smiled half-heartedly. *How am I going to tell him?*

As they drove to the restaurant, the air was heavy with tension. Unbeknownst to the other, they both felt it in their own way.

"Sorry I was late, by the way. I got a little behind at work today. My dad and I are training my stepbrother and some things take him a little longer right now."

Knowing that he was referring to Evan, Jenny smiled unexpectedly as she pictured him in her mind, his messy hair and stained white t-shirt; then quickly wiped it out of her mind. *Stop it Jenny. This isn't the time!*

"Oh, yes. I remember you telling me that he was moving here. How has that been; having another brother in the house? It must be busting at the seams over there." She giggled.

Caleb wasn't amused. "In some ways, it's like I'm slowly being pushed out of my own family. I know Dad is happy, and Laci is great, don't get me wrong. Her kids are too, but I do feel a bit lost these days. I think that's why I'm really looking forward to leaving. Finally, free to do my own thing for once and not follow my family's path, ya know?"

Jenny nodded her head, "That makes sense."

Finally arriving at the restaurant, they walked inside and settled at their table.

Jenny's nerves were on edge and part of her could barely think about food, so she broke the small talk. "You will love school, Caleb. I know it." She replied; fully aware she used a singular pronoun in her statement.

He tilted his head. "Wait. Why did you say *'you'* will love school? I thought we were both going?" Confusion now written all over his face.

Ugh! He's going to be so upset with me! How can I tell him? I don't want to hurt him, but if I don't tell him, I'm hurting myself. I hate this!

"Yeah, about school," she hesitated, then pushed on. "I won't be going with you, Caleb. I've decided to stay here and keep working, maybe take some online classes. I'm so sorry!" Jenny's chest felt like there were a hundred cement blocks on top making it nearly impossible to breathe. "I'm not ready. I don't want to leave, Caleb."

Caleb couldn't believe what he heard. *Is this really happening?* He was quiet, unsure how to respond.

"Did you hear me? Are you upset? I'm so sorry." She added.

He snapped out of it. "No, no, no! I'm not mad at all, Jenny. I am surprised, no doubt, but not upset. Are you sure about this?"

"I am. I've been praying about it for a while now and this feels right. I dreaded telling you, so afraid you'd be mad." Jenny's heart was beginning to lighten.

Caleb looked down at the table, playing with his napkin. Only half of his problem had been solved by Jenny's decision. He still had his part to do. "Jenny, there is something that I wanted to talk to you about tonight, too. Looks like this is confession night," he chuckled quietly.

"Sure, what is it?"

The waitress interrupted, of course, taking their orders, then Caleb continued. "I'm not sure how to say it really. I think you're an amazing person, Jenny. I really do," he stammered.

Jenny knew exactly what he was about to say and was truly relieved. "But," she added, then finished his sentence, "...you think we should break up and date other people."

"Why are you smiling? And how did you know?"

"One, it was obvious where you were headed. Two, I feel the same way."

"Seriously? You wanted to break up?" Caleb's heart sank a little knowing she didn't want him anymore, which was silly, considering he wanted the same thing.

"Look. I knew I wasn't going to be leaving for college. I also know that we are both young and independent, and you need to be free to date other girls while you're away and meet new people. We both should! The last thing you need is to have someone pining away for you back home. This is an exciting new chapter in your life, Caleb. Enjoy it!"

"Wow. I don't know whether to be happy or sad right now. You seem really good with all this." *Almost too good with it,* he thought. *I wonder if she's already met someone. Nah.*

"I think it's okay to be both. I know I am."

"Well, that's good to know. At least I'm not alone in my confusion and angst," he laughed.

Jenny laughed too, and the two of them enjoyed their dinner as they shared fond memories and good conversation, celebrating their newfound status as 'just friends'.

"Before we go, my mom has a part-time job opening at the winery to help her with events. Since you're staying in town now, would you be interested in working for her? I told her I'd ask a few of my friends, but I think you'd really like it."

"Off-topic here, but did you just call Laci your 'mom'? That's a first!"

Caleb smirked. "Yeah, I can't event recall when I first wanted to say it, but I held back, more embarrassed than anything, I guess. Not sure why. It finally felt right though."

"Hey, no arguments from me. I think it's cool. But to answer your questions, yes, I would love a chance to talk with her about the job. I adore Laci! I've always wanted to learn how to plan events and parties like she does! If I'm being honest, that part has always been a bit more appealing to me than even the culinary side of things," she replied. *That also means I'll get to see Evan a lot more! Please let me get this job!*

"Cool! Well, I'll give her your number and she can call you. Will that work?"

"That would be awesome, thanks Caleb. For everything."

"Truth be told, it's I who should be thanking you. You're pretty amazing, Jenny. I am probably crazy for letting you go." He shook his head, wondering if he was truly making a mistake.

Her eyebrow raised. "You didn't let me go dude, I left on my own. Gracefully, of course," She said in fun, then laughed her quirky laugh.

"That you did." He added with a smile.

Caleb drove Jenny back to the coffee shop, then hopped out and walked her to her car.

"Wow. Guess this is kind of a goodbye then, for a while at least. I didn't anticipate this part. Honestly, I figured we'd break up, you'd slap me or say a few mean things; we'd eventually make up and be friends again, and I'd still get to see you around campus," he said with a chuckle. "Now the whole thing feels weird."

Jenny reached out and pulled him into a tight hug, tears falling on his shoulder. "I'll miss you too, but we'll always be friends. You're not getting rid of me that easy."

Caleb pulled away and looked her square in the eyes. "Jenny —" he started.

She suspected she knew his next sentence, however. "Don't, Caleb. This is the right decision for both of us, okay? Trust me. Now go and become a great chef, okay? Just promise me that when you open your own restaurant, I'll get my meal for free when I stop in to try it out." The tension broke with her silly comment and Caleb laughed.

"Deal. And I'll even throw in a free drink or two when you learn to like wine."

"Not sure that will ever happen, but I'll work on it. Who knows, maybe your mom will teach me a thing or two about wine when I start working for her. Well, *if* I get to work for her."

"Something tells me you will. I'll make sure of it. Oh, and there is one more thing. You already know my stepbrother is working there now. Ignore him. He's a nice guy and all but can be a bit full of himself at times. Hopefully it won't be too bad, and I doubt you'll see him too often anyway."

"Thanks for the advice. I'm sure I'll be fine and will hold my own if I encounter such a predator." She winked, secretly anxious for the opportunity to encounter his brother at the winery. "I need to get home. Be careful traveling okay? Will you be home for Thanksgiving?"

"Not sure yet. I doubt it. I'm hoping to get a part-time job while I'm up there and may not be able to get away that soon, but maybe Christmas. I want to be here when the baby is born for sure. Have fun, Jenny. I hope you'll be happy here."

"I already am," she replied. They hugged one last time and went their separate ways.

Jenny sat in her car, and for a moment, wondered if she was missing out on a big adventure at college. Deep down though, she knew this was the right decision, and had a feeling that she was about to begin her *own* big adventure right here at home.

* * *

LATER THAT EVENING, Caleb came home and found the whole family in the movie room watching a marathon of Harry Potter movies and chowing down on bowls of his dad's famous popcorn. Evan lay snoring on the floor, unaware of it all.

"Ugh. I am *not* going to miss these magical movie nights

that's for sure," he mumbled under his breath. He swallowed and felt the lump in his throat, knowing full well his words were mere words. Travis heard him come in and jumped up, wrapping his arms around Caleb's waist, as was his norm. "I'm gonna miss you big brother."

"Hey, sport. I will miss you too," Caleb and Travis had grown pretty close over the last year and although he wouldn't admit it to anyone, he enjoyed having a little brother for the first time.

Mitch got up to get refills on popcorn and stopped to chat with Caleb, putting his hand on his shoulder. "How'd it go tonight, son? You okay?"

"Yeah, yeah. It went surprisingly well. Turns out she isn't going to school at all, and she ended up telling me it was okay to date around. Weird, huh? I'm a little sad I guess, us ending things and all, but it was the best for both of us."

"Wow! Why her sudden change about school, did she say?" His dad asked.

"Umm... not in so many words. She wasn't feelin' it, I guess. Plus, she likes her job and is happy here at home. Some kids don't need to leave to find their purpose. Believe it or not, I think she wants to work for Mom."

"What?" Mitch was even more confused now, turning to Laci for some explanation. "Lace!" He shouted at her over the movie.

She looked up, her brow a little furrowed. "What? This is my favorite part, when the pink-suit lady gets her payback!"

"Lace, the kitchen, please?" He waved her to join them.

"Fine." She scooted to the edge of the couch and got up. "If he only knew how hard it was to get off that sofa. I need a dang crane to get me up, these days," she mumbled to herself.

"Do you want us to pause it, Mom?" Emma asked.

"No, sweetie. You can keep it going, we'll be right back."

Laci waddled into the kitchen to find Mitch standing with

his arms closed and a pissed-off look on his face, which was very rare when it came to her.

"What's wrong? What'd I do?" Laci asked, truly clueless as to what it could be.

"When were you going to tell me that you're hiring an assistant?"

"Well, it came up today. Your mom suggested it, for your information. She thought it would be good for me to have some help with my events so I could get more rest and not have to run around so much." Laci's 'mad voice' kicked in, as did her frustration with being asked the question in the first place.

"My mother? You two certainly did bond today, didn't you? What else are you not telling me?" Mitch seemed genuinely upset by their newfound friendship, for some reason.

"Why are you getting so upset about this? It's your mother, Mitch! I figured you'd be over the moon happy for us, knowing how hard it's been since we met. We finally make a breakthrough and you're going to accuse me of keeping secrets?" Laci huffed, then swallowed her words. The taste was a tad bitter, knowing she was in fact keeping a secret from him. The first one ever. It wasn't hers to tell though. Maggie needed time.

Caleb needed to interject and was kind of upset at his dad for acting like such a baby. "Dad, Laci asked me right before I left for my date if I would ask some of my friends about a part-time job. Since Jenny isn't going to school now, I thought—"

Laci interrupted, shocked by his comment. "Wait, Jenny isn't going to school with you? When was someone going to fill me in? Is that because of the breakup? Is she upset with you?" Laci spouted.

"Hold on! Let me finish, Mom. Yes, she is okay, really. She wants to stay here and completely understood about the breakup part; she even seemed relieved, to be honest."

"Well, that's good, I guess. So, she's interested in working for me?" Laci's eyes lit up, all excited about having an assistant.

"Yeah, she flipped out about the job, said she would love to learn from you. I guess she's always wanted to be an event planner or do something like what you do."

Mitch waved his arms like a flagger bringing in a plane. "Hey, you two, can we get back to my original question here?"

Laci looked at Mitch and brought her hands up to her hips. "You know, if you had waited a little longer, I would have told you tonight when we normally do most of our talking… in bed."

"Whoa, you two. TMI!" Caleb shouted. He put his fingers in his ears and walked out of the room. "I'm going to change clothes on that note, before you two get all mushy."

Mitch and Laci couldn't help but laugh at Caleb's reaction, then Mitch let out a big sigh and pulled her close. "I'm sorry, darlin'. I don't know what got into me. I'm not upset about it, it's just odd that you didn't tell me about wanting to hire someone. You never keep stuff from me," he said softly. "I'm glad you found someone to help you out around here though. My mom is a pretty sharp lady." He smiled.

"She is. So is her son." Laci got up on her tiptoes and gave him a quick kiss. As she walked to the kitchen, her phone vibrated in her pocket. She pulled it out and saw Maggie's name.

Laci turned around and looked at Mitch, and he mouthed *"Who is it?"*

She pointed at him and silently replied, *"Your mom,"* before walking down the hall for added privacy.

"Hi Maggie," Laci answered, anxious to hear how her date had gone. "How are you?"

"Is Mitch nearby?" Maggie asked so she would know what or what not to say.

"Yes, we're having family movie night tonight. This is Caleb's last night at home for a while." Laci figured the general small talk would bore Mitch if he were trying to eavesdrop. She looked his direction as he walked away.

Whispering, Laci began the interrogation. "Well, how did it go?"

"It was a wonderful evening, sweetie. He said I looked very nice too, so thank you." Maggie's voice told the story of her excitement more than anything.

"You are beautiful on the inside, Maggie, that's what he saw. The outside is a bonus."

"Well, I felt better about everything knowing I had your advice and encouragement."

"So, where did you go?" Laci asked, checking down the hall to make sure Mitch hadn't come back within earshot.

"He took me to a fabulous Indian restaurant and then we ended up at a winery south of here. They had a band and we even danced!" Maggie said with a giggle.

Laci could hear Maggie's smile loud and clear, and it warmed her heart to know that she finally trusted her as a confidant. She was also finding it difficult to keep from laughing out loud along with her but kept it inside as best she could. "I'm so happy for you, Maggie!" Laci replied quietly. "Will you see him again?"

"I definitely will, and actually..." she paused, then whispered "He's staying the night." She blushed. "Do you think it's too soon?"

Did that woman just tell me what I think she told me? Laci's eyes popped open to the size of Jupiter, and she threw her hand up over her mouth, shocked at Maggie's words. *I cannot un-see that image now. Not possible! Lord help me!*

Laci cleared her throat quietly. "Maggie, you're a grown woman. How you choose to live your life is up to you, no one else. I think it's kind of sweet actually." Laci smiled, genuinely happy for her mother-in-law. "I'm so glad it went well. Now you can tell Mitch." She added.

"I'll tell Mitch soon, sweetie, I promise. I need to make sure this is the real thing first."

"You're only dating, Maggie. I don't think you need a lifetime commitment before you tell your son. Trust me, he's going to be okay with it. He's a big boy. Even if he's not, he'll get over it eventually."

"Yes, I know. There's a little more to it than that, but I'll explain to all soon."

Laci was confused by her comment, and a sense of concern bubbled in her belly, along with the indigestion from the tacos she'd enjoyed earlier, and the baby of course.

"Is everything okay? You know you can tell us if it's not. We are your family!"

"All is well my dear, don't you worry. Now go back to your sweet family and enjoy your night with them," she replied. "Oh, and Laci," she added.

"Yes?"

"I do love you, my darling girl. Thank you for being there for me through this."

Laci's heart swelled and she could barely reply. "I love you too, Mom. I was honored to be the one you came to. Did you want to say goodbye to Caleb?

"Yes, dear. Thank you!" She replied.

She walked down to the end of the hall, quickly wiping a few stray tears from her face before anyone could see, and as she turned the corner to go back into the living room, she nearly knocked Mitch over. He had been hovering during their entire conversation, and obviously a bit anxious to know the nature of Maggie's call.

"Caleb!" Laci yelled out, covering the phone with her hand,

then looked at Mitch. "Your mother would like to say goodbye to her grandson." She explained.

He barreled down the stairs and around the corner. "What's up?" Caleb asked.

"Here, take the phone. Grams wants to say goodbye before she goes to bed."

Caleb gave her a weird look. *She hardly ever talks to my Grams, let alone on the phone,* he thought, then took the phone. "Hey Grams, how are you?" He asked, walking away.

Mitch looked at Laci and shook his head in complete disbelief of what had transpired. "Let me see if I got this right," he began, pacing around a one-by-one square foot area of the floor. "For the last year, you and my mother have avoided one another, been sickeningly sweet to each other out of spite, and sometimes even ignored one another completely. After the miscarriage, you started being cordial, almost friendly to a degree, but nothing earth-shattering. Over the past twenty-four hours however, you two have been chattin' like a couple of house hens and now she's calling you on the *phone*? For the love of Pete, *please* tell me what on earth changed, Laci?" He put his hand on his forehead. "Don't get me wrong, darlin', I love seeing the two of you having a real mother and daughter connection with each other, it's awesome! Can you blame me for being a little curious on how this all came about, though?"

Laci looked down at the floor and swirled her toe around in a circle, gathering her thoughts. She sighed. "Mitch, you know that I love you with all my heart, but your mom is going through something right now that only another woman would understand, and she came to me for help. So, I was there for her and it changed everything! That's all you get. For now, at least. I'm not going to tell you anything more because it's not my story to tell. Everything is fine, don't worry. You're gonna have to trust me on this, okay babe?"

He brushed her hair back from her brow and cupped her face in his hand. "I love you too, and hearing you tell my mom 'I love you' gave me more joy than you can possibly know. I'm glad you could be there for her, I really am. I'm just not used to being kept in the dark. It feels weird."

She leaned in closer to him and slid her arms around his neck. "Your mom needs this to stay between us for now, ok babe?" She asked in a soft voice, then kissed his soft lips ever so slightly.

His mouth turned up in a little smile. "You're doing that thing again. Stop it."

She kissed him again. "What *thing* would that be, exactly?" She kissed him again.

"You know good-and-well what *thing*," Mitch replied, then returned her kiss, firm and passionate.

Laci felt the goosebumps rise on her arms and when Mitch pulled away, he smiled, proud of his ability to give her chills.

"Well, if that's how you're going to respond, then I'll have to keep secrets from you a little more often," she giggled. He gave her 'the look' and she rolled her eyes. "Just kidding, dear." She winked at him.

"Look. Your mom will tell you when she's ready, babe. Can you hang out in the dark a little longer? And don't you *dare* ask her anything about anything, you hear me, Mitch Young? I don't even want her to know I gave you a *hint* about there even *being* a thing."

"That was a lot of 'things' to remember," he joked. "...but yes, I can hang out in the dark a little longer, as long as I have you close by in case I get scared." He winked playfully, then added one more kiss for good measure.

About that time, a loud voice bellowed from the other room. "Come on you guys! The movie is almost over!" Emma shouted.

Then Travis ran around the corner and slid on his sock-feet right into Mitch's side.

"They're in here kissing each other again! Yuck!"

Mitch laughed, picked up Travis and threw him over his shoulder, tickling him. "One of these days sport, you won't be saying 'yuck', trust me."

"Whatever," Travis replied. Mitch put him down, then Travis grabbed them both by the hand and dragged them back into the living room.

Caleb had already changed and was on the floor eating Travis' popcorn. They sat down on the couch, and Travis and Emma were immediately on top of them, snuggling under their arms. Laci looked around the room, taking in the precious sight of their blended family all together under one roof for one last night. She knew it would be some time before that would happen again. A tear rolled down her cheek and her chest tightened at the thought. Caleb's departure the next morning would be difficult without a doubt. Mitch squeezed Laci's hand to comfort her. She knew he felt it too, even stronger as it was his son about to leave, but they didn't dwell on it. Rather, their hearts overflowed as they cherished the moment.

CHAPTER 4

Laci sat up and decided to get out of bed after tossing and turning the last few hours.

"Lace, come back to bed," Mitch groveled from his side of the bed. "We have another hour at least."

She walked around and kissed him on the cheek. "You'll sleep better if I'm not causing seismic mattress tremors, trust me. I'll go start breakfast. Big day ahead," she whispered in his ear.

"Uh-huh. Big… day," he mumbled, still half asleep.

She tiptoed out of the room and into the hall, still dark in the wee hours of the morning, and only a sliver of light from the downstairs nightlight as her guide. She flipped on the light in the kitchen and turned on some soft music on her phone. Cooking to music was a must in her kitchen and usually calmed the baby too. He was already starting out this day extra jumpy. A few months ago, it was cute and fun, but now it was downright aggravating.

In the quietness of the morning, she took a few minutes to have a conversation with the big guy upstairs as she started frying the bacon. Laci's 'God talks' were far from traditional prayers, it was more of an open conversation, and her trying to make sense of the world as it was. Some days she was humble, extra thankful, and did her best to listen to Him for a while, trying to learn the day's lesson. Other days, it was a mish-mosh of her rambling on and on about a dozen things for which she wanted Him to handle on *her* timeline, or asking for forgiveness for all the stupid things she had done, asking for patience, or yelling at Him for this and that, getting angry when things didn't work out as she'd hoped. She was very open with Him. Then there were the sweetest moments, like that morning, when it felt like God was physically there in the kitchen with her and she could reach out and touch Him.

That morning, she sang quietly to the song playing on her phone, then lifted up each member of her family, ending with Caleb and his new journey that was about to begin. *Hard to believe he won't be around anymore, and even harder to imagine him as a chef.* She smiled at the thought. But he was over the moon when he got his acceptance letter from the New York Institute of Culinary Education. All he could talk about for weeks after was his restaurant and what kind of menu he would create. He was finally going for his dream, and Laci was so proud of him.

In the short time she and Mitch had been together, Caleb had been their biggest cheerleader, even when times were tough during her cancer fight. He gently nudged Mitch to keep fighting for her, and she was grateful for that support. Kids don't always want or like a new person in their parent's life, but Caleb always had an open mind and heart. Laci realized how much she would miss him, his sweet demeanor, and his silly jokes. A few tears fell from her eyes down to the hot griddle, sizzling right along with the bacon.

From the corner of her eye, Laci caught a glimpse of

someone entering the kitchen. She quickly wiped her tears and turned to see Evan walk in, shoulders slouched.

"Morning, Mom." He yawned.

"Hey sweetie. Why are you up so early?"

"Couldn't sleep. Then I smelled the bacon."

Laci laughed. "Bacon always does it, huh?"

"That and coffee." He chuckled softly.

"It's almost done. Can you fix me a cup too, while you're over there?"

"Sure. What time is Caleb's flight?"

"I think they're leaving at five thirty, flight leaves at eight. Speaking of which, I need to go roust them."

"You'll miss him, huh? Is that why you were crying? I saw you wipe your eyes."

"I certainly will. He's been a big help to me and Mitch, but now I have *my* baby here, and that makes me very happy." She smiled. "Mitch will be sad for a while, too, with Brad and Caleb both gone now, so be patient with him, okay?"

"Sure. That's easy. I know it won't be the same having me instead of Caleb, but I'm glad for the chance to get to know him better. I know this might sound weird, but I don't miss Dad as much when I'm here. Is that bad?"

Laci came around the counter and stood next to him, her arm now around his back. "Sweetie, no! Of course not. Your dad is watching over us, trust me. I know for a fact he is glad you have someone to lean on. He knows you're happy and that's what he would want more than anything. Are you happy, being here?" She asked for reassurance.

"Yeah, definitely." He turned around and fixed their coffee. "I know it's only been a couple of days, but it feels right; like this is where I belong now, ya know?" Evan said, then handed her a steaming cup of coffee.

"Thanks, sweetie. I do know what you mean. That's what it

feels like when you are exactly where God wants you, in His will."

"Cool." He smiled and did that crazy thing with his eyebrows knowing it would make his mom laugh, and she did.

"You're a nut. I'm going to run up and make sure everyone is awake. Watch the bacon for me?"

Mitch and Caleb finally stumbled into the kitchen several minutes later. The rest of the kids followed behind and bellied up to the snack bar, yawning and still half asleep.

"Let's say grace," Mitch said.

They all bowed their heads as Mitch asked a blessing on the day ahead, and Caleb's travels. Emma was crying before he could finish.

"Okay you guys, no tears okay?" Caleb asked. "I'm not leaving forever, geez! I'll be back the week of Christmas unless Mom has our baby brother earlier."

"Hey, don't jinx it, Caleb Young!" Laci squealed, then giggles rippled around the table.

Breakfast chatter ensued, then everyone got up and dragged themselves to the front door, slugging along like a bunch of sloths. Goodbyes were hard.

Mitch broke the ice. "Come on guys, get those hugs in."

Travis walked over and wrapped his arms around Caleb's waist, as was his custom. "I'll see you soon, sport." Caleb had a soft spot for his little stepbrother. He started to choke up but cleared his throat to ward off any embarrassing emotions.

"We can play Minecraft online, right?" Travis grinned up at him.

"I'll play when I can, bud. Gotta get my homework done first though, okay?"

Emma inched her way over to Caleb. "Get over here, sis." But she wouldn't look at him. Caleb reached over and lifted her chin. "You better text me and keep me posted about Isaac, you hear me, girl?"

Laci's eyebrow raised at Caleb's comment. She hadn't heard anything from Emma about this Isaac guy before. *Emma likes a boy? What's this about? Why hasn't she told me?* Laci's heart sank a little at the realization that her little girl was growing up and *'mom'* seemed to be moving out of that familiar place where Emma would tell her everything. Now wasn't the time to ask questions of course, so she filed it away for another time.

"Shhh! Not here, dork." Emma slugged his arm and grinned, her cheeks now red from embarrassment. She couldn't believe Caleb said his name out loud. Emma looked over at her mom hoping she hadn't heard but was sure she had. It was almost as if her consciousness could sense her mom's disappointment, not having shared any news of the new guy yet, which was unusual. Her mom was truly her best friend and she told her everything, but this was different. Emma had waited to divulge the details in fear she wouldn't approve. She brushed it off, gave Caleb a tight hug goodbye, and walked away.

Todd and Evan took their turns shaking hands and giving Caleb the 'we-don't-hug-because-we're-too-cool' handshake. Laci couldn't help but giggle under her breath as they all wandered back to their rooms.

Mitch took Caleb's bag to the car and gave him and Laci a minute to say their goodbye.

"You excited?" she asked.

"Yeah. Nervous too, though. Kind of wish Jenny was still going, ya know?" He replied.

"Have you talked to her since your dinner together?"

"We texted a couple times last night before bed, but just random stuff. We're in a good place. Friends."

"I'm glad, and thanks again for telling her about the job. I'm excited to see her again. I'm excited for you too! You're going to love college, Caleb. Soak it all in and spread your wings. You'll be running your own kitchen before you know it."

Caleb chuckled, "Thanks La—, I mean Mom... I will admit; it feels kind of cool to say that word again. Different, but cool."

Laci took a breath to keep herself from blubbering. "Well, I am honored to be a surrogate mother to you sweetie. I know your mom is looking down and so proud of you. I am too. Give me a hug, your dad is waiting."

"Hey, Mom?"

"Yeah, sweetie?"

"Thanks for," he paused. "...for loving my dad and coming into our lives. You sort of made everything better. I hope you know that. He's probably the happiest I've seen him in years, and I kinda like being a big brother." Caleb blushed.

Laci smiled from ear to ear and pulled him into a bear hug, as much as possible without squishing baby Young. "You're so welcome! Now go on! Get out of here before your clothes get damp from all my tears. I love you, Caleb. Son."

"I love you, too," he replied with a sweet smile.

He picked up his duffle bag from the floor and opened the front door. Mitch stood quietly on the porch waiting for them to finish, smiling like a Cheshire cat as the rain drizzled down behind him.

"Be careful driving, okay? The roads will be slick this early in the morning." Laci urged.

"Your rain will bring me good luck as always, darlin'," he replied. "Now come here and kiss me goodbye so I'll warm up!" His sweet, southern accent always made her heart leap in her chest.

Laci wrinkled her brow and smiled. "Warm up?"

"Yes, your kisses warm my heart, don't ya know?"

"Mitch Young. You are too much! My how I do love you

though," Laci kissed his lips, still cool from being out in the morning air. "Bye love."

"Bye. I'll text you when I'm on my way home."

Laci shut the door behind him and closed her eyes listening to the quiet of the house as the rain fell harder. Walking back to the kitchen, she peeked in the living room and found the kids sacked-out on couches and sprawled across the floor. *Early mornings never were their thing.* She smiled and decided they had the right idea. It was nap time.

* * *

AT THE AIRPORT, Mitch helped Caleb inside with his bags and got him checked in. The hardest part was now upon them.

"Looks like this is it, pops." Caleb said jokingly. It helped him ward off the emotional stuff.

"Pops, huh? Man, I must be getting old," Mitch replied. "I know you don't like this part, so I'll keep it short. You know that you are my whole world, and I love ya. Please know that I'm here for you, son, for anything, anytime. You call and I'll be there, understand?"

"Yeah, Dad. I know. You're in good hands now that you have Laci in your life. You two are so happy together, and I couldn't have asked for a better stepmom. You did good."

Mitch laughed softly. "Well, thank you. You had a big hand in us being together. I wouldn't have made it after your mom died if it hadn't been for you and Brad. You two saved me so I could save Laci. Now is your time though. Focus on you! It's a new beginning for you, Chef. Enjoy every minute of it, okay? Be good in all you do, for yourself and others. Remember that, Caleb."

"I couldn't do it any other way. You raised me right. I'll miss you all so much, but I know this is right. Someday you'll be eating in my restaurant!"

"I can't wait, son. Now give me a hug and get on your way. You'll be boarding soon."

Caleb dropped his carry-on bag and wrapped his arms around his dad for an extra-long, tight bear hug. A tear escaped down his cheek. "I love you, Dad," he whispered.

"I love you, Caleb. Go get 'em, son. You'll be great!"

They pulled apart, Caleb picked up his bag, then turned and walked away without looking back.

Mitch watched him until he was out of sight, passers-by walking around him on every side rushing to make flights. But he stood motionless, unable to hold back the tears as they slid down his cheek. *He's turning into such a good young man, but I never knew it would be this hard watching my baby boy leave the nest,* he thought to himself.

"You did good, Karen. *We* did good," he said softly, speaking out loud to his late wife. He wiped the tears away with one swift swipe of his shirt sleeve, then returned to the car, heart heavy-laden.

* * *

TIME WAS GROWING short until Baby Young's arrival, so the day after Caleb left for school, Laci called Jenny to see if she could start right away. During their brief, yet pleasant conversation, they shared several things they had in common and Laci could already tell they would work well together. She somewhat expected to anyway, having met Jenny a few times when she and Caleb had dated. He would bring her in the house once in a while for short visits, but they never stuck around long; always on the go as most kids were. When she and Caleb decided to part ways though, her heart sank a little. Jenny seemed to be the type of girl Laci had always envisioned as a daughter-in-law someday; kind, sweet, and a little sassy, which was a crucial trait to have in the Young family. Regardless, Laci was happy to finally have an opportunity to get to know Jenny better.

A few days later, she sat in her neatly decorated office, tucked away from the hustle and bustle of the house, and planned out the first day with her new assistant. The room was filled with the sweet smell of a pumpkin spice jar candle burning in the corner, adding a warm glow in the early morning darkness. She leaned back in her chair and rested her hands on top of her belly, taking in the quiet of the moment and admiring her office. It was one of two places that brought her joy, the other being her writing room. The walls were painted a light shade of caramel brown and a comfy couch sat against the back wall, strewn with small decorative pillows in all shapes and shades of teal, brown, orange and dark yellow. Her favorite part though was the wall stickers carefully placed around the room; famous book quotes and words of inspiration, each one bringing a smile to her face when read. Her favorite one being, *'everything will be alright in the end, and if it's not alright, then it's not the end,'* coined from one of her favorite movies, *The Most Exotic Marigold Hotel.*

It was almost September, and Laci's mind was already drifting towards fall and how to decorate for the upcoming holidays. With the right décor, she could transform her everyday office into a veritable haunted house for Halloween, or Santa's workshop at Christmas. *There is nothing like a few fall leaves and pumpkins to get us in the mood!* This year however, she would definitely need Jenny's help. *Won't we little one?* She said out loud, smiling and patting her tummy.

Evan came around the corner, still half asleep, and ducked inside her office. He wasn't quite used to early mornings yet.

"Hey sweetie. Aren't you bright eyed and bushy-tailed!" Laci giggled.

Evan grunted in reply and sat down on the couch.

"Up late?" She asked.

"Not that late. One a.m. I think." He yawned and leaned his head over on a pillow.

"Ev, you've got to start getting more rest. Mitch needs to know he can count on you."

He lifted his head up from the pillow. "I know, Mom. I won't let him down, I promise. I just couldn't sleep, stuff on my mind."

"Everything okay?"

"Yep. Still adjusting to the new schedule, I guess. I really like being here though."

"Good. Mitch says you are doing very well too. I'm proud of you, Ev."

"Thanks," he replied and managed a half-smile.

JENNY HAD ARRIVED a few minutes early and made her way to the winery. She located the 'Office' sign and followed it around the corner. She heard voices, and since the door was open, she simply knocked softly on the door trim and peeked her head inside.

Laci looked up as she walked inside. "Jenny, sweetie, welcome! Perfect timing. Come on in!" Laci stood up and greeted her with a hug. "You can meet my son. Evan, this is Jenny. She'll be helping me with the events and here at the office until the baby comes."

Evan popped up off the couch as his mouth dropped open. At the same time, Jenny's eyes widened, a smile now spread across her face.

"What in the world are you doing here?" Evan asked, surprised.

Laci raised an eyebrow in a very Spock-like manner. "You two know each other?"

Evan smiled. "Umm, yeah. Well, sort of."

Jenny laughed softly. "Yeah, we met last week when he strolled into the coffee shop five minutes before closing and spilled his drink on my clean floor." Then she looked back at Evan and winked.

"Now that was an accident and you know it," Evan replied in his defense; his cheeks flushed. "Plus, you threw me off with that soymilk if I recall." His face recoiled from the memory.

"Yes, yes I did. You also said I could use *any* milk remember?" She added.

Evan laughed. "Yeah, I guess I did."

Laci sat back and smiled as the two of them bantered back and forth, the connection taking place was more than obvious, and she couldn't help but think how much they reminded her of herself and Mitch when they first met. She never saw Caleb and Jenny look that way either, not even once.

"Okay you two, we're burning daylight. Jenny we should probably get to work, and Evan, I *know* you have somewhere to be," she grinned.

"Yes Ma'am, Mrs. Young," Jenny replied, a little embarrassed by her behavior. *Why does he get to me like that?* Jenny thought to herself. *First day on the job and I'm already distracted!*

"Evan? Scoot." Laci shooed him toward the door.

"I'm going, Mother." He turned and looked at Jenny one more time. "Bye, Jenny." He grinned and walked out.

With Evan finally gone, Laci offered Jenny a seat. "Now then, I guess I should go over the job with you and make sure you still want it," she smiled.

"Yes, Ma'am. That would be great." Jenny replied.

"First things first, please call me Laci."

"Yes, Ma—, I mean Laci." Jenny laughed.

"Good. Now that that's settled, does Evan know you are Caleb's ex-girlfriend?"

Jenny looked down at the floor. "I'm not sure, to be honest. I was planning on telling him soon."

"Well, if I had to guess based on what I saw, I think he may have a *bit* of a crush on you, so you might want to tell him before you leave today. Never start a relationship off with a secret sweetie." Laci winked at her.

Laci's sweet smile helped put Jenny at ease, but she still felt awkward. "There's no relationship or anything. I promise. I mean I barely even know him, and even if I did like him, I would never let that get in the way of doing my job." Jenny's face was bright red.

Laci laughed and put her hand on top of Jenny's. "Sweetie, it's okay. Why don't we get to work and focus on something else for a little, hmm?"

"That sounds great." Jenny smiled nervously and they began their day.

* * *

"Hey Mitch, what label goes on this box?" Evan asked.

Mitch walked over and turned the box on its side. "See this code here? Anything with YV-MOS is the Moscato. YV-MER is the Merlot. I'll make you a cheat sheet for now, but eventually you'll memorize them."

"What's the number after the code?"

"That's the year we bottled it. None of them are very old yet, so that's why we store the newest bottles in the cellar and let them continue to ferment and age." Mitch explained. He liked that Evan was showing a genuine interest in the business.

"Can I ask a non-winery and somewhat personal question?" Evan asked.

"Sure. What's up?"

"Is my mom's new assistant Caleb's ex-girlfriend?"

Mitch laughed. "I take it you met Jenny?"

"Yeah. I actually met her a couple of times before at the coffee shop."

"I see. Well, to answer your question, yes. She is Caleb's ex-girlfriend. They broke up the day before he left for college."

"Why did they break up?" Evan paused. "Sorry, that's none of my business. You don't have to tell me."

"I won't go into details, but they were simply better friends. Jenny was supposed to go away to school with him but changed her mind. She wasn't ready. And to be honest, Caleb was ready to spread his wings and date other girls. It was mutual from what I could tell. Why do you ask?" Mitch asked, even though he already knew.

"Aww, no reason really. I met her in the coffee shop when I got into town. She seems nice and definitely feisty." Evan smiled, fidgeting with a bottle sticking up out of the box.

"She does seem nice. Caleb never talked much about her to be honest." Mitch's curiosity was now piqued. "I hope you don't mind if I ask, but was Jenny the new *friend* you went to see on your lunch that day?"

"In all fairness, sir, I didn't have any idea she was Caleb's girlfriend," Evan said, defending his intentions.

Mitch threw his head back in laughter. "Ev, it's okay. I wasn't accusing you of anything, I promise. Listen," he paused and sat down next to Evan, putting a hand on the back of his shoulder. "As far as I'm concerned, she's free to date whomever she wants now, as is Caleb, and you."

"I'm not interested in dating her, sir. She's really nice, that's all." Evan quickly stood up and grabbed some Moscato labels, then went back to work.

"Whatever you say, slick," Mitch replied softly, shaking his head with a smile. "It might not be up to you though," he added.

"What do you mean?"

Mitch looked Evan in the eye. "God has a way of putting people in our lives when we least expect it, for reasons we can't always see at first. He put your mom next to me on that plane two years ago, and in my wildest of dreams, I could have never imagined how my life would change the way it did after that. Simply have fun, and have a little faith, that's all," Mitch said in his rich southern tone. His sincerity came through loud and clear when he spoke of Laci, she was everything to him, and he made sure everyone knew it.

"Yeah. I think I know what you mean. Thanks, Mitch," Evan answered, a smile on his face.

* * *

JENNY GRABBED her insulated lunch box then walked over to the wedding barn, still decorated from the previous weekend wedding. Inside, she looked around in awe of the neatly positioned bales of hay that lined the walls, rafters donned with strings of lights, and soft white strips of tulle draped from one end to the other, wrapped in ivy and fake orange baby roses. Fake flowers were easier to see in the tulle and lasted much longer. Her mind wandered to a place where she herself would walk down an aisle someday with the man of her dreams, picturing Evan next to her. *What? No way! Good grief I don't even know the guy. Why on earth would I think of him?* She jeered at her own thought, then sat down on a bale of hay. Before she could take a bite of her sandwich however, Evan walked in and sat down next to her, pulling an apple out of his jacket.

"How is your first day going?" He inquired.

"Hmm, let's see. Pretty good I guess, outside of you almost getting me fired this morning!" She took a bite.

"What do you mean *I* almost got you fired? You're the one who poked at me first." He chuckled, but was slightly flustered by her comment. "And by the way, when were you going to tell me that you and Caleb were dating?" He added.

She swallowed her bite, but a lump crept into Jenny's throat at his words, realizing the time had come for an explanation.

"I told you I would tell you the next time I saw you, but this is the first time I've seen you! I didn't figure it would be here."

"Well, we're here now, so fire away, coffee girl." He smiled his cheesy grin.

"Look. When I met you, I had already made up my mind to break things off and tell him I wasn't going to school. That's why I asked you to not tell him we'd met. I didn't want it to complicate things. When we broke up, he told me about this job with your mom and I needed the money, plus it's exactly what I want to do someday," she explained.

"Working at a winery?"

"No, silly. Planning events!" She laughed. "And I'm sorry I didn't have a chance to tell you sooner. Are you upset?" She wrinkled her nose and mouth, awaiting his response.

"No way! You have to do what's right for you, and that's exactly what you're doing. And now I get to see you more." He leaned over and bumped her shoulder with his.

Jenny's mouth turned up slightly at his touch, but then it disappeared. "Let's get something straight, Jeep-boy, "

Evan's eyebrow raised. "Hold up. What happened to Jeep-man?"

"Well after that display in front of your mom today, you're now Jeep-boy," she grinned. "But just so we're clear, I'm here to work and I don't need a distraction, especially one like you."

Evan turned his face toward hers and moved in closer. "Now

why would *I* be a distraction, Miss Jenny?" He smiled and stared deep into her eyes.

She picked up her lunchbox and stood up. "Stop, Evan. That's exactly what I mean right there. This? You and me?" She pointed back and forth between them. "It can't happen. Not now."

"Well that's dandy with me!" Evan stood up; his brow furrowed. "What makes you think I wanted *us* to happen anyway? I've got news for you, I'm not the least bit interested. I am focused on my job too, Miss Sassy-pants. Nothing more." Evan tossed his apple core on the ground. "Have a great first day, Jenny," he said as he stomped off.

Jenny sighed and shook her head. *That's not exactly how I wanted that to play out. Ugh! He's so stubborn!* She brushed it off as best she could, but there was something about Evan she couldn't quite explain, something that made her feel he was meant to be in her life, almost as if there was a force pulling them together. She sat back down and finished her lunch, and went back to work, wondering if she had lost her chance to get to know him better.

Jenny returned to the office and Laci immediately noticed something was a little off, starting with Jenny's smile. It was no longer there. *Why do I sense this has something to do with my son?*

"Everything okay, sweetie? Have I bored you to death already?" Laci dug in, anxious for details.

Jenny shook her head back and forth. "No way. I can already tell I'm going to love working here with you, Laci. I can't say that Evan is very happy about me being here though."

"Evan? Why would he not want you here? He seemed pretty happy about it earlier this morning."

"I think he might like me, and I don't want to mess things up with this job. I also kind of told him I wasn't interested and that... well, that *we* couldn't happen," she explained.

"Well, that's very professional of you, and I appreciate you wanting to keep things platonic while you work here. But sweetie this is a family-owned business, not corporate America. If you like Evan and he likes you, then what's the harm in developing your friendship and let things happen naturally? Providing you don't let it interrupt your work, of course." Laci winked.

A little smirk appeared on Jenny's face. "Okay, to be honest, I do like him. I have liked him since he walked into the coffee shop." She rolled her eyes and stood up, pacing the office floor. "And I can't believe I just told you that. You're not only my boss, but you're his mom!" Jenny plopped down on the couch and buried her face in her hands, groaning out loud. "And I really liked Caleb too, Laci, please don't think bad of me! Evan is so different though."

Laci couldn't help but laugh. "It's okay! I always knew you liked Caleb, and I could immediately tell you liked Evan, that was not hard to miss. I promise I won't tell, just try not to worry about it. Why don't you take the fall décor out of storage and get your mind off things."

Jenny looked up. "Sounds perfect," she replied.

I think things around the office are going to be extra fun this fall! Laci thought with a little smirk on her face.

As the day went on, Laci and Jenny got to know one another better and worked on the office, decorating it with strands of fall leaves, baby pumpkins, and all things orange, yellow and red. It was the beginning of Laci's favorite time of year, and of course she had the added excitement of baby Young on the way, but despite that, she had an unsettled feeling deep in her bones, as if something unexpected was coming. She brushed the feeling away though and enjoyed the day with Jenny.

* * *

THE WORKDAY AT ITS END, Jenny hopped in her car and left. She saw Mitch and Evan walking up the driveway and gave them a wave as she passed by.

Evan shook his head, still frustrated about how things went with Jenny earlier that day.

Mitch grinned. "Don't worry, Ev. It's only the first day. Things like this take time. Girls like to be wooed, slow like molasses."

"I'm not wooing her. I don't have time anyway, and she's busy too. Besides, Caleb would hate me."

"Caleb doesn't get a say in this, and even if he did, he'll get over it. You have to do what you think is best."

"Why does that sound like hard work?" Evan asked.

Mitch stopped in front of the door and looked Evan in the eye. "The good ones always are and usually worth every bit of it." He winked. "Now let's go get cleaned up for dinner."

* * *

"HEY BABE!" Laci squealed as Mitch entered the kitchen, a big smile on her face.

"Oooo, Momma is happy! Must have been a good day with your new assistant." He said, and wrapped his arms around her tummy, kissing her soft lips.

"We had a great day. She is so smart, Mitch, and full of great ideas. She's perfect for this."

"Good! Because we all know that if Momma's happy," Evan turned to Mitch, and continued in unison, "everyone's happy." They laughed.

"Alright, you two. Get out of here! I need to finish dinner." She slapped Mitch on the tush.

"What are we havin', darlin'?"

"Your favorite; salmon and rice."

Mitch danced a little 'Charleston'. "Mmm, mmmm. I'll be back in a minute to help you."

"You'd better." She winked, flashing him a smile.

A few minutes after the guys headed upstairs, Laci's phone howled like a wolf, a special ringtone that Laci had designated for Mitch's mom. *Ooops. Suppose I'd better get that changed now that we're friends and all.* She giggled at the thought.

"Hi, Maggie."

"Laci, dear?" Maggie panted.

"Mom, are you okay? You sound kind of winded."

"I'm fine dear, just out shopping for Mitch's birthday present. What should I get him?"

Laci burst out laughing. "You're shopping a little early, aren't you? Did you find a sale on power tools or something?"

"It's only a few days away dear, I don't want to show up empty handed." Maggie replied.

Worry wrinkles appeared on Laci's forehead. "Mom, his birthday is in April. You have eight months, sweetie."

Laci's memory flashed to the day that Maggie almost took her medicine twice, now this. She knew deep inside something wasn't right.

Maggie didn't reply, there was only silence that seemed to last forever. "Maggie, are you okay?" Laci asked.

"Yes, dear. I'm so sorry to bother you during dinner." Her voice was low and muffled. "I wanted to get a jump on my shopping for next year," she added with an uncomfortable laugh.

"Well, of course. That's always a smart idea. I wish I had time to do that myself, but it never seems to work out." Laci tried to make the conversation as normal as possible.

"Laci darling," she paused, "let's keep this between us if that's not too much to ask."

Laci was unsure how to respond, not wanting to upset her

any more than she already was. "Mom, I need to know what is going on. I don't think you're being honest with me."

Maggie sighed heavily. "I'm fine, but I may be having some mild memory loss. It's nothing serious though, trust me. I'm going to be fine, dear. Don't worry, okay? And please Laci, don't tell Mitch. I'll talk to both of you soon, I promise."

"You swear you'll tell us soon? I can't keep secrets from him, Maggie. He's your son. He deserves to know."

"Yes, dear. Please, give me a little more time. It's not that bad, trust me."

Laci exhaled quietly, closed her eyes and shook her head. "I am trusting you to be honest with me, Mom. I love you, but if anything like this happens again, I am going to tell Mitch. Is that understood?"

"Of course. But I'm fine, really. I'm so glad you called me Mom."

"I didn't even think about it honestly. It simply felt right." Laci smiled. "Do you want to join us for dinner? It's almost done." Laci hoped she would say yes, then maybe open up to the idea of telling Mitch about the memory loss *and* the boyfriend.

"I'm here with Richard, so I think we'll have dinner out tonight. Thank you though."

"Okay, Mom. Have a good night, okay? And be careful." She added, then hung up.

"Who was that?" Mitch asked.

Laci jumped sky high when she heard Mitch's voice behind her.

"Sorry, darlin', didn't mean to scare ya." He smiled and kissed her on the cheek.

"Oh, your mom called to say hi," Laci said, then quickly grabbed her belly as the baby gave her a little kick. *Mercy, little one. Is this your way of subtly reminding me that I'm keeping a secret?* She thought.

"Why did you tell her to be careful? Where is she?"

"She's shopping at the mall, but I say that to everyone, kind of a mom habit, I guess."

Mitch raised his eyebrow. "If you say so. You and baby okay there? That kick looked painful."

"Yes, we're fine. Now wash your hands and season the salmon." Laci was grateful he didn't dig any deeper about his mom's call. "How was your day?" She asked, changing the subject.

"Good! Pretty sure Evan is crushing on your new assistant." Mitch laughed. "She must have burst his bubble at lunch though, he came back to work all pouty, but very focused. Not much on chit-chat after that."

"Wow. Her first day and we already have an employee romance brewing." Laci giggled. "I'm not exactly sure what happened at lunch, but Jenny lost a little of her spunk too. They'll figure it out eventually."

"Could be more of an employee scandal if they're not careful." Mitch replied.

Laci tilted her head. "Why do you say that?"

Mitch shrugged his shoulders. "Not sure how Caleb will feel about her and Evan taking up with each other so soon after they broke up, ya know?"

"Hey." Laci put her hands on her hips. "Caleb and Jenny broke up on mutual terms. They are all free to do as they please. Plus..." she paused.

"Plus, what?"

"Plus, I'm pretty sure she is sweet on him too. I'm positive she is."

"Women's intuition, huh?" Mitch inquired.

Laci winked. "Something like that."

"You know more than you're letting on, don't you?"

"Maybe." She smiled and kept Jenny's words to herself.

"And I suppose this is some sort of girl-pact isn't it?"

"Something like that." Laci giggled, knowing Mitch was beyond frustrated with her vague answers, but that's what she loved the most. She leaned in and sealed her secrets with a kiss on his warm, soft lips.

"I guess I'm okay with that. For now." He kissed her again.

CHAPTER 5

By late September, the leaves were already transforming from green to various shades of gold, orange and red, announcing the arrival of fall. Things were getting busier all around the winery as grapes arrived for crush season and with only two months left until the Christmas tree auction event for the Breast Cancer Center, Laci and Jenny were extra busy lining up tree designers, sponsors, and already registering guests. Not only was the big Christmas event approaching soon, so was Laci's personal event, the arrival of baby Young. Her belly showed it too, growing larger by the day.

Jenny and Evan were also getting more comfortable with each other, and of course Laci and Mitch encouraged it by making sure they had plenty of things to do together around the winery. But despite their efforts, Evan still hadn't gotten the courage up to tell her how he felt.

That day, the barn was hotter than usual. It was already eighty degrees in the shade, which was rare for that time of year. Laci and Jenny had finished up their errands, so she sent Jenny to go watch the guys load grapes on the conveyor belt.

That was always Laci's favorite part to watch when she first came to the winery and began learning about the business.
"What am I going to watch them do again?" Jenny asked, somewhat confused.

"It's the thing they use to crush, squish, and stem all the grapes. Trust me, it's neat to watch." Laci smiled.

"Okay, okay, if you say so." Jenny walked away, rolling her eyes once she turned the corner.

"Watching Evan act all macho while him and his stepdad play with grapes isn't exactly my idea of fun." She mumbled under her breath and walked to the barn.

The school bus dropped Todd off at home, and he met Jenny as she was leaving. "Where you headed, Jenny?" He asked.

"I guess I'm going to watch grapes get crushed. How was school?"

"Pretty crappy actually. Failed a stupid test." Todd kicked the dirt in frustration.

"Hey, it happens, Todd. Don't be too hard on yourself. You'll bounce back," she replied, trying to encourage him.

Meanwhile, Travis and Emma ran outside the house to greet him. "Hey Todd! Let's go to Gram's house." They shouted.

"Okay, that actually sounds pretty good. I'm not in the mood to do homework yet anyway."

"Well, you all have fun! I have to go watch some grape-squishin' action." Jenny laughed and walked toward the barn.

"See ya, Jenny!" They all shouted in reply.

Todd and Emma hopped in the side-by-side (Travis called it the mule) and took a short ride to Grandma Maggie's house. They enjoyed visiting her after school from time to time. On many occasions she would have a batch of homemade snicker doodles still baking in the oven, filling her house with the sweet aroma of cinnamon and vanilla. When they pulled up in

Maggie's drive however, Todd noticed the front door was wide open. He looked over at Emma, one eyebrow raised.

They hopped off the mule and walked inside.

"Grams!" Todd yelled. "Whatcha got the door open for?"

There was no reply. "Let's split up and look for her, Emma," Todd said.

"I'll head to the kitchen. You check the living room." Emma replied and she went her way. There was no sign of Grams, but she had been there. The counter was a mess, covered with flour, sugar and broken eggshells, which was odd. Grams was a neat freak and typically cleaned as she went along. Emma noticed a bowl of cookie dough still sitting out, so she opened the oven hoping to find a batch already baking. Instead of cookies however, Emma found something quite different.

"Todd!" Emma yelled, quickly turning off the oven. The blanket clumped inside on the top rack was starting to smolder. Emma was scared. She grabbed her phone and dialed her mom.

"Hey sweetie! How is Mag—," Laci began.

"Mom! You need to get over to Grams right now!" Emma shouted.

"What's wrong, Emma?" Laci's anxiety building in her chest.

"Grandma tried to bake a quilt. Something isn't right!"

About that time, Todd ran into the kitchen and saw the surprise in the oven. "Holy Mother of Pearl! That's going to be a bit chewy." Todd's use of sarcasm helped calm him.

Emma threw her hands up in the air. "Well get it out!" She yelled, still on the phone. "Sorry, Mom."

"It's okay, Em. I'm on the way," Laci replied, and hung up.

"Mom's on her way. Please tell me you found Grams!"

"Yeah, she's ok. I found her outside working in her flower garden. I'll go get her in a minute."

Emma exhaled in relief and sat down on a barstool. Meanwhile, Todd grabbed two oven mitts and pulled the hot blanket out onto the floor. Emma was ready with a cup of water, and as she sprinkled the top of the blanket, it hissed, then skinny puffs of white smoke flew into the air.

Laci's car screeched to a stop in front of Maggie's house and she waddled as fast as she could inside. When she got to the kitchen, Grams was sitting at her table with the kids, drinking a cup of tea to calm her nerves.

Emma ran over and threw her arms around her mom's waist. "It's okay, Em," she hugged her tight then kissed the top of her head.

Maggie looked up at Laci from the top of her cup, then slowly placed it back on the table. "I know what you're thinking, and I can promise you I'm fine. I simply forgot about starting the cookies, that's all." Maggie said in her defense.

Todd looked at Grams with one eyebrow raised. "Was there cookie-dough in that quilt, Grams?"

"Why no, silly! I—I—" Maggie stuttered in search of an answer. "I was cold and wanted to heat it up for a minute. I went outside to water my flowers and lost track of time, that's all."

Laci picked up the now damp quilt and held it up, it was riddled with tiny black holes, singed by the heat. She looked at the kids and managed a closed-lipped smile.

"Kids, why don't you go outside and give us a minute. Please?" Laci's look was all they needed, and they immediately walked outside.

Laci sat down at the round, antique wood table and took Maggie's hand in hers.

"Mom, do you remember putting the blanket in the oven? It's also 80 degrees today. How were you chilly? Tell me what's going on, and I need you to be honest with me, okay?" Laci asked in a soft voice, gently squeezing Maggie's hand.

"Mitch's dad made this table for me forty years ago. It was

the first thing he ever gave me that he'd made with his bare hands." Maggie said in her sweet southern belle tone, avoiding the subject at hand. She ran the palm of her hand over the tabletop, feeling every groove and crack. Small tears rolled down her cheekbones, leaving tracks in her blush.

"We're going to get you some help, Mama. I have to tell Mitch now, you know that, right? This could have ended badly today, and you scared the kids to death." Laci's words weren't meant to be harsh, but they cut Maggie deeply, although she knew she was right.

"No, Laci, don't! Not yet, please. It was an accident. I will never do it again, I promise." Maggie begged.

Laci took a deep breath, then exhaled. "Maggie, if something else happens, I will *have* to tell Mitch, do you understand?"

"Yes, dear, I do. But you see that's also why Richard is moving in soon."

"Richard, your boyfriend, is moving in? And he knows about everything?"

"Well, I don't know if boyfriend is really the right term for him. More of a companion and friend, and yes, he knows. He wants to help. He does care about me a great deal, and I him."

Laci sat back in the chair and folded her arms. "Huh. So, let me get this straight. Richard is a sort-of boyfriend, whom Mitch doesn't know about, and he's moving in to help you because you're having memory issues, which Mitch *also* doesn't know about," she sighed. "The secrets are starting to pile up here, Mom. I don't like it."

"I know, dear. I don't blame you. I just need more time, please." Maggie pleaded.

"You keep asking for more time. Time for what?"

"Time to figure out exactly what I'm dealing with here. Then I'll tell all of you together. I promise."

"You have until the end of the month. I can't keep this from him anymore. He will never forgive me." Laci's eyes were sad, wanting to protect her mother-in-law, but in her heart, she knew she was betraying the man she loved. Time was growing short.

They walked outside together, arm in arm. "Let's go kids! Grandma needs her rest." Laci shouted, then gave Maggie a hug goodbye. Once the kids were in the mule, Laci turned to them, "This stays between us for now. Deal?"

"Deal," they replied in unison, then they took off and Laci hopped in her car and followed them home.

* * *

EVAN FINISHED LOADING a crate of grapes into the feeder when he noticed Jenny walking up to the barn. The sight of her nearly took his breath away as he took in her beauty, but in the midst of his daze, he missed the first rung coming down the ladder and fell to the ground, landing with a hard thud.

Jenny saw him fall and screamed out his name as she ran to his side.

"Ev! Evan! Are you okay?" She shouted, now on her knees next to him. He wasn't moving though or breathing that she could tell.

"Mitch!" Jenny screamed. "Help! Evan fell!"

She looked around for Mitch but didn't see him anywhere. Jenny couldn't wait any longer for help. She leaned over Evan's head and began giving him mouth-to-mouth resuscitation as best she could. A few seconds went by when she heard a rumble coming from Evan's chest. She sat up and watched his face as it came to life. His smile was now ear-to-ear and he began to laugh.

Mitch ran up behind them, but in all the commotion, they

didn't notice. He saw Evan's smile and decided to stay back and see what transpired.

Jenny's face however, still wet with tears, slowly transformed from fear and concern, to anger and rage, which of course came spilling out. "Evan Kramer! You asshole! How dare you do that to me! I don't cuss, look what you made me do! Ugh!" She stood up and stomped around him, spewing a few more choice words, then finally noticed Mitch standing off in the distance, watching the scene unfold with a smile on his face.

Jenny looked him in the eye. "How long have you been there? Are you going to stand back and do nothing? You think this is funny, don't you?" She continued to rant and pace around, stomping harder with each step. "Ugh, men!" She exclaimed and walked.

"Jenny, wait!" Mitch yelled. Jenny turned around with her hands on her hips. "I'm sorry I laughed." He said, but she didn't reply and kept walking.

Mitch bent down next to Evan, still laying on the ground, but he was no longer laughing.

"Did you really knock the wind out of your sails, son, or were you teasing the poor girl the whole time?" He asked.

"Yes, I was really out of it, Mitch!"

"Okay, okay, don't get all defensive on me," Mitch laughed.

Evan rolled his eyes. "I admit, it only lasted a minute. I thought it might be fun to see how she'd react. Guess I screwed up, huh? Once she started mouth-to-mouth, I couldn't hold back laughing! To be honest, I figured you'd run over and then I'd magically 'wake up'," he said, using air quotes with his fingers at the reference.

"Well, I get wanting to have a little fun with her, but it went too far. You'd better hop up and go make things right," Mitch replied.

"Yeah, I guess you're right." Evan tried to sit up, but immediately he felt a crushing pain inside his chest. "OUCH!" He groaned.

"Ev! What's wrong?" Mitch leaned over and put his hands under Evan's shoulders for support.

"I don't know. I'm not faking, Mitch. It really hurt when I tried to sit up!"

Mitch tried to help him up. "Okay, let's go on three. Ready?"

"Ready."

"One, two, three."

Evan pushed himself up as Mitch lifted, taking as much weight off him as possible.

"UG-H-H-H! It hurts Mitch!"

"Lay back down, Ev. Slowly. I'll call an ambulance." Mitch laughed quietly in the moment.

"I hear you," Evan groaned through his teeth. "This isn't funny anymore."

"Well, it kind of is, seeing as how this was all to impress a girl. Poetic justice."

"I suppose you're right."

Jenny took a few minutes to cool off a little, then made her way back to the office. It was empty, which was a relief, but she no sooner sat down to collect her thoughts when Laci walked in.

"Hi, Jenny," Laci greeted her, but her thoughts were still caught up in the events that had just transpired at Maggie's. "How did you like the grape crusher?" She asked, void of any emotion.

Jenny laughed sarcastically, too wrapped up in her own frustration to notice Laci's state of mind. "Ya know, it might have been kind of cool had your son not fallen off the ladder and faked being unconscious to poke fun at me!" Jenny stood up, still fuming as it replayed in her head. "Or maybe he was hoping

I would give him mouth-to-mouth and try to steal a kiss! Pretty chicken way to go about it, if you ask me."

"What? What are you talking about?" Laci asked.

As Jenny paced the floor, Laci's phone rang. "Mitch? What's this about my son faking a fall?" Laci inquired, exhaustion evident in her voice. About that same time, an ambulance siren blared as it pulled swiftly into the drive. "I hear sirens, Mitch. Why do I hear sirens?" Laci's tone and her blood pressure both now elevated. She stared out the window in shock. *Is this really happening? What else, Lord?*

"I think the crazy kid cracked a few ribs trying to impress your assistant." He chuckled.

"What? I'll be right there!" Laci hung up and grabbed the keys.

"Let's go, Jenny. Loverboy apparently wasn't faking *all* of it." They hopped in the golf cart and drove over to the wine barn. As the EMTs loaded Evan onto the gurney, Jenny ran to his side.

"I'm so sorry, Evan! I thought you were faking!"

"No, Jen, I'm the one who's sorry. I really did fall, but I was having some fun at your expense too, and that was wrong," he breathed in. "UGH!" he moaned in pain.

"Don't talk. Rest." Jenny took his hand.

"It was stupid I know. I only did it to be closer to you."

Jenny laughed. "Well, maybe next time you can ask me out on a date."

Evan laughed too, but his face contorted in pain. "Ooo, ouch. Yeah, I'll try that next time."

Laci and Mitch stood back to give them a moment, then looked at each other and smiled. "I think my boy has a crush," Laci said softly.

"He looks like I feel when I look at you."

"How's that?" She asked, eyebrow raised.

"Hopelessly in love."

She took Mitch's hand. "That's a good look on you," she winked.

As he looked at her in that moment however, Mitch noticed Laci's pale skin-tone and tired eyes. "Speaking of which, you're not looking so good right now, darlin'. You feel okay?" Mitch asked in his sweet, southern tone that Laci loved.

"I'm fine, tired mostly. It's been a long, busy day."

"That settles it then. You are going home to rest. That's a perk of being the owner, ya know? I can order you around." He winked, then kissed her on the cheek and whispered an 'I love you' in her ear.

She replied in kind, but she was worried about her son. "What about Evan?" Laci asked, watching as they loaded him into the ambulance. "You'd better go with him, Mitch. I wouldn't fit in that little wagon anyway, and Jenny can meet you both at the hospital."

"Nothing like a little tragedy to bring a couple closer together, right Mrs. Young?" Mitch stated in jest.

"Nothing indeed. We certainly know all about that don't we, Mr. Young?" She giggled, remembering the challenges she and Mitch encountered before they could finally be together. At times, it seemed impossible that their love would overcome the many obstacles, but standing there together at that moment, looking down at her tummy and anxiously awaiting the arrival of baby Young, she was grateful for each and every one they faced. It was the next challenge that worried her the most, however, and she carried her worries about Maggie back to the house without a word, waiting for the truth to come out.

As for Evan, not much can be done for broken ribs of course, but he soaked up all the attention and care that Jenny could give while he was recovering. And it was thanks to those broken bones that the two of them got a fresh start and began to grow closer. They shared lunches together, did chores around the winery together, and Evan started showing up more and more at the coffee shop during Jenny's breaks and picking her up after work. She began sticking around Evan's house later in the evenings, too, sometimes they walked to the barn and stayed up until the wee hours of the morning talking about all kinds of things. They played cards and watched movies, laughing at all the same parts and truly enjoyed one another's company. Evan was becoming the most important part of Jenny's world and seemed to be everything she had hoped for in a guy. There was only one small problem... he hardly ever showed her any affection or treated her like he even *wanted* her to be his girlfriend. Jenny wasn't sure what to do about it, so she simply stayed quiet and enjoyed being with him when she could, whatever their status.

"WHAT ARE you going to be for Halloween, Jenny?" Her co-worker asked.

"I haven't thought about it much, to be honest. It's still two weeks away. I've never really gotten into Halloween," she replied.

"You and Evan should go as Dorothy and the Scarecrow, seeing as how he still can't find the brains to ask you to be his girlfriend," her co-worker jested.

Jenny managed a half-hearted laugh. "Yeah, that's a good one." But to some degree, her friend was right. *Does he even want me to be his girl?*

Halloween finally came however, and although she and Evan didn't dress up or go to some big party, they planned a night together watching spooky movies and sharing popcorn in Evan's basement apartment. Jenny couldn't wait to spend the evening with him, and in anticipation had her hair fixed earlier that day. It wasn't a fancy date, but Jenny wanted to make a good impression nonetheless. There were times when Evan definitely had his 'dimwit' moments though, as Jenny called them. Those not-so-few, but always classic times when he would find a way to aggravate every nerve in her body without an ounce of effort. Like that night when she arrived at his house. He escorted her down to his room and opened the door. The smelly-sock odor nearly knocked her over, but she didn't care. They were together and that's all that mattered. She took off her hood, anxious for him to notice her hair. *Boy did he ever notice*!

"You do something to your hair?" Evan asked, squinting at her as if the sun were in his eyes.

"Yeah, I had it fixed today." Her face beamed with pride.

"What was wrong with it before? Did you change the color?" He asked with a smirk on his face.

After his genius remark, Jenny shoved his arm and nearly knocked him to the floor. *Silly me for thinking he would know what 'fixed' meant aside from the obvious animal-related term!*

"What'd I say?" Evan asked, surprised by her response.

"Ugh! You can be the most insensitive, bone-headed moron sometimes!" She yelled as she stormed around his room, arms flailing and still talking to herself.

Evan stood there; jaw open and baffled by what had transpired, then watched her walk out of his room. *I guess she didn't get that I was joking. What is it with girls being so sensitive about their hair!?* He said to himself, then watched as Jenny did a one-eighty turn and stomped back downstairs and into his room again, standing directly in front of his face.

"It just so happens that when girls get their hair fixed, it means they probably like it. And even if you don't, it wouldn't have killed you to say something nice!" She yelled.

Evan looked her square in the eye. "I never said I didn't like it, did I?"

Jenny stared at him in silence, sucked in a breath of air about to talk, then exhaled without a word. Her eyes wandered up and around, realizing those exact words never actually left his mouth. "Not exactly, but you certainly implied it."

Evan busted out laughing, unable to hold it in any longer. His laughter infuriated her even more of course. "What are you laughing at?" She asked, fuming mad and on the verge of tears.

He walked over and put his arms around her waist, pulling her close. "I'm laughing at you, your fire and spirit. You're even more beautiful when you're feisty and yelling at me. And for the record, I may not have noticed your new hair-do right away, but I happen to think you're beautiful inside and out, old hair, new hair, I don't care! The minute you walked up to the counter that night at the coffee shop and got all sassy with me, my heart was yours. So, if you don't mind, I'd like you to be my girl and I'd really like to kiss you right now!" He said with a firm voice, smiling.

"Umm," Her mouth dropped open and she tried to reply, but Evan was too fast for her and moved in to steal a long, passionate kiss.

Jenny's head was a little fuzzy when they parted, but once she regained her composure, she opened her eyes and smiled. "Wow. Jeep-man has skills," she giggled. "Does this mean we're official?" She asked, her cheeks glowing a bright shade of pink.

"Well, that depends. Will you officially be my girl?" Evan smiled.

"Yeah, yes! Absolutely! I thought you'd never ask." Jenny giggled.

"I can be a bit dimwitted at times."

Jenny's eyes popped open as if he'd read her mind. "Yes, you certainly can be," she agreed with a smirk. Every nerve in her body was in tune with him as she leaned in for another kiss.

As she enjoyed his embrace in that sweet moment, Jenny realized that even in his most dimwitted moments she was more in love with Evan than she could have ever imagined. *How is it even possible after only a few short months?* She thought.

Three horror flicks and two tubs of buttered popcorn later, the evening had come to an end. Evan walked Jenny to her car and held her close. "You've gotten to me, Coffee Girl. And I'm head over heels for you. I hope you know that."

She leaned her head back into his arm. "Really? I'm so glad! I'm crazy about you too, Evan. I am so happy that I made the decision to stay home instead of leaving for college."

Evan smiled, but then his face went bleak. "Ugh. Speaking of that, we haven't exactly talked about Caleb and how we're going to tell him. Think he'll hate us?" Evan asked, already worried about his stepbrother's pending reaction.

"Look, Ev... Caleb and I were simply better friends than a couple. It was a decision we made together. He wanted to date other girls and we didn't click romantically. No sparks, ya know? He can't really be upset about us."

"That doesn't mean he won't be. I'm trying to prepare for it, that's all."

"Let's not worry about that right now, okay? I'd like to enjoy *us* for a bit if that's ok." She replied.

"Yes, ma'am," Evan replied, and kissed her softly.

JENNY WENT HOME, still on cloud nine from Evan finally admitting his feelings. She flopped down on the bed and stared at the ceiling, grinning from ear to ear when her phone rang, startling her. When she looked at her phone, she'd hoped it was Evan, but that was not the case. Caleb's name flashed across her phone and her heart sank.

"Hey there, Caleb." She answered in her best fake-happy greeting.

"Hi, Jenny! Hey, I know it's late. I'm sorry. Wow it's so good to hear your voice. I'm sorry it's been so long since I've called. I got so busy with studying for finals and getting projects done, I lost track of time. How are you? You sound great!" He replied.

"I'm great actually! I love working with Laci at the winery too. We are planning her big Christmas event for the Breast Cancer Center. I'm learning a lot."

"Yeah, that's her favorite event. That and Christmas itself. Did you get to help her decorate the office?"

"Yes. I've never seen so many tubs of decorations in my life!" She laughed at the thought, then realized how much she used to enjoy Caleb's company. He was always easy to talk to.

"That's Laci alright. If I didn't know any better, I would think she's really a Christmas elf."

Jenny laughed, but Caleb's chit chat was becoming a little forced at that point.

"What's going on, Caleb? Did you call for any certain reason?" Jenny asked, urging him to the point.

"Not really. Missing home and friends, I guess. Are you seeing anyone? Sorry, you don't have to tell me. That was rude. You sound happy. I've really missed you, Jenny."

"I am happy. I love working at the winery with your step-mom. She's kind of amazing and I'm learning so much from her already. Everyone misses you around here too, Caleb. Are you liking school?"

"I am. It's hard work, and I have a job at a local restaurant that I love, but it's a lot of hours. I was hoping to come home and surprise everyone at Thanksgiving but looks like that won't happen now."

Jenny's eyes popped open at his words. *What a mess that would be if he showed up and saw Evan and me at the dinner table together.* She thought to herself, then sighed in relief that his plans wouldn't go through. "Well, I know it's hard being away, but you're doing what you love and one day you'll look back and be grateful you made this choice to go after your dream."

"I'm not so sure every choice I've made is working out so well, like breaking things off with you. I'm not so sure that was the right thing to do. Would you ever give me another chance, Jenny?"

Jenny froze in shock, unable to reply to his question. She certainly wasn't prepared to tell her ex-boyfriend that she was falling in love with his stepbrother yet! *What do I do now?* She thought. *Keep your cool, Jenny.* She talked herself off the ledge and took a breath.

"Caleb, you're so sweet. I miss you too, but I think you're homesick. You and I both know that we weren't a good fit, and you needed to focus on your future. Crystal Creek is my future, I'll never go anywhere and do big things like you will. You'll meet a wonderful girl someday that loves trying new, exotic food as much as you do," she laughed, remembering all the gross foods he used to make her taste. "As for me, I took a break from dating altogether actually. I have some good friends, but for now that's all I want." She bit her lip after the lie oozed off her tongue.

Caleb sighed quietly. "Well, maybe you're right. It's hard being away on the holidays. I do miss you though. I hope that dork of a stepbrother hasn't given you too much grief while you have been working there," he joked.

She smiled. "Evan? Gosh no! Honestly, we hardly ever see each other," Jenny replied, hoping her lie sounded somewhat convincing.

"Good. I figured he'd have his paws all over you the day after I left."

Jenny spilled out a half-hearted laugh, rolling her eyes as they talked. "Well, I hate to cut this short, Caleb but I'm really tired. It was nice talking to you though. Will you be here over Christmas break?"

"That's the plan, I really want to be there when the baby is born. Hard to believe I'm going to have a little brother or sister."

"Well, Laci and the baby are doing really well. I'm sure your dad keeps you updated though. Good luck with finals." They wrapped up with a goodbye and hung up.

Her rant ensued. *"Ugh! What is going on here, Lord? Are you having fun torturing me from up there? What was he thinking, calling me so late? And why now? Why would he think breaking up with me was a bad choice? Things are going so well with Evan! How do I break something like that to him? Ugh!"* She kicked her legs up and down, slamming them against her bed throwing a mini-hissy fit. *"I am so grateful he won't be home at Thanksgiving. That would have been a disaster! At least we have a little more time to figure out how to tell him before Christmas."*

Jenny's melodramatic outburst was probably a little much, but warranted. Her initial thought was to tell Evan that Caleb called, but it was after midnight. Besides, things were still new between them and finally moving in a good direction. *If I tell him about Caleb, it could ruin everything!* She thought, and decided to keep it to herself. Her little secret.

CHAPTER 6

Time seemed to pass faster during the holiday season. With November nearly half over, Laci was feeling the pressure of her big event later that week, plus Thanksgiving dinner looming the following week. She held tight to the hot cup of coffee to warm her hands as she reviewed the day's tasks on paper from top to bottom before Jenny arrived. Those early mornings were her favorite time to soak in all of God's blessings and listen to His words. Laci's faith had only grown stronger through all the trials that she and Mitch had faced in the past, and the one that lay ahead would be no different. Maggie's episodes were growing worse, not better, and Laci felt a deep sense of sadness when she thought about her condition. She needed to tell Mitch the truth once and for all, but struggled with the promise she had made to Maggie. Still, it was getting harder and harder to hold it in. She resolved to wait until the timing was right and went back to her thoughts for the day ahead.

That morning was especially chilly outside, nearing frost temperatures as the November rain fell softly on the ground.

Laci never wavered in her belief that good things always followed the rain, they really did, and of course her love of the rain translated to falling snow in the winter. It had been years since she had seen a white Christmas and had requested one many times in her conversations with God. She was hopeful this would be the year, and honestly needed it more now than ever, with everything going on. Soon the arrival of their little one would be a reality. *What a sweet gift it would be to see snow this Christmas with you being born, huh little guy?* She said to herself and her baby belly, still unable to focus on work. It seemed almost foolish, but after Hannah saw Laci holding a baby boy in her dream that past summer, Laci believed it would become a reality. It sounded even crazier as she thought about it again, but didn't care and clung to that hope more than ever.

A long week of prep for the Christmas tree auction event was in store, but she was confident it would be a success. Having Jenny by her side had been a tremendous help. Unfortunately, that week was also Laci's birthday, which she tried hard to ignore and pretend like it didn't exist, but Mitch wouldn't allow that to happen. His antics had already begun.

"Laci, are you in your office?" Mitch yelled from the tasting room across the hall.

Laci looked up from her desk and laughed. "Yes, Mitch. I'm enjoying a quiet moment with my coffee!" She replied. "What do you want?"

"Come here! I have something for you!"

Ugh. If he only knew how hard it was for me to get this whale of a tail up out of my chair, he wouldn't be asking me to come to him! She scooted up close to her desk and placed her hands firmly on each side, pushing herself up slowly out of her chair, then waddled to the tasting room.

It was dark inside as she approached the door.

"Where are you, Mitch?" She peeked inside and looked around.

Suddenly, the lights flipped on and Mitch, Evan, Jenny, and the kids stood around a big slice of Key lime cheesecake covered with little white candles. Laci screamed, and Emma immediately pulled out a can of silly string and commenced to spraying it in the air, the streams of sticky red twizzles naturally fell in her hair.

"You guys scared me to death!" Laci squealed, smiling from ear to ear and overjoyed at the display. "My favorite breakfast food—cheesecake!" She walked over and scooped a big bite off with her finger, like it was icing on a cake.

"That's only a small part. Here is your real gift," Mitch replied, then they all scooted apart, revealing a shiny new espresso machine sitting on the bar behind them. It was the 'La Pavoni' Italian espresso machine, the *crème de la crème* of machines; the one she had dreamt about ever since tasting that first cup of espresso in Italy on their honeymoon.

Laci gasped for air and her hands flew up to cover her mouth in shock at the sight of it sitting in front of her. To no one's surprise, the tears started to flow, and she walked over to Mitch, pulling him into her arms. "Thank you! You're amazing, you know that?! Where on earth did you find this?" She squealed, then continued to hug everyone else around her.

Her love of coffee was a close second to Mitch and her kids, and she wasn't ashamed. She ran her hands over the shiny, red machine, admiring it as if a rare gem unearthed for the first time, her mouth hanging open in amazement. She also knew the price tag of that machine, and quickly proceeded to give Mitch a piece of her mind as the reality of it set in.

"Mitch Young! What on earth possessed you to do this? We can't afford this! We have a baby coming, and he needs diapers and a new tricycle, and tuition to Harvard! What do you want me to do with this? It won't even fit in our kitchen, and we certainly can't remodel," she continued to ramble.

Meanwhile, Mitch slowly walked over to her, then reached up and gently set one finger on top of her lips. "Ssshhhh. Stop talking and stop worrying. Enjoy it, Lace. I know it's a few days early, but you'll be so busy this week. I wanted to give it to you now. Happy Birthday, darlin'," he whispered, then leaned down and kissed her tenderly. His warm lips made her weak in the knees and in that moment, she melted in his arms.

"I'm sorry," she replied. "I love it. I truly love it. You know I do! But where are we going to put it, Mitch?"

"It's not for the house," he replied.

"What do you mean?"

"I thought you might be able to turn part of the wine-bar into a coffee bar. I know you've always wanted that and figured this would help get you started." Mitch's eyes smiled as he told her, excited to help her dream come true.

"I don't deserve you. How on earth did I get so lucky?" She cried, holding him tight and taking in the moment.

"Get a room, you two!" Evan shouted, laughing.

"Oh whatever. Get to work, all of you! But thank you so much. I love you guys!" Laci replied, overjoyed by her surprise.

After everyone had their fill of cheesecake, they all went their separate ways. Todd took the kids to school and Jenny and Evan headed toward the warehouse to stock bottles.

"Wow, look at that! We're all alone, Mrs. Young," Mitch said in a playful deep, sexy voice. He pulled Laci into his arms and danced back and forth with her, silent music playing around them.

"Look at them, Mitch," Laci said, watching Jenny and Evan walk away, hand in hand.

"I'm kind of busy looking at you." He winked.

"Stop it, babe," she giggled. "I'm serious. Look at them! What do you see?"

"I see a couple in love," he replied, then took his hand and turned her head toward him so their eyes met. "I also see a stunningly beautiful woman in front of me that still makes my heart flip over inside my chest. Not too many men are as lucky as I am, ya know." He pulled the silly string off her hair and tossed it to the floor.

Laci blushed, then took his face in her hands and lifted herself up on her tiptoes, kissing his soft, warm lips. She could taste the salt of her tears as they trickled down between them.

"You okay?" He asked.

"I'm better than okay, love. I never want you to leave me. Please don't ever leave me, Mitch!" She cried harder, suddenly scared by the random thought of losing him someday.

"Where did that come from? I'll never leave you! Never!" He hugged her tight, not wanting to let go although they both knew work was waiting. "Although... work awaits," he added.

She sniffed, wiping her face with her sleeve. "I know. Thank you, Mitch. For everything."

"You're welcome, babe. You deserve all of it and more. I love you!"

"I love you, my Creepy Stalker Crawdad-Fan." She smiled.

"I love you, too! Way to pull out the oldie but 'goodie'. You haven't called me that in a long time!" He laughed.

"Seemed like the perfect time. You are kind of creepy with all those silly strings in your hair."

"Yeah," he laughed. "Guess I'd better get cleaned up and get to work."

"And I should get what's left of this cheesecake to my office for safe keeping," she laughed.

"That's the only reason you love me, isn't it? The cheesecake," Mitch joked.

"That, and the espresso machine. I'm a new woman now!"

"Women and their machines," he replied with a wink.

Laci rolled her eyes and slapped him on the arm playfully. "Have you heard from Caleb this week?"

"Yeah, I called him last night after we finished filling bottles. He's doing great, seemed a little hyper even. They are running their own mock-restaurant and he's top of his class so far."

"That's great, Mitch! Do you think he'll come home for Thanksgiving?" She asked.

"No, I asked him about it. He said he had to work and couldn't get out of it. He will be here for Christmas though."

"Awww, that's too bad. I get it though. It's a busy time for restaurants. Well, Christmas will be here before we know it, starting with this event! We are packing everything at lunch so bring Evan with you. Now I need to get to work. Shoo!" She smiled.

"Going, going! Bye love. See you at lunch!" He blew her a kiss and went on his way.

OVER THE NEXT couple of days, after they relocated all the supplies to the Red Lion Hotel, she and Jenny went into full event mode. Jenny was amazing, and it was nice to see Evan pop in to see her, sneaking kisses behind the trees. *Life is good, little one. It's my favorite event, favorite time of year, and I'm sharing it with everyone I love. Nothing could spoil this week!* She said to herself, a big smile spread over her face, giddy and unable to contain her enthusiasm.

* * *

MAGGIE and her Ladies Auxiliary friends took turns sharing stories and laughing together around the dinner table at Max's

Place, their favorite restaurant in town. Maggie yawned, suddenly quite tired, and decided to leave a little early.

"Hey ladies, I think I'm going to head home if you don't mind." She stated.

"You feel okay, Margaret?" Gladys asked, one of her dear friends.

"I'm starting to feel my age, I guess. Kind of tired tonight."

"Well, be careful driving home," Gladys replied.

"I will. I'm so sorry about my blunder earlier tonight."

"It's okay! It happens to the best of us, Mags!" Another friend replied.

Maggie stood up from the table, grabbed her purse and started to walk away, but stopped and turned around. "By the way Janet, please tell Leo I said hello, okay?" And she walked away.

Gladys and the ladies all looked at one another with a puzzled look on their faces, bewildered by her comment. "Gladys, Janet hasn't been at this table in over ten years. And who is Leo?" One of the ladies asked the group.

"Leo was Janet's first husband, over twenty years ago." Gladys replied. Most of the ladies wouldn't have known that, except for her and Maggie since they were in the original group. At that point, Gladys was now quite worried about Maggie's state of mind.

"I'm sure she was just tired and a little confused. It happens more and more at our age, unfortunately." Helen added, then changed the topic.

The ladies continued to banter on about this and that after Maggie left, enjoying their dessert, but after a while Gladys couldn't ignore the gnawing feeling in the pit of her stomach that something wasn't right.

"I'm going to step outside and make sure Maggie made it to her car, ladies. I'll be right back." Gladys announced. Once outside, she looked down both streets to ensure Maggie had left. As she feared however, she spotted Maggie's car parked on the adjacent street. She walked over to the car and put her hand on the hood. Cold. She had never made it to the car, and Maggie was nowhere in sight.

"Maggie!" Gladys shouted. She turned the other direction. "Maggie, where are you?" She shouted again. Only silence replied.

Gladys pulled out her phone and dialed Laci's number.

* * *

LACI'S EVENT was a huge success, raising nearly $300,000 for the Breast Cancer Center, which would provide free mammograms for women who couldn't afford them. After her own experience, she had committed herself to becoming an advocate for this cause as it helps women get diagnosed sooner, and what was accomplished at her event would probably save hundreds of lives. Laci was overwhelmed to be a part of it, and now exhausted from the planning of it. She and Jenny were finally able to sit down as the guests continued to dance and enjoy the end of the evening.

"Well, we did it, girl! You were fabulous tonight. Every guest and vendor was happy, and every single detail went off without a hitch!" Laci exclaimed in joy.

"Thank you so much! I had so much fun, Laci. It was amazing. I recall one little hitch though; when that sugarplum tree almost fell over on Dr. Keip," she giggled.

"Yes, I almost forgot!" Laci laughed out loud. "I don't think he realized the ornaments were wired on the branches, but he wasn't about to leave without checking to see if that angel was an authentic WWII-era ornament, by golly."

Laci threw her head back in laughter as she remembered the

scene but was interrupted by her phone buzzing. She didn't recognize the number, and thought about ignoring it, but something inside told her to answer.

"Hello, this is Laci."

"Hi Laci, this is Gladys, your mother-in-law's friend from the Auxiliary." Gladys' voice was shaky.

"Hi, Gladys. How are you?"

"Well, I'm not sure yet. Is Margaret with you?"

Laci had to think a second about who Margaret was, not used to hearing her full name, then it dawned on her. "Oh, Maggie? No, she's not here. Why?"

"Her car is still here at Max's but she's nowhere to be found. She left over thirty minutes ago. She said she was tired and wanted to get home early."

Laci stood up as chills ran down her spine, panic now evident on her face. Mitch was next to her and looked up to see her face transform and knew immediately that something was wrong. He sat up on the edge of his seat, waiting.

"Gladys, please stay there. Mitch is right next to me and we'll meet you there. Have you called her cell yet?"

"No. After I saw her car, I called you. " Gladys sniffed. "Laci, you may not know this," she stammered, "but her memory isn't quite..." her voice trailed off.

Laci sighed. "I know, Gladys. It's getting worse. We'll find her, okay? Don't worry."

"It's getting cold. Please hurry." Gladys pleaded, and hung up.

Mitch stood up and turned to Laci, worried and anxiously awaiting the news. "Lace, what's wrong'? What is it?" He asked.

"It's your mom, Mitch. She's missing. We need to go. I'll explain everything on the way."

The color drained from Mitch's face. "What do you mean? Missing? Where was she?" He asked, then grabbed his keys and jacket.

Laci grabbed his hand and squeezed it tight, nearing tears but held it in. "We need to go. I'll explain everything on the way," Laci repeated, and took him by the hand as they hurried out to the car.

EVAN AND JENNY had overheard the conversation, unable to figure out what was going on.

"Mom, what can we do? Is she okay?" Evan asked.

"Sweetie, Maggie is missing. I don't know much yet, but I'm sure everything is fine. Could you and Jenny get things wrapped up here and pack everything in my car? Here are the keys." Laci's hand shook as she handed over the keys.

"Of course. I'll get Jenny home then come help search for her." Evan replied.

Jenny's heart sank hearing the news. "Laci, how can I help?"

"Thank you, sweetie. You're helping me just by getting things done here. You've worked so hard today, and I couldn't have done it without you. Go home, rest and pray we can find her." Laci hugged her neck. "Evan, we'll call you as soon as we know more. Love you."

Laci and Mitch quickly left the hotel and within minutes were on their way to Max's restaurant. It was the ladies' favorite place to have their monthly dinner.

Mitch's mind drifted as he drove, unable to focus. "Lace, please tell me what's going on. What are you not telling me, and don't say 'nothing'." He pleaded in a soft, low tone.

For the next several minutes, Laci explained everything that had transpired in the last few months with his mom, starting with her forgetting her meds that day at the house, up through the blanket incident.

"I don't understand why you didn't tell me earlier, Laci.

That's not like you. You never keep things from me!" Mitch's voice level rose, wrought with frustration.

Laci broke down, unable to hold it in any longer, knowing that she had been wrong to keep all of it from him. Her hands shook as she talked, then Mitch reached over and squeezed them tight to calm her down.

"She begged me, Mitch. We had finally reached this wonderful point in our relationship; she was confiding in me. She trusted me, and I couldn't break her trust! It meant too much to me. She asked me to wait and let her tell you herself, and I waited. But I also didn't—" her voice broke. "I didn't realize it was this bad."

"We'll find her, darlin', and get her the help she needs. I promise."

Ever since they met, Mitch always had a way of reassuring her that everything would be alright, even in the worst of circumstances. "I know," she tried to smile. "There's one more thing," she added.

"Good grief! What else could there be?" He asked, shaking his head back and forth. Laci could tell his compassion was wearing thin.

"Your mom sort of has a boyfriend. A guy named Richard. Do you know him? I guess they are getting somewhat serious." Laci's head hung low.

Mitch busted out laughing, which was not the reaction she was expecting given the tense moment at hand. "Richard Westmore?" He continued to laugh. "They have been friends for years! He was my parents' attorney. Surely you're joking."

"I'm not. They go to dinner regularly, and I think they're even having sleepovers. She even asked me for advice on what to wear on their first date."

"Was that what you two were giggling about that day she was over for lunch?" He recalled.

"Yes, it was! That was the day that everything turned around for us. She was as giddy as a schoolgirl getting ready for that date, you should have seen her." Laci smiled.

"That's better."

"What?"

"Your smile. I love your smile, darlin', and I needed to see it. Listen, I want my mom to be happy, trust me. I'm not sure Richard is the answer, but if she's happy then I'll have to get used to it. I'm not sure I like it, but let's concentrate on finding her right now and go from there."

Laci nodded in reply.

THEY PULLED into Max's parking lot and saw Gladys, the other ladies and about ten men standing outside the restaurant. The temperature had dropped faster than expected, and as they walked past Maggie's car, Laci noticed it was already covered with frost. Gladys ran over to Laci and took her by the hand.

"I knew you could draw in the men, Gladys, but where did you find all of them?" Laci smiled, trying to lighten the moment.

Gladys winked. "I simply made a few calls to some of my buddies with the Rotary Club and they were more than happy to help search. Richard is here too. He looks a little upset though. You might go talk to him."

"Thanks, Gladys. You're amazing and having all these extra eyes to search is wonderful! I'll go talk to Rich." She replied, then headed outside.

Richard stood under the old black light post in front of the restaurant, a worried look on his face. Laci couldn't help noticing how handsome he was in his jeans and a zip-up sweat-shirt. He had a large, firm build, aside from a little pooch in the middle; a neatly trimmed salt and pepper mustache and beard, and his eyes sparkled a bright blue in the light shining down. It was easy to see how Maggie would be attracted to him, but she got the feeling there was a lot more to Richard on the inside from hearing Maggie talk. He smiled at Laci as she walked up, and somehow in that simple act he conveyed a sense of hope.

"How are you holding up, Rich?" She asked.

"Aww, I'm good Miss Laci, don't you worry about me. We need to find this little gal of mine, I know that for sure." Rich's voice was deep but had a Santa-like jolliness to his tone. It made Laci smile.

"We will, Rich. I knew you were someone special when she showed up at my house a few months ago, all excited about your first *official* date, and worried about what she was going to wear," she said, a quiet laughter rose in her throat.

"That lady can light up a Texas stadium with her smile, ya know? I think I was as nervous as a cat in a room full of rocking chairs that night myself. Didn't want to disappoint her, that's for sure."

"Well you didn't. She called me later that night and was on cloud ten. I could tell then that she was over the moon for you," Laci paused as she collected herself, saddened by the memory. "I have to ask though, did you or do you know that..." she began, but was unable to finish her sentence for the tears.

Rich patted Laci on the back to give her some sense of comfort. "I knew all along, Miss Laci. She and I have been friends for many, many years. She suspected it some time ago, and when we started seeing each other for lunches and movies as friends, she confided in me. I already had my suspicions. She was starting to forget details of where or when to meet me. When I'd correct her, she became frustrated and angry with herself. I didn't mind though, mainly because I have loved that woman for quite some time, although I never let it be known until recently. I'm not sure why I wasted so much time living life without her," he shook his head in disbelief. "Anyway, when she finally shared it with me, I immediately asked if she wanted to move in with me so I could help take care of her when things start to get bad. She refused of course, stubborn woman," Rich chuckled softly. "She finally agreed to let me sleep over though, and now we take turns at each other's house. I was out of town on business this weekend and just got back. I knew she had dinner plans with the ladies, so I wasn't too worried when she wasn't home. That group always goes long, but for some reason I didn't have a good feeling inside tonight. I'm so grateful Gladys called me." Rich's raw honesty touched Laci's heart. It was the first time they had ever met, yet he seemed like someone she'd known for years.

"I'm so glad she has you in her life, Rich. We're going to find her, and I expect to see both of you at my Thanksgiving table next week, you hear me?" Laci added, then hugged his neck.

"Yes, Ma'am, we'll be there." Rich replied.

Laci took Richard over to Evan and introduced him as Maggie's friend, leaving out the mushy details for now, and suggested he join Evan's search party.

Mitch whistled to get everyone's attention and gathered them around the restaurant entrance. Even Max himself was outside, ready and willing to search.

"Well folks, thank you for coming. My mama seems to be having some memory loss and she's gone missing. I'm sorry to get you all out in the cold, but she's walking around out there, and we don't have much time. Temperatures are dropping fast. Laci and I will keep trying to call her cell phone, but in the meantime please call me or Laci the minute you see her or find anything that might help us locate where she might have gone. She has lived in this town all her life, so she could literally be anywhere. You'll need to drive around a bit, but you may need to get out and yell her name along the side roads," he paused and inhaled deeply. "One last thing. I can't thank you all enough for helping us tonight. Please be careful out there." Mitch was being strong for everyone, but his face couldn't hide the fear. The search teams broke up into groups of two and three per vehicle and each one drove off in a different direction to search.

Mitch walked around to open Laci's car door, kissing her softly before helping her inside.

"Gladys is going to stay here with a few other ladies in case she comes back here okay?" Laci said. The smoky white puff of her breath now visible, making the cold temperature even more obvious.

"That's great, Lace."

Mitch got in the car and they were off. "Max even agreed to keep doors open and the food hot for us. We're going to find her, Mitch." She reached over and took his hand.

Ten minutes.

Twenty.

Thirty.

No calls from the search teams, and still no sign of Maggie anywhere. It was like she had vanished into thin air.

* * *

MAGGIE SHIVERED. Her legs ached and she felt as heavy as though sandbags were being dragged behind her as she walked down the dirt road, dazed and unaware of her surroundings. Then, as if woken from a deep sleep, she suddenly stopped, blinked several times, and started searching around for something familiar. There was only darkness in every direction though. Panic stricken, she fumbled in her purse and pulled out her cell phone, nearly drained of battery power.

"Twenty missed calls. Dear Lord." She looked up into the night sky. "Where am I?" She asked out loud, then dialed Mitch's number with her cold, nearly numb finger.

* * *

MITCH'S PHONE lit up as it rang, the word 'Mama' displayed in bold on the screen. He scrambled to answer, pulling the car over to stop. "Mama? Thank God! Mama, where are you?" he shouted in the phone.

Maggie's breathing was heavy and labored. She stammered and had a difficult time getting her words together. "I, umm... it's dark and well, I'm not sure!" She exclaimed, clearly frustrated.

"Mom, are you hurt?"

"I don't recognize where I'm at! I'm so scared!" Maggie's voice shook.

"What do you see? Anything, a street sign, a statue, buildings, anything?" Mitch's heart raced. "Mom? Are you there?" Mitch shouted.

"Yes, dear. But I don't see any of those things," she paused and Mitch heard her soft crying on the other end.

"Mom, it's going to be okay. Tell me where you are!" Mitch was growing more frustrated by the minute.

Laci reached out her hand and whispered. "Let me talk to her."

She took the phone. "Mom? This is Laci. I need you to help us, okay?" Laci's soft, sweet voice seemed to calm Maggie somewhat.

"Please don't be made at me, Laci! I'm so sorry." Maggie cried softly.

"We're not mad, Mama, we just need to find you, okay? Talk to me and tell me what you see."

Maggie stopped and turned slowly, taking in her surroundings. The road was damp. To her right, trees. To her left, trees. Her heartbeat sped up as she peered down the dirt path in front of her. No cars. No lights. Only a thick shroud of darkness surrounded her. Her breathing sped up in her nervous state. "Laci, I can't tell where I am. It's nothing but trees." Her voice quivered. "Nothing is out here! My car is nowhere around, I honestly don't know how I got here."

"Okay, Mom, stay calm. Don't move, find a spot to sit by the road if you can and tell me the last thing you remember from tonight." Laci asked her simple, easy to answer questions as not to overwhelm her anymore.

Maggie sat down and curled her knees up around her, then closed her eyes. "Gladys and I had dinner with the ladies, we were laughing about our hairstyles over the years," she mumbled.

"Yes, Gladys said you all had a good time. That's great! What else?"

"We were at Max's place. He made cannoli's for us."

Laci smiled. "You're doing great, Mom. Keep going!"

"They wanted to stay longer, but I was tired, so I left early. So tired..." Her voice began to fade.

"Mom, stay with me! You left early. Then what?"

"It's cold, Laci." Maggie whispered.

"I know, Mama. Hold on! You didn't take your car. It's still at Max's. Did you walk down a street?" Laci asked, trying her best to get a clue to where she was.

"I walked home. I wanted to go home."

"Are you on a road?"

Maggie looked down. "I was, but not anymore. I turned down the path next to the gas station."

"That's great, Mom! What gas station?" Laci smiled, overjoyed that they now had some idea of the direction she headed.

"It was so dirty, though. Daddy needs to get over there and clean that place up." Maggie added without hesitation. In her mind, a memory had sparked; not of today, but a yesterday long ago.

Mitch watched as the smile on Laci's face dissipated. "What's wrong?"

"Hold on a minute, Mom." Laci pulled the phone away and covered it with her hand to muffle her voice. "She said that the gas station was dirty, and that *Daddy* needs to get over there and clean it up." Tears rolled down Laci's cheek at the realization of how much Maggie's state of mind had worsened.

"That's it!" Mitch said with energy.

"What?"

"She's not heading home, to her house now, she's headed to her *first* home with my dad. It sits way back off Vermont Road in the country. He built it for her with his bare hands. She even helped him occasionally. She'd always said those years out there in the country were some of the happiest years they had together, before my brother and I were born." Mitch recalled.

Laci uncovered the phone. "Mom, we are getting closer. Can you find the side of the road by the station and watch for us?" She asked.

But there was no reply. "Mom, are you there? Mom!" Laci yelled.

"Hurry, Mitch! She's not answering me!"

"Give me the phone and I'll keep trying her back. You call everyone and let them know to meet us at the old Hickory Hill church out past the old filling station. She can't be far from there."

Laci made all the calls, then watched out her window as they drove past the gas station, complete with the old, tall gas pumps with round signs on top of each one that used to identify the brand of gas. The windows were broken, and every other board had a hole in it. The old awning now hung down, dangling from one big nail, and the rust-covered Coca-Cola signs were still fastened on tight to the one wall that still stood intact. Laci imagined it was a bustling place at one time, young men pumping gas for young ladies, innocently flirting as they worked, and old men standing around talking about their crops or the weather, or how much work they all had to do at home. Women probably sat on benches out front, gossiping about their neighbor's laundry still on the line or comparing their peach cobbler recipes. A simpler time in many ways. *I'm sure that time holds great meaning for Maggie, and longs to be back there with her husband, which is why her mind took her there so easily. It's her home.*

Mitch pulled into the gravel lot at the church and kept trying to call Maggie's phone. It went straight to voicemail. *Where are you, Mama?* He said to himself.

"Still no answer?" Laci asked, and reach out to hold his hand.

"Nothing. I think it's dead."

"She can't be far, Mitch. We'll find her."

"I know."

THE HEADLIGHTS BEAMED COMING up over the hill, and once the small group had arrived, they assembled and made a search plan.

"Hi everyone. Well, we have some good news and some bad news. My mom finally called, and she remembered walking past the old filling station that my dad used to own. She's not exactly in her right mind, I'll warn you. We believe she has Alzheimer's and it's gotten bad here recently. She tried to walk home tonight, but instead she went looking for her very first home about four miles back in those woods. There wasn't much left of the house last time I was there, which was years ago, a few boards and pieces of an old porch, so it won't be easy to find. It's dark and cold, and she could be anywhere. I still have a vague recollection of where it should be, but let's group up and stay about five feet apart as we walk toward the house in case she veered off the route. Keep your cell phones on and call me if you see her. Her cell is dead, so we have no way to reach her. The church is unlocked, and Gladys and Laci will be inside warming things up."

Mitch led the group out to the edge of the woods, and they flanked off in their teams as he'd instructed. Laci and Gladys opened the church and turned up the heat, then started a pot of coffee.

"How long have you all known about Maggie's condition?" Laci asked.

"Not long really, and honestly we didn't realize it had gotten so bad. It's been such a gradual thing, but last week at our bridge club, she walked into the kitchen to fill a plate and then asked all of us why we brought *leftovers* instead of full dishes. She had no recollection that we had already eaten dinner an hour earlier. We kind of laughed it off of course, thinking she was being funny, but we soon discovered there was nothing funny going on at all." Gladys replied.

"I've known for some time but kept it quiet at her request. I didn't even tell my husband, her own son! I'm sure he's furious at me for keeping it from him. What kind of daughter-in-law am I, Gladys? How could I keep that a secret?" Laci added, her tone laced with regret.

"Maggie can be extremely persuasive my dear, don't beat yourself up. You were protecting her in your own way and honoring her wishes."

"They have to find her. I'll never forgi—" Laci squealed and grabbed her stomach. "Ahhhh!" She yelled, bending over.

"Laci! Oh, my heavens! Are you in labor? Darlin' please tell me you're *not* in labor!" Gladys yelled in a panic.

Laci tried to calm herself by doing breathing exercises, short breaths in and out, slowly exhaling each time. "No, I'm okay. Stress can trigger contractions sometimes." She continued to breathe slowly.

"Lay down on one of the old pews, sweetie. You need to rest." Gladys looked around for something soft to put under her head but found nothing. "Good grief. If we were in a good Catholic church, I'd get you a kneeling pillow, but these Baptists have absolutely nothing, doll. I'm sorry." Gladys added in her sassy, southern tone.

Laci laughed. "I bet they have a fridge full of good food though," she joked. "It's okay. I'll be fine. I have five weeks to go and he's *not* coming out if I have anything to say about it!"

Calm down little guy. If you can, I can. Deal? She said to herself inwardly.

CHAPTER 7

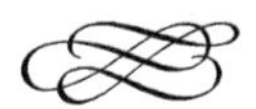

Several minutes into the search for the old house, there was still no sign of Maggie and the temperature was steadily dropping. Mitch and his team had been walking in the direction of Mama's old house but had no idea if anything recognizable would still be visible, especially in the black of night.

Mitch's phone rang. "You find her, Evan?" He asked, hoping for good news.

"Not yet, sorry. We found her cell phone though, which means she can't be far, Mitch."

"Okay, we'll head toward you. Shine your lights when you hear me okay?" He asked, then turned and walked toward Evan's path yelling Maggie's name the entire way. The fog settled over the grass like a quilt of smoke, swirling around with every footstep.

"Mitch, over here!" Evan yelled as he saw lights from the Mitch's search party.

Mitch looked to his left and saw flashlights bouncing around, so he picked up the pace as he walked to Evan's group.

"Any sign of her yet?" Mitch asked, out of breath.

"Nothing yet. Sorry," Evan replied. "Here is her phone. We found it over by that big stump." Evan shined his light on it.

Mitch walked toward the wide tree stump. It stood about waist-high, taller than most, and noticed some markings on the side as he got closer. He squatted down on his knees to get a better look, and it was clear that Maggie had stopped there for a reason. He brushed away some moss to see the initials MA followed by a 'plus' symbol, then the initials JY, and the date. John Young and Maggie Anderson, carved in the side of the tree over fifty years ago, the day before they got married. Mitch took a deep breath, then stood up and called his mom's name as loud as he could. The group spaced out a bit and kept pushing forward as Mitch led them deeper into the woods. They had probably walked another fifty feet when he stopped in his tracks.

"What is it Mitch?" A fellow searcher whispered.

"Everyone stop and be very quiet please," he shouted.

They immediately stopped and silence followed, but only for a second. He heard it again a short distance ahead; a soft whimper. *It's her I know it!* Mitch ran toward the sound and the others followed. Her cries grew louder. Finally, Mitch could see her silhouette and ran faster. As he got closer, he tripped and fell over a broken board, once part of a white picket fence. When he looked up, Maggie was crouched down on the ground, clinging to rotten wood post, a remnant of her old house. He stood up and rushed over to her, wrapping her in his arms.

Maggie screamed. "No! Daddy's coming home. Leave me alone! Who are you?"

"It's Mitch, Mama. Your son. Don't you recognize me?"

"Let go of me! My son is a baby, you're a man! Leave me alone or my husband will take care of you when he gets home." She yelled.

Mitch's breathing increased as his heart began to beat faster, somewhat in shock at her state of mind. He wasn't even sure what to do next. He didn't want to scare her or make her worse, but he knew he had to get her out of the cold.

"Mama, I need to get you home. You're safe now," he whispered, a tear escaped the corner of his eye.

Maggie looked up with tears streaming down her cheeks, "Brad? Oh, my sweet, baby boy!" She exclaimed.

"He thought it best not to correct her and simply agreed, but his heart sank in the reality of the moment. "Yeah, Mama. It's Brad."

"Where is Daddy? He should be here by now. Take me to Daddy!" She cried out, then collapsed into Mitch's arms, now completely unresponsive.

He laid his forehead on Maggie's and wept. "He'll be here soon, Mama." He lifted her up and carried her back to where the group was waiting.

"Grams! Is she okay, Mitch?" Evan asked, relieved they had found her.

"She's passed out on me. Can you call your mom and have her send an ambulance to meet us at the church?"

"I'll call right now! Will she be okay, Mitch?"

"Physically yes, but that's about all I can be sure of right now."

As they walked, Maggie mumbled more nonsense, floating in and out of consciousness. Richard rushed up to her. "Maggie!" He exclaimed and took her limp hand. The flashlights cast enough light that he could see her eyes. She looked at him without any response. Mitch knew how hard that must have been for him.

"I'm sorry, Rich," he said.

Richard remained silent, saddened at the severity of Maggie's condition, but well aware this day had been coming for some time. "She heard me. The Maggie we know and love is still in there." He walked the rest of the way by Mitch's side so he could help carry her if needed.

That was the most difficult walk that Mitch had ever taken with his mom, and as the group trudged through the cold woods, his mind raced with 'what if's' and 'what now's'. He'd never seen his strong, sassy mama so fragile and helpless before, clearly unable to manage life on her own now. *It's time to call Brad,* he thought.

The church was now in sight and the ambulance was waiting out front. Laci and Gladys stood on the steps keeping watch then Laci saw them and exclaimed. "Mitch!" She ran to his side; Maggie was laying in his strong arms like a little child with her head resting on his shoulder.

"Hey, darlin'," he replied.

Maggie's eyes were glassy, moving back and forth but never focused on any one thing. The EMT rushed up and took her from Mitch's arms. "She's in shock," he yelled to his partner. He laid her on the gurney and checked her vitals. "Breathing is shallow, heart rate is seventy-five and dropping. She's not shivering. Hypothermia is setting in. Let's get her inside!" He shouted to his partner as he strapped her in, then they quickly pushed her into the back of the ambulance. "Will you be riding along, sir or following behind us?" He asked.

"My wife and I will follow behind if that's alright," he replied.

"Okay. We'll take good care of her. See you there."

"Thanks guys."

Gladys walked over to them and put her arm around Mitch. "She's tougher than she looks, Mitch. Don't forget that. She's going to be okay." She smiled, offering encouragement as best she could. "And you'd better get this little lady checked out as well. She may not tell you, but I will. She had some false labor pains earlier while we were waiting on y'all." Gladys looked at Laci apologetically.

"Gladys!"

"I'm sorry sweetie, but you need to get that baby checked out. You've been under a lot of stress with all of this and it's taking a toll on you both."

Laci dropped her head in defeat. "I know."

"Thank you for telling me, Gladys. You're right, she is far too stubborn and would have pretended everything was fine." He hugged her in thanks.

The back door of the ambulance closed, and the driver walked around front. "We're headed out, sir." He said.

"Right behind you. Thanks so much!" Mitch replied.

Evan was listening in the background watching everything transpire, then walked over and hugged his mom and Mitch. "Call me as soon as you know something okay, Mom? I'm going to call Jenny and let her know we found her."

"We will, sweetie! The kids are at the church lock-in, don't forget. We'll fill them in tomorrow. You might have to pick them up, but I'll let you know."

"Yeah, whatever you need. Go! I love you!" He replied.

Mitch shared a quick 'thank you' and 'goodbye' to the faithful group of friends and loved ones who helped in the search; most had stayed to make sure she was safe, then they headed for the hospital.

The emergency room was filled to the brim with crying babies, patients waiting to be seen, and family members sleeping as they waited on their loved ones. The smell of bleach and sawdust made Laci nauseous as they waited at the desk. Mitch gave the nurse Maggie's name and she escorted them back to her room.

"They're still checking her out and putting in some IV fluids. The doctor will be in shortly." The nurse commented.

Laci inhaled quickly and grabbed her belly, her other hand in a death grip around Mitch's arm.

"Laci!" He shouted and turned to her.

"They are only Braxton Hicks contractions, I'm fine," she replied through clenched teeth, breathing faster and faster to ease the pain.

"Let's have the doctors make that decision, okay Lace? It's been a stressful night. You and our baby are my whole life, and I need to know you're okay!" Mitch stressed.

"How far along are you, dear?" The nurse asked.

"I'm due on Christmas day," Laci replied.

"Alrighty then, we're definitely going to have you examined, okay?" She helped Laci to a chair. "I'll be right back. You just breath and relax, sweetie." A few minutes later, she returned with another nurse and got Laci into a room.

Laci submitted to their wishes, of course. Mitch was at the end of his rope after seeing his mom go through all she had that night, and she knew it would ease his mind knowing the baby was okay. *It will ease mine too. Please let our baby be okay, Lord! Maggie too.* She thought to herself.

"Are they going to be okay?" He asked with concern.

The nurse turned and laid her hand on Mitch's shoulder gently. "We're going to get your wife and the baby both checked out thoroughly, Mr. Young. Why don't you stay here with your mom while we get her situated and I'll come back to get you soon. We're going to be in the room right next door," she replied in a sweet, calming tone.

"Yes, ma'am."

Laci looked at him and silently mouthed the words 'It's ok. I love you,' then they walked her through the door and closed it behind them.

Mitch watched from the hall as they disappeared into the room. He stood motionless, and at that moment, became completely overwhelmed by everything going on around him. He dropped his head and took a few deep breaths before walking back into Maggie's room.

"Mr. Young, I presume?" The doctor asked in a thick British accent. He stood about six-foot-tall, sporting a white doctor coat and stethoscope, and smelled of a strong Drakkar-like cologne that nearly knocked Mitch over as he approached him to shake his hand.

"Yes, I'm so sorry I didn't see you come in. My wife is being seen next door so I'm going between the two," he replied in a weary tone. "I'm Maggie's son, and please call me Mitch."

"Nice to meet you, Mitch. I'm Dr. Edwards. You seem a bit gutted with everything you have going on tonight. Why don't you take a seat and give yourself a minute to breathe, then tell me what transpired tonight that brought Maggie and your wife in to see us."

"Gutted would be a very accurate term. Never heard that one before though."

"Sorry, my British slang comes out now and then," he chuckled.

Mitch smiled in reply, then did as he asked, explaining the events of the evening in as much detail as he could.

"You've been through the proverbial wringer tonight indeed. I can't imagine what you're feeling, but let me at least tell you what's going on with your mum, shall I?"

"Yeah, that would be great. How is she?"

"Well, this is what I know so far. She's definitely suffering from shock and some hypothermia from being out in the cold so long, but that's already getting better. Physically she seems fine. Her blood pressure is good, and her heart rate is going back up, which is a good sign. We drew some blood and will run a few tests to make sure everything looks good there. She wasn't really responsive to any of my questions when she first arrived, which is typical for someone in shock, so we gave her a mild sedative to help her sleep, so it will be a little while before she becomes responsive again. You mentioned she spoke as if she was in the past. Has she been having memory issues long? Has anything else like this ever happened before?"

"It has, but I didn't know about it at the time. My wife has noticed her memory slipping a few times over the last few months, but she didn't say anything to me at my mom's request. She's a stubborn woman, much like my wife," Mitch chuckled softly. "She didn't want to worry me I guess and didn't think it was all that serious." Mitch shook his head back and forth still in disbelief of the situation at hand.

"It's too early to tell without running all the proper tests, which we'll do, but it definitely seems she may be suffering from Alzheimer's. Was this her first severe episode?"

"She had another bad one a few weeks ago. Apparently, she accidentally tried to bake a blanket or something, instead of cookies; said she was trying to get the blanket warm. Anyway, she walked outside to water her plants and forgot all about it. My kids found the blanket smoldering in the oven, could have caught the whole house on fire."

"Yes, that's common as the disease progresses, and that helps confirm my suspicions then. She'll need constant attention and care from this point on, I'm afraid. She won't be able to drive or go anywhere alone. I'm going to admit her tonight so I can run some more tests to verify everything, and then we'll meet again tomorrow morning to discuss a plan together, okay? We'll do whatever we can for her, Mitch. I promise. I must tell you though, that this is only the beginning. It can be manageable, but I look for it to worsen in the next few weeks even. I don't want to be all doom and gloom. She'll have good days ahead too, so enjoy every one of them while you can," he said, almost in a way that sounded he knew from personal experience. "Now go check on your beautiful wife and see how she and that little baby are doing. The nurses will keep her comfortable and I'll see you in the morning. They'll let you know when she's being moved up to a room. Until then, try not to worry. It's going to be okay," he added, and gave Mitch a sympathetic pat on the back.

"Thanks, Doc. Guess it's going to be a long night." He forced a half-smile and walked out. He walked over to Laci's room and found her nurse-free, for which he was thankful; finally, alone for once. The baby's heartbeat was coming through a speaker on the baby monitor strapped to her belly, loud and strong. Mitch smiled.

"Mitch, honey, I am fine. Go sit with your mom and don't leave her room, okay? If I need you, I'll have the nurse come get you, silly." Laci smiled and squeezed his hand.

"I have orders from the doc to come check on you, so I'm here on official business." He chuckled. He sat on the edge of her bed and took her hand. "I love you so much darlin'. I'm so scared! I need my two favorite girls to be okay." He leaned forward and hugged her neck, then began to weep softly.

Laci could feel his warm tears fall on her shoulder. "I know babe, I know," she whispered. Her arms wrapped around him tight, trying to comfort him the best she could. His body trembled in her embrace as he let go. She was helpless in that moment, and her tears followed. Mitch had been through so much already, and his mom was always his rock. She was there for him when he lost his first wife to breast cancer, and when he almost lost Laci to the same disease. It hadn't been that long since the miscarriage of his and Laci's first baby. On some level, he had even lost Brad, in a sense, when he moved so far away. Brad was his brother, but also his best friend, and Laci knew it had been hard running the business without him by his side. Now he's about to lose his mom to this ugly, horrible disease!

When is enough, enough, Lord? Haven't we had our share already? She said to herself, having it out with God as was her custom. In that moment though, she heard the words echo in her mind. His reply was one simple phrase. *Have faith.*

She smiled, then pushed Mitch up so she could look him in the eyes. "We're going to get through this, do you hear me? That's what the Young family does, that's what your mom taught you, to be strong and face whatever comes your way head on. God is still in control and He won't let us go through this alone. You hear me?"

Mitch sat up and rested his forehead against hers. "I hear you, darlin'," he replied softly, and cleared his throat. "I guess I'd better get back to Mama."

"Yes, she needs to see a familiar face when she wakes up, and tell her I'll see her soon as they get this baby monitor off me."

"Sounds good. I'll tell her." He blew her a kiss and walked out.

The room was silent for a brief moment after Mitch left, too quiet. Laci's breathing became faster and faster as she began to drown in the thoughts and emotions that flooded her mind. Fearing for Maggie's future, heartbroken for Mitch as he watched his mom suffer, nervous about their baby who was to arrive in a few short weeks, and even anxious about Thanksgiving dinner next week and what that day would bring after all this. *Obviously, I need the itty-bitty-committee to show up and give me some options here, Lord! That's how we get through the crazy times, right?* She thought to herself. It was too much, and her heart raced to keep tempo with her mind, pushing her to tears.

There was a soft knock at her door.

"Come in," she said in a cracked voice.

The door opened and a little old man holding a bible walked through. Laci looked up at the ceiling. *Prayer is your answer for everything! There's no negotiating with you is there? I still like my itty-bitty-committee... just sayin'.* She mumbled in her head.

Her visitor was most likely the hospital chaplain, but Laci didn't think they offered visits to the ER patients unless there were dire circumstances. *Is there something you're not telling me about my fate, because if you're calling me home, I'd appreciate one last steak dinner!*

"Hello Miss. My name is Steve, I'm the pastor at a local Christian church. I like to visit ER patients when I can. Mind if I visit for a bit?"

"Of course, Pastor. I'd appreciate the visit actually." Laci wiped the fresh tear stains from her face.

"I can't help but notice the red eyes and wet cheeks. Is there anything I can do? I'm happy to listen or pray with you if you aren't up for chatting." He patted her hand softly.

"Aww, thank you. I'm a tad stressed I guess." Laci began, then shared the Cliffs Notes version of everything that was going on in her life, fighting back the tears.

He listened patiently, then took her hand and prayed with her. "You have much on your plate, my dear."

"I didn't really notice." She chuckled softly, wiping her eyes.

"Don't lose heart, my dear. You will have more challenges ahead as you walk through this season, but don't ever forget to look up and have faith that God will see you through it. He'll show you what you need to see when the time comes, all you have to do is ask, and believe," he added, and went about his way.

Laci was somewhat puzzled by his comments, knowing he was trying to be an encouragement, but left her wondering all the same. He had no sooner walked out of her room when a sense of great peace fell over her, which is something that had been missing for quite some time. Despite the challenges that lay ahead, she smiled then closed her eyes, finally able to rest.

* * *

A COUPLE of hours had drifted by before Maggie was placed in a room. She was still sound asleep. The doctors conducted a thorough exam on Laci and the baby as well and both were doing fine, but the baby's heartrate was elevated so they admitted her for observation as well. Not a typical practice, but in light of Maggie's condition, the doctors decided to put them in the same room in the hopes it would help ease Maggie's mind when she woke. She even slept all night even in the midst of all the nurses coming in and out to check on them.

Before Mitch realized it, the sun began to peek through the blinds above the couch, which also served as his bed for the night, although sleep had kept its distance as he watched over his girls to make sure all was well. His back couldn't take any more however, so he stood up, splashed some water on his face at the sink, and decided to take a walk to stretch out the kinks while they were both still asleep.

The waiting room was quiet, filled with the aroma of fresh coffee brewing. A hint of a once-strong perfume still lingered in a few places though and reminded him of how his grandmother smelled when he visited her as a child. He thought it funny how certain odors or smells could bring about such strong memories, like the scent of peppermint always made him think about his dad and how he always carried a pocket full of mints, popping them in his mouth all day long. And the smell of this hospital itself, remembering how much he'd hated it when he'd been watching Karen wither away and die from the cancer. His phone rang, and he was thankful for the interruption.

"Hey little brother, how's it going?"

"It's too early to tell," Brad chuckled.

"You're definitely up early."

"I couldn't sleep. How is she? Anything new since last night?"

"No, not yet. She's still sleeping, and I expect the doctor will be by shortly. The sedative really knocked her out. I'll call you as soon as I know more though."

"Sounds good. How is Laci doing? Baby okay?" He asked, obviously not wanting the call to end.

"Both are good, man. The baby's heart rate has gone down so that's great news. I'm glad they kept her overnight to be safe. We need this one to be okay, ya know?" Mitch's throat closed up, and he swallowed to keep his emotions at bay.

"I know, Mitch. And he will be, or she," Brad replied with a chuckle.

"Thanks, Brad. I'd better get back to the room. Once the doc comes in and we figure out the next steps, I'll call you back and we'll make a plan as best we can."

Brad was silent.

"Brad? You there?" Mitch asked, concerned.

He cleared his throat. "Yeah, I'm good. Sorry. This is a lot to take in, that's all. I can't stand being so far away, Mitch."

"I know man, but there is nothing you could do any different if you were here, trust me. She is healthy overall, so that's good. As far as the extent of her Alzheimer's, we will have to take it day by day. The doc's tests will hopefully tell us more."

"Alright. Keep me posted and tell her I love her." Brad's heart was in his throat, trying to hold it together.

"I will, brother. I will. Stay positive, and tell Hannah I said hello. We miss you guys." Mitch added.

"Miss you all too, man. Talk soon."

* * *

EVAN WANDERED into the kitchen and made his coffee, still sporting his PJ pants and favorite old t-shirt, trying to sort through the previous night's search and rescue. He'd hoped it was a dream, but that was not the case. Maggie wasn't his blood relative, but he had grown to care for her in the short time he'd been there and already thought of her as a grandparent in many ways. The hardest part though, was seeing his mom so upset by the whole situation. She had been through so much and was finally in a good place for once. It sucked.

Evan smiled at the doorbell's chime, knowing Jenny was on the other side. He hurried to the door to find a shivering Jenny, in her brown, fuzzy sweater, jean overalls and her favorite snow boots to stay warm.

"Good morning, beautiful," he said, gazing at her with the door wide open. He couldn't help but think how lucky he was to call her his.

"Mornnnningggggg." Her teeth chattering uncontrollably. "You gonna l-l-l-let me inside there, Jeep-boy? It's k-k-k-kind of chilly out here." Her breath visible as she talked.

"Sorry! Yes, get in here! I'll help." Evan chuckled, then scooped her up and carried her inside, wrapped tight in his arms.

She giggled out loud and wrapped her arms around his neck. "Ev! Put me down!" She squealed as he bounced through the front door, her teeth still chattering.

He sat her down but kept her tight inside his arms for added warmth. "This is the best 'good morning' I could have ever asked for," he said with a big grin and leaned down and softly kissed her cold, pink lips. That's when he knew. *She* was the one, his one. The love he felt for Jenny welled up like a volcano inside his chest, desperate to erupt and make it known. In her eyes, he saw everything. She was in every crack and crevice of his future—of their future—and the realization nearly stopped his heart.

Jenny giggled softly.

"What?" He asked, a cute smirk on his face.

"Nothing! That was *quite* a good morning kiss—very unexpected."

"Is that bad?"

"Are you kidding? On the contrary, it was amazing! I can't seem to get enough of your kisses." She smiled.

"Well in that case, there are many more where that came from. We should probably eat first. You hungry?"

"Starving! You cooking?"

"Me? Ha!" He forced a fake belly laugh. "You are the budding Chef. I was thinking you would cook while I sit back and watch TV. Isn't that how it works? The woman cooks while the man watches?" He winked, messing with her.

Jenny reached out and slapped his arm playfully. "Ahh, so you won't be mad if I burn your eggs then, right? Which would be hard for me since I'm a pretty good cook and all. Heck, for that comment, I'll even go the extra mile and spill hot coffee in your lap." She flashed him a big, cheesy grin.

Evan's smile vanished however. "Ev? You okay? I was just messing around, silly. What's wrong?" Little worry lines on her brow.

"No, no, it's all good. I like that you are sassy and dish it back to me. I just can't stop thinking about Grams. Sorry. I know it was bad timing, not sure what came over me honestly."

"I get it, trust me. Don't ever be sorry for what you feel, Ev. We had a long night last night, even longer for you and I know it wasn't easy to see her like that. It's going to be okay, though." She said in a calm, reassuring voice.

"Thank you. I'm so lucky to have you in my life, Jen. I don't ever want to lose you."

She pushed herself backward, moving out of his embrace. "Why would you say that?"

"I don't know. I'm not fancy or rich or sophisticated in any way whatsoever, especially not like Caleb. Guess I worry you'll wake up one day and figure out I'm not who you want, or that you'll want him back."

Jenny took a deep breath. She had been more than a little on edge ever since Caleb had called and asked her for a second chance, probably to the point that Evan sensed something was off. It was hard to keep it from Evan, and she wondered if it was time to simply come clean. *No, Jenny. It's better to keep this to yourself,* she thought. *I told him where we stand, and he was fine with it. Why rock the boat?* Justified in her thoughts, she let it go.

"Ev, I was never truly happy with Caleb or our relationship; not like I am with you. He's a great guy, and we will always be good friends, but I don't want him back! He didn't really treat me like his girlfriend anyway. It was always about Caleb, and what suited him. You are the man I want!" She gently laid the palm of her hand on his cheek, then leaned up to seal her words with a kiss.

Evan brought her close, reveling at her soft touch. Her sweet kiss was the last kiss he ever wanted to know. She was the one he was meant to love, and he had to tell her. They parted and Evan brushed her hair back from her eyes. He inhaled a breath of courage, then whispered, "I love you, Jen. I am in love with you! I can't hold it in any longer." At the same time, a sense of relief and utter fear settled in his chest, uncertain of her reply.

Jenny's eyes widened in her shock of his declaration. It was all she could do to contain her joy and her heart nearly leapt out of her chest, her face beaming. "What? I didn't think you would ever feel this way!" She caught her breath. "I love you too, Evan Kramer" She exclaimed as her lips quivered and the tears fell from her eyes. She jumped into his arms and hugged him tight, kicking her legs in joy. "Woohoo!"

Their lips met again; their hearts finally in sync to the rhythm of new love.

Evan cleared his throat and smiled. "Coffee?" His cheeks flushed.

Jenny smiled. "Sounds perfect."

They walked into the kitchen, still reeling, when Jenny noticed the house was abnormally quiet. "Where is everyone?"

"Mom and Mitch stayed all night at the hospital with Grams and the kids had a lock-in or something at the church last night."

"How is she doing, have you heard anything?"

"No, not since last night. They were running tests and she was resting."

"Is there anything we can do? Should we go up there?" Jenny asked, feeling guilty about not doing more to help.

"They need to talk with Maggie's doctor first and figure out what is going on, so it's probably better to give them some privacy. I'm worried that it won't be good news though."

"We have to put our faith in God and let Him handle the details. Life is hard, but God is still good. We tend to forget that at times."

"I'm not too proud of it, but my faith has been fairly non-existent over the last few years. It was easier to shut God out after I lost my dad. He was my best friend. Then, Mom got cancer and that added fuel to the fire. I'm not gonna lie, I was flat-out pissed off at God. It wasn't fair! Now this?"

"I'm sure that was hard. I can't even begin to imagine, but good has come out of it. Your mom met Mitch. You moved here and met me, and now we have each other. I want to help remind you of all the good that God can still do; that He *is* doing. You have to look for it, though. You have to believe." She beamed a bright smile.

Evan looked at Jen's sweet face and marveled at her beauty, like she held pure sunshine inside. "How do you do it?" He asked.

"Do what?"

"Stay so positive, always find the good in things even when they aren't good?"

Jenny wrapped her arms around his waist. "I guess because I've been given so much. I've had more blessings than I deserve, and I've also been forgiven of much. That makes it even easier for me to forgive others and give them even a small piece of what I was given."

"I suppose you're right. It might take me a little longer to get here, but I'll try."

"Take all the time you need. Last I checked, our God is a patient God. And speaking of which, Laci is going to lose patience with me if I don't get all our stuff unpacked today so I'd better get to work."

"You make me so happy, Jen. Every day. I need you to know that," Evan said with a smile.

Jenny's smile disappeared. *It's time,* she thought.

"Ev, there's something you need to know."

CHAPTER 8

Mitch came back into the room carrying a cup of hot, steaming coffee for Laci, knowing she would need it to get through the morning. Sunlight glistened on her cheek as she slept and Mitch couldn't help but admire her beauty, inside and out. A soft kiss to her forehead helped stir her awake.

"Good morning, handsome," she mumbled in a groggy voice, sniffing the air around her. "You brought me coffee?"

"Mornin', darlin'. And yes, I brought you coffee."

"Good coffee?" She raised up and scooted forward on the bed.

He chuckled at her coffee-snob request, which he loved about her. "Not quite, but hopefully it's better than nothing. Unfortunately, there isn't a Starbucks within range." He brushed the hair from her eyes. "You're beautiful, you know it?"

Laci nodded in utter disagreement, but Mitch had a way of keeping her centered, grounded, and always made her feel like a treasured gift rather than a possession or a toy to control. She was his girl and loved that about him more than anything.

"Thank you, but you are biased." She winked, sipping on her coffee.

"And will happily remain biased for the rest of my life, darlin'." He picked up her hand and kissed the top, as he often had from the very day they met.

"Good, because you're stuck with me, babe."

He smiled. "Did you sleep okay?"

"I slept better after the 4am vitals check. Before that, not a wink. You?"

"I've had better nights. Miss you by my side. Doesn't feel right."

"Aww, babe. I know how hard this has been for you. I'm so sorry I made it worse."

Mitch's face was worn and tired, worried about the unknown that lay ahead. She took his hand in hers. "Remember what I told you last night? She's going to fight this as hard as she can, and we'll get through it together," she whispered, trying not to disturb Maggie's sleep.

"I have no idea if she'll be able to take care of herself, her home, go shopping again. What if she gets lost again? The doc said she wouldn't be able to go anywhere alone. What do we do next?" He tilted his head back and rubbed his eyes and forehead.

"We wait and talk to the doctor when he comes in this morning, see what he recommends. Maybe we need to pull Richard into the conversation. He loves her you know, and he has been taking care of her this whole time."

"Yeah, I gathered that. Why would she keep that from me and Brad?" Mitch's brow furrowed at the thought. "Why did you?" He added, recalling her own secrets from him.

"I think she was worried about what you would think of her being serious with someone other than your dad; that you wouldn't approve, and it was her place to tell you, Mitch Young, not mine. You know that." Flustered by his comments,

Laci turned her face away from him and tried to crawl out of bed.

"Hold up, you're not about to get out of bed, darlin'. I'm sorry. I was out of line." Mitch cupped his hands around her cheek, and he leaned in to give her a kiss, but she turned away.

"Aww, come on, Lace. Don't pout," he said, then poked a finger around the ticklish spot on her side, trying to force a smile or laugh.

"Stop it, Mitch. I'm not playing," she said sternly, then cracked a smile, unable to hold it back.

He turned her face toward him again. "I'm on edge, and I'm sorry. I know you were simply honoring my mom's wishes. Honestly, I don't know what to do."

She leaned forward and kissed him softly. "I'm sorry too, I shouldn't have made this about me. I know you're going through a lot right now. The doctor will be here soon, and we'll make a plan, okay?"

"How is it you always have a way of making everything sound less overwhelming?"

"It's a God-given talent, very hard to learn." She winked.

"Ah, I see. Well, the job is all yours." He smiled.

She sipped her coffee. "Ah, this isn't too bad actually. You're so good to me."

"That's *my* job. Gotta take care of two of my favorite girls, ya know." He smiled and kissed her forehead again but was quickly interrupted.

"WHERE AM I?" Maggie shouted in a panic. "How did I get here?"

Mitch jumped up and ran to her side. "Mama, it's okay. I'm here." His voice calm and reassuring.

"Mitch, sweetie! What's going on? Why am I in the hospital?" Maggie's eyes began to bounce all around the room, trying to get her bearings. She spotted Laci in the bed next to her. "Dear

Lord Laci! Sweetheart, what are you doing here? What is going on, you two? You're wearing a hospital gown, are you okay? Dear Lord. Is the baby okay?" She tried to sit up, wanting to get out of bed but fell back against her pillow, still dizzy.

Mitch smiled, both pleased and relieved that she recognized him and was being her normal, feisty self. "Mama, I need you to calm down. I'll explain everything."

"Ugh. Well someone had better start explaining that's for darn sure."

Laci chuckled softly. "And she's back," she mumbled.

"Mama, do you remember anything about last night?" Mitch rubbed her arm softly to help calm her down.

Maggie's face went blank at first, then her brow furrowed, straining to remember something. "I don't," she replied. "What happened, Mitch? What's wrong with me?" Her voice quivered.

Within moments of her question, the nurse came in to check her vitals, and right behind her was Maggie's doctor.

He walked over to Maggie's bed and shook her hand. "Good morning, young lady. I'm Dr. Edwards. How are you feeling this morning?" He asked in his rich British accent.

Mitch stood up to shake his hand. "Morning, Doc, she's awake but she doesn't remember anything, and we haven't had a chance yet to explain what happened."

"That's okay, Mitch. I'm rather glad I could be here for the conversation. I hope that's alright."

"Absolutely. Whatever is best." Mitch sat back down next to Maggie and took her hand.

The doctor pulled up a chair. "Margaret, can you tell me the very last thing you can remember before you woke up this morning? Take your time, dear."

Laci crawled out of bed and sat on the other side of Maggie as well, for support.

Maggie was out of sorts, of course, but she took a deep

breath and smiled, pulling herself together as she always did. "Let's see." She rubbed her forehead. "I was going to dinner at Max's to eat with my lady friends. Girls night out, ya know." She smiled. "We do it every year."

"That's right, Mama." Relieved she could recall her dinner.

"What did you eat?" The doctor asked.

Maggie smiled. "Oh, well that's easy. Max's famous tortellini soup, of course."

"That sounds delicious! Can you tell me about what time you left dinner?"

"I...," she paused, her eyes searching for the words. "that's odd. I remember feeling a little ill and left early, but I don't actually remember leaving the restaurant. I remember being cold." Maggie's voice shook as she began to panic. "What's wrong with me? Mitch, what happened?"

The next several minutes they walked Maggie through the events that transpired after she left Max's. Every detail. None of which Maggie could recall.

Mitch squeezed his mom's hand and smiled. "We're going to get you through this, Mama."

Maggie took a deep breath. "Well, what's next then? I'll do whatever needs to be done so you all don't have to worry about me."

Dr. Edwards patted Maggie's hand. "You're a sassy one, Ms. Maggie. Not going down without a fight, I like that in a woman." He winked.

Maggie giggled. "Watch it, Doc, you're pretty charming with that accent and all, but I got a man and he might get jealous."

"He's a very lucky man indeed. Will he be coming in today? I'd like to meet him."

"I don't know," she snickered. "Apparently I don't know much these days."

In seconds, the room was filled with laughter at Maggie's

little joke on her memory and made the future a little less scary for a moment.

The doctor folded his hands across his lap though, then his serious face returned.

"That's the best way to handle this, Margaret. Live, laugh, and enjoy the time you have." His kind smile didn't help.

"So how long until I can't remember anyone or anything? I want the truth."

"Alzheimer's is an unpredictable disease, and if there were no extenuating circumstances you would most likely have years left until that time came. Unfortunately, your brain scans show thinning blood vessels and the blood flow to your brain is greatly reduced compared to most people your age. This, along with the Alzheimer's, point to something called Rapidly Progressive Dementia. It's somewhat rare, but I reviewed everything and had my colleagues in London review your results as well. They agreed. With RPD, your symptoms will progress much faster than the average Alzheimer's patient. I can prescribe a few meds to help you cope and slow down some of the symptoms, but they won't help for too long. The worst is yet to come, and it could be two weeks or two years. Unfortunately, every patient is different. I'm sorry, Maggie, but based on what you've already experienced, I would estimate your quality of life will deteriorate quickly and I'm afraid and you'll need around-the-clock care to make sure you don't harm yourself or others. Eventually, perhaps a memory care facility."

Mitch's mouth dropped a little and stumbled back into the wall, not expecting the doctor to paint such a bleak outlook. He knew it wouldn't be easy to hear, but the reality was ten times worse. "Mama, no," he whispered to himself. Laci took his hand and squeezed it tight.

"It's going to be alright, Mama. You won't be alone and we're not putting you in a home, ever!" Laci said.

Mitch let go of Laci's hand and paced the floor to let off a little steam, still shocked from her diagnosis. It didn't seem possible.

"Mitch, come back here. I know you're upset sweetie but try and relax." Maggie patted the empty spot next to her on the bed, nudging him to sit down. "You have a baby on the way, and I have Richard. He loves me, ya know." She smiled proudly. "I won't be a burden to you and Laci and your family. I will make the best of it for as long as I can, and once I reach the point where I can't look at you and see my baby boy anymore, then Richard will know what to do and do what's best for all of us. I don't want you to worry, with the baby coming."

"I know, Mama. I understand, but I still wish you had told me about all this earlier. I could have—"

"You could have what? Fixed me like you try to fix everything?" She put her hand over his. "There is nothing for you to do, baby, except live your life and let me do the same. This can't be fixed."

"She's right, Mr. Young. The best thing to do is help her live comfortably and try to enjoy every day she has left to the fullest. The way God intended."

Mitch's head tilted sideways at the doctor's mention of God and smiled. It was nice to hear.

"We can do that, Doc." Mitch wiped a tear from his eye then leaned over and hugged his mom's neck as tight as he could.

A knock at the door broke the tension in the room, and Richard walked inside.

"Hey everyone. I hope I'm not interrupting. I just wanted to check on my lady," he said with a big smile, never taking his eyes off Maggie once he entered the room.

Maggie's face lit up like a Christmas tree. "You're right on time, my dear. Come in. This involves you, too."

They updated him on Maggie's diagnosis and talked through

all the options, which he took like a champ. Richard smiled and took Maggie's hand.

"Well, it sounds like I get to keep my eye on the love of my life for as long as she'll have me."

Maggie's eyes spilled over with tears. "Rich, I can't let you waste your life on me. You need to live your own life; I'll be fine in one of those homes."

Richard got off the bed, then bent down on one knee. Mitch and Laci's faces lit up with shock as they watched the scene in front of them.

"Margaret Anne Young," Richard started, "I have loved you every day for the past twenty years, and more. Now I finally have a chance to make it official, so why don't you quit being so darn stubborn, and marry me already?"

Maggie's smile was wider than the Texas plains and tears slowly traced their way down the tiny wrinkles in her beautiful face.

"Well, if you insist." Her voice cracked as she spoke.

Richard stood up, smiling, and threw his arms in the air.

"Finally!" He shouted.

Mitch and Laci laughed, enjoying the sweetness of the moment.

"You know I can be very demanding, right?" Maggie added.

"I wouldn't have it any other way. I love you, Mags." Maggie took his hand and placed it on her cheek.

"I love you too, Richard," she said. "Thank you for never giving up on me."

"I never will, Mags. You're my girl."

"We're keeping it simple, getting a justice of the peace, right? I mean like *Monday*. I'm not waiting any longer than necessary to be your wife!" She smiled.

"You read my mind, love." Richard grinned and leaned in to give her a little peck on the lips.

The doctor stood up to leave. "I don't think I've ever witnessed a proposal in a hospital before."

"Trust me, Doc," Laci chuckled, "declaring love in a hospital room is a regular thing for this family."

They all laughed, knowing that Mitch and Brad had done the same thing.

Dr. Edwards took Maggie's hand. "Well I was honored to share in the moment. You've got a splendid man there, Ms. Margaret." He smiled.

"Thank you, Dr. Edwards. So, what now?"

"Well, you seem to be doing fairly well today. I'll want to see you in my office once a week going forward to monitor your progress. Can you do that?"

"I certainly can." She smiled and looked up at Richard, stars still in her eyes. "And when I can't, he'll be there to help me."

"We're going to help you through this, Margaret. You have my word." The doctor shook hands with the family, then walked out.

No sooner had he left, and another doctor walked in to check on Laci and the baby. After a quick exam, she, too, was given the green light and released to go home.

"Looks like it's time to get my two favorite ladies' home." Mitch smiled.

"And just in time for Thanksgiving too. It's going to be a busy week!" Laci replied.

"I hate to break it to ya, darlin', but you are *not* going to make a big, fancy dinner this year."

"You watch me, Mitch Young. I plan on having one of the biggest spreads you've ever seen! Hot dogs, tater tots, nachos… the works!" She winked at him and laughed.

CHAPTER 9

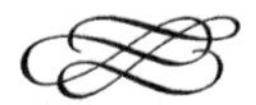

Laci peeked at the clock for the third time. Five-thirty a.m. Ten minutes since the last check. Knowing there was a full day ahead however, and baby Young already kicking and tossing in her tummy, she got up and started her day.

Traditionally, before Laci and Mitch were married, Thanksgiving was always a day of parades, cooking, eating, watching football games all day and napping off and on. After her battle with breast cancer though, and eventually marrying Mitch, it had become a non-traditional day filled with very little if any TV, and lots of fun music. *I even sneak in a few Christmas carols when can, I can't help it!* Laci smiled to herself. There was still cooking and eating, but now it was focused on being simple and stress-free. No more all-day on her feet in the kitchen, and then spending all afternoon cleaning up and washing dishes. Now, Mitch cooked alongside her as they laughed and cut up with one another. They threw together a few side-dishes and homemade pies, then bought the turkey and dressing already smoked and ready-to-eat so they could eliminate some of the hassle. It was a day they shared together from beginning to end.

Mostly, it was fun again. She and Mitch laughed and played in the kitchen while they cooked, playing trivia or watching a Christmas movie. The kids usually sat around and played games at the table while they cooked, too. It had become a family day in every sense of the word. This year would be the first without Brad and Caleb however, so it would definitely be much quieter than normal.

After brewing some coffee, Laci put some cinnamon rolls in the oven and took a few minutes to sit in her bay window to take in the view of the wooded surroundings. Living in the log cabin that Mitch's uncle had left them gave her such joy, and it had become a home like no other place she had ever lived. It was peaceful, but more importantly, filled with love and joyful moments despite the challenges they'd had along the way. Laci had made the big bay window her own little 'happy place'. The window seat overflowed with colorful pillows and an old handmade afghan her grandmother had given her years ago. Books and magazines were stacked all around, making it easy to find something that suited her mood. Between the forest animals that roamed outside, the blooming flowers in spring, tall maple trees with their colorful leaves in fall, and a perfect view of the rain, she needed nothing more. It was her time for self-reflection, and the ever-important conversations with God. *It's time for a little java with Jesus on this beautiful Thanksgiving Day!* She thought and curled up in the window to take in the view.

From the corner of her eye, she spotted a family of deer not far from her window. The doe stopped and turned its head toward Laci, staring at her for what seemed an eternity. *For heaven's sake, she's looking right at me. So beautiful. What are you thinking, mama deer? You look sad.* Laci froze, holding her coffee cup steady so as not to scare the doe away. She was a beautiful, magnificent creature. If Mitch were there, he would be saying how nice it would look hanging on his wall downstairs. *Ugh! Men. You aren't a trophy deer, are you? You're kind of freaking me out a little though, I have to admit.*

The baby suddenly hard kicked inside Laci's belly and Laci jumped to catch her coffee before it spilled. At that, the doe ran away as fast as she had come.

"Well good morning, little one. Guess we had better get some breakfast in us, huh?" She said out loud as she walked into the kitchen.

Mitch came around the corner, sniffing the sweet, cinnamon aroma that filled the air.

"Morning, darlin'" He said softly. "Breakfast smells amazing! Let's eat."

"You're as bad as the kids, Mitch Young."

"Guilty," he laughed. "Speaking of which, I'd better get a cinnamon roll before they wake up and see them."

"I was about to pull them out of the oven. Be patient there, my love." She grabbed an oven mitt.

He moved in front of her and took the mitt out of her hands, then leaned in to kiss her softly. "Why don't you let me take care of that for you?"

"You can take care of that and anything else you want, babe." She winked.

"Don't you dare get me started, darlin'. Not while there are cinnamon rolls in the oven." He laughed.

"So, you're saying you'd rather have a cinnamon roll than me? Okay, I see how this works." Laci joked, turning up the music a little to give the kids a nudge. It was almost time to get started on the cooking, her favorite part.

Mitch opened the oven, pulled out the rolls, threw the mitt on the counter then turned around and pulled her close. He wrapped his left arm around her waist, then took her right hand in his, dancing her around the kitchen to the Christmas Waltz playing in the background.

"Happy Thanksgiving, my love," he whispered softly in her ear. His hands moved behind her head and he pulled her gently into him, his kiss sweeter than Carolina tea. Laci's heart fluttered being inside his arms, and goosebumps popped up all over her body. It sometimes made her sad, but Mitch could move her in ways her late husband never could, and he didn't even have to touch her to make her heart flutter. One look was all it took. They slowly danced as he gently nudged her backwards until she was pressed against the counter. He rubbed his hands up and down her back, then slipped his warm hands under her shirt and caressed her breasts.

Laci moaned softly as his hands roamed, her body growing more and more excited at his touch.

"Morning!" Evan shouted, then yawned as he entered the kitchen half-awake, not realizing he was interrupting a moment.

Laci let out a sigh as Mitch hurriedly pulled away with a quiet giggle.

"Well," she cleared her throat. "Good morning, Ev!" She wiggled out from behind Mitch and fanned her face.

"Cinnamon rolls done?" Evan asked, still clueless.

"I need to add some icing, slick, hold tight," Mitch replied. He kissed Laci on the cheek. "You sit down, darlin'. I'll take care of it. You seem a little flushed." He winked, then pulled out a chair at the kitchen table for her.

Within the next hour, the rest of the kids were up, and everyone was gathered around the table, scarfing down cinnamon rolls and coffee, discussing the to-do list for the day ahead.

"Alright gang, what do you say to a little touch football outside to get the day started? It's a beautiful day!" Mitch slapped his hands together and rubbed them, ready for a fun little competition.

"I'm in!" Evan replied.

"Gee, that sounds like *so* much fun, but I think I'll stay in and help mom cook." Emma rolled her eyes.

Laci laughed. "Well you boys have fun, and don't get hurt, please?"

"Where's the fun in that?" Mitch laughed in reply, kissed her on the cheek and they all headed outside.

Thanksgiving Day had officially commenced.

Emma ran up to get dressed, but Evan lingered behind, waiting for everyone to leave.

"Hey Mom, do you mind if Jen comes over for dinner? Her mom isn't feeling too well."

"Of course, sweetie! We would love to have her. Always," she replied, but felt there was something more going on. "You seem kind of off. Everything still good between you two?"

"Yeah, we're great! I just wanted to ask you a quick question."

"Of course, shoot." Laci continued to clean the table.

"How did you know that Dad was the one? Or Mitch?"

Laci immediately stopped moving and stood straight up, her eyes as big as seashells. She was fairly sure her heart had stopped too, at the shock of his question. *Are you kidding me right now!? Where did this even come from, they've known each other for like a minute, maybe a minute and a half! Lord, please don't let him be thinking what I think he's thinking.* She took a deep breath and calmly replied.

"That's a big question." She fanned her face, now beet-red, as she formulated her answer. "It was different for both I guess. Your dad was definitely the one I was supposed to be with, but not for the reasons you probably think. We had a wonderful life and we loved each other, I miss him every day. For me though, there was always something missing."

Evan smiled a nodded. "You never did go overboard on the affection with Dad. I kind of remember you two even had some trouble along the way. Didn't he sleep on the couch a few times?" He chuckled.

Laci smiled. "Yes, he did. Every relationship takes work though, even if you're head-over-heels in love. Sometimes couples need a break from each other. That doesn't mean the love is gone."

"That's how you look at Mitch. Head-over-heels. That's not the way you looked at Dad. Does it feel different?"

"Yes. It probably sounds bad, and I don't mean it to, but everything is different with Mitch. He makes my heart flip!" She said, glowing. "I don't know how else to describe it really. When we are apart, it feels like half of me—more than half—is missing and it almost causes me a weird physical pain in some ways. I miss him and my heart aches when he's not with me. It did from the very start. I never actually had that with your dad. I loved your dad very much Ev, please don't misunderstand, and not a day goes by that I don't miss our life together. But I don't remember missing him when he went away for work, which makes me sad. When Mitch is gone, nothing is right in my world until he is back by my side. I guess that's the best advice I can give to you, Ev, if your world is brighter and feels more complete with Jenny in it, and she makes you feel like you could do anything, then you would be crazy to ever let her go."

"Thanks, Mom. I'm glad you and Mitch are so happy together, I really am. You make it look so easy."

Laci burst out in laughter. "Oh, mercy, no! Looks can be deceiving, and we've had our share of ups and downs even in the short time we've been married. I will admit though, that this is the happiest I've ever been. There is no one in the world that I'd rather be with or spend my life with than Mitch. He's my best friend. Please don't think badly of me for saying that. I will always love your dad very much."

"You weren't really *in* love with Dad though, were you?" Evan asked with some hesitation, not completely ready for the answer.

She dropped her chin as a heavy sadness filled her heart. "I'm sorry to say I wasn't. There is a big difference between loving someone and being *in-love.* Trust me. No matter what you decide, make sure you are *in-love,* okay? You'll know."

Evan reached over and hugged his mom, knowing how hard this conversation was for her. "I will. I love you, Mom. I could never think bad of you for that. Thanks for being honest with me though."

"Are you going to propose to Jenny?" She asked with tears in her eyes.

"Don't panic, Mom. I'm simply mulling over some things, that's all." He kissed her forehead.

"I'm proud of you, Ev. You are such a wonderful young man." Laci's tears flowed. "Jenny is the luckiest woman in the world as far as I'm concerned, well next to me of course," she giggled, "and if she makes you happy, then go for it!" She smiled.

"I think it's Mitch and me who are the lucky ones, mom. And I will definitely go for it." He replied.

Laci watched her son walk out of the room. Not long ago he was such a tiny thing who used to reach up to her with his little arms and say 'awaanna hode you', squeezing his hands open and closed over and over again until she picked him up. Now he was a young man beginning a new journey in life and love. She smiled then wiped the tears from her face and went about her day.

EMMA FINALLY DECIDED to show up and helped set the table for dinner. Laci recited the names of those who needed place settings.

"Mitch, me, Evan, Jenny, Todd, Emma, Travis, Maggie and Richard."

She sighed at the thought of Maggie, slowly losing herself a little each day. Even in the last week she'd had several more episodes, but overall seemed to be holding up okay.

"Hey Mom, what if I wanted to have a friend over for dessert or something?" Emma asked, her cheeks a shade of soft pink.

"Well, I don't know. Who would this mystery guest be?" She smiled.

"A friend. His name is Isaac. He's really nice mom, and he's a year older but he is the cutest and really smart."

"I was wondering when you would get around to telling me about him. Why did you wait so long? You even told Caleb about him before he left and didn't say a word to me! You have a crush on him, don't you?"

"It might be more than a little crush, and I told Caleb because he didn't make fun of me or tease me. I figured you'd be upset."

"Aww, sweetie, I would *never* have made fun of you! I'm glad you're telling me now though. So, tell me all about him!" Laci pulled out a chair and sat down, motioning to Emma to sit beside her.

"Okay, he's tall, and plays baseball, but he likes all the same music as I do. He's in my math class, and...," Emma talked on and on about her crush and Laci couldn't help but smile watching her face light up as she shared. It didn't matter what the rest of the day would bring, those moments between both Evan and her sweet daughter were, by far, the best of the day.

"I guess we'd better set out an extra dessert plate from the sounds of it." She replied.

Emma jumped up and hugged her mom's neck. "Thank you,

Mom! I'll go call him! I love you!" She yelled as she took off to her room.

"Well, back to work I guess." She laughed to herself.

Mitch and the boys came back inside from their game and he joined Laci in the kitchen to help with dinner. The turkey was warming in the roaster, pies were in the oven, and the aroma of sage, pumpkin and cloves filled the air.

"You heard from Mom yet, today?" Laci asked.

"Richard called. It's been a good day so far and they'll be here soon."

Laci wrapped her arms around his neck. "It's going to be alright, babe. Let's give her the best Thanksgiving Day ever."

Mitch kissed her soft lips. "So we shall."

* * *

Caleb slowly pulled into the driveway and inched his way up to the house so no one would hear his car. He got out and quietly walked up the porch then knocked on the door.

"I think Mom's here, darlin'!" Mitch yelled as he opened the door. Shock and joy spread across his face as he saw his son standing there. "Caleb! Son, what are you doing here?" Mitch grabbed him and pulled him into a bear hug, slapping him on the back and squeezing him tight, took his bag and walked inside.

"Lace! Look who I found at the door!" Mitch shouted as he escorted him into the kitchen.

"Who is it? I can't leave the pie filling!" She replied.

Mitch and Caleb snuck up behind her as she stirred. Caleb reached around and covered her eyes.

"Ah! I can't see the pudding, who is it? Hurry, tell me before it burns!"

Caleb uncovered her eyes and peeked around so Laci could see him. "Hi, Mom." He smiled.

"CALEB!!!!" She shouted and threw her arms around him. "Sweetie! It's SO good to see you! What are you doing here? We thought you had to work at the restaurant all weekend." She hugged him again, tears rolling down her cheeks.

"I wanted to surprise all of you. Figured this was the best way. I almost told Jenny when I called her last week but decided to surprise her, too."

Mitch put his arm around him. "Welcome home son. We are *thrilled* to have you home." He patted him on the back. "Let's get your stuff put away so you can change and relax before dinner. We are going to have a full house today."

"Where are the kids?"

"They're in the family room playing games. I don't think they heard you come in."

"Great, I'll surprise them after I change."

Laci continued to stir her pie filling, then suddenly gasped in panic as she realized that Caleb probably had no idea his ex-girlfriend was not only dating his stepbrother but had grown quite serious in the time he had been away at school. *You're going to surprise them alright.* Laci rolled her eyes up. *Lord, give me strength!* She said to herself as they left the room, now a little worried about how the day would play out once the truth was revealed. *This will definitely be a Thanksgiving dinner to remember. I'm sure Caleb will be gracious though. They broke up after all.* She shook her head, already doubting her words. *Any other surprises you want to throw at me today, Lord? Bring it on! What else could go wrong?*

CALEB CHANGED clothes and settled in, then came downstairs to surprise Evan and the kids as they sat around the family room playing spoons. He smiled as he watched them from the door, thinking how nice it was to be home with his plus-sized family and how much excitement Laci and her kids had added to the house.

"Hey!" Caleb interjected in a loud voice. "You all need to scoot over and let the master play," he said with a big cheesy smile.

Evan looked up at Caleb and his mouth dropped open in shock. "Wow. Hey brother, what's this? I didn't think you were coming home until Christmas?" Evan got up and shook Caleb's hand to welcome him home, but inside he was already nauseous. *Oh boy, this is not going to turn out well.*

"I got the weekend off and was missing everyone pretty bad, figured I'd surprise y'all."

"Awesome dude. Well, get in here." Evan replied. It's not that he didn't like the guy. He *was* his stepbrother after all and they always had a good time hanging out, but it was hard to be excited, wondering how he would take the news. Caleb squished himself onto the bench seat at the table and they dealt him in. Laughter arose and all was well. For now.

* * *

THE TABLE WAS SET. Music was playing softly, and the candles were lit. It was almost time for dinner. Maggie and Richard had arrived, and she was doing okay so far, apart from being a little tired. The doorbell rang again, and Evan answered the door. It was Jenny, and Evan quickly stepped outside on the porch, closing the door behind him.

"Well, Happy Thanksgiving to you too." Jenny said jokingly. "What is going on? The dinner is inside, correct?"

Evan's face was somber and immediately Jenny knew something wasn't right.

"What's wrong, Ev? Is Laci and the baby okay? Maggie?" Jenny asked.

"They're all fine. Caleb is here, Jen."

"What?" She exclaimed. "He told me last week he wasn't coming home for Thanksgiving!"

"Last week? He called you? Why didn't you tell me?"

"It was no big deal, and we're still friends remember? I don't have to tell you every little thing that happens to me, Evan." Jenny's defensive state escalated.

"I know that, but when it comes to Caleb saying he's coming home for Thanksgiving you should have told me!"

"He wasn't supposed to, that's why I didn't say anything! He said he had to work, I swear."

"What else did he say? That's the only reason he called?" Evan knew better.

"He was homesick and needed to talk to a friend. That's all, I swear."

"He's still in love with you, isn't he?"

"No! I don't really know. I don't think so. He was never in love with me to begin with, not to my standards anyway. Why are you freaking out about this? We need to be honest with him and get it out in the open."

"So how do we do that, huh? *Here Caleb, have a slice of turkey, and oh by the way I'm in love with your ex-girlfriend. Happy Thanksgiving, buddy!*" Evan tried to make light of the situation, but his attempt was unsuccessful.

"He's not a bad guy, Evan. He's your stepbrother, and we broke up, remember?" She paused.

"Well of course he's not. I know that. It's still awkward though, and I'm worried he'll think I stole you away from him despite that fact. I am literally breaking 'bro-code' here, big time."

She laughed. "I love you, Evan, not Caleb, and although you

frustrate the crap out of me, I wouldn't have it any other way! Caleb will be fine. Bro-code doesn't apply here, so why don't we go inside where it's warm and have a nice dinner? We'll figure it out, okay?" Jenny's voice softened, and she scooted closer to Evan. She wrapped her arms around him and poked out her bottom lip.

He laughed. "Stop it, Jen. This is serious. It could end badly, you know."

"Let's talk dessert. Pumpkin or pecan?" She said, trying to divert his attention as they walked inside.

MAGGIE AND RICHARD made their way to the table, and the kids followed behind them. Laci saw that Jenny had arrived and gave her a hug.

"Have a seat, sweetie. Do you want sweet tea or water?" Laci asked

"Tea is fine, thanks."

"Evan, can you help me in the kitchen?" She asked, giving him the 'eye'.

"I KNOW what you're going to say, and no, I have no idea what to do!" Evan stated.

"He doesn't know?" She asked.

"Well, NO, mother! When was I supposed to tell him? I didn't really expect to see him on Thanksgiving Day!"

"Oh boy, this dinner will be one for the books." Laci looked up to the ceiling. "Lord, be with us!"

Emma popped into the kitchen. "Mom, Isaac is here. Can he sit at the table with us?"

"I thought he was coming for dessert?" Laci asked, exasperated.

"His family already ate, they have to eat early since his dad works. Is that okay?"

"Sure, sure. Have him come on in. The more the merrier!"

"Thanks, Mom! You're the best!" Emma shouted as she ran off to meet her guest.

Laci sat down to catch her breath, blowing the bangs out of her eyes. *'You're the best, mom', 'let's have a few more guests over mom'; heck let's throw in the Hickory Crawdad team while we're at it!* She mumbled quietly to herself.

Mitch crept around the corner and found her sitting at the empty kitchen table. "Hey, darlin'. You okay?"

She tried to laugh but didn't quite pull it off. Instead, she offered a half-smile. "I'm good, I just need a minute," she said as the tears began to fall.

"What is it, sweetie?" He sat down and took her hands in his.

"It's been a long day that's all. Is everyone about ready to eat?"

"They're wandering into the dining room as we speak. Do you need anything? I knew you would overdo it once I let you host dinner. You can't do anything half-way can you?" He laughed softly. "That's one of the many things I love about you – you always make everything look so beautiful and special for everyone."

"Well, it's not exactly working out that way this time, and you're right, it was too much. But I wanted this one to be extra special for your mom, that's all. You never know," Laci's voice trailed off, trying to hold back her tears.

"Hey, it's okay and I can't thank you enough for all you've done, but you need to take care of yourself and our baby, okay? That's the most important thing right now. Promise me you'll sit down after dinner and let me, and the kids take care of the cleanup. You're not allowed to touch so much as a dish towel. Do I make myself clear, Laci Young?"

"Yes, yes, I promise. I won't touch a dish towel. Emma's crush is here now, and I'm pretty sure he's more than a crush though. Oh, and Evan asked me how I knew you were *'the one',"* she said using air quotes.

"Calm down, darlin'. They're big kids now, and if it's meant to be, it will be, right?" Mitch leaned over and kissed her softly. "Now let's go eat this delicious meal, shall we?" He helped her up out of the chair, pulling her in for a quick hug and kissed the top of her head. "Happy Thanksgiving, Lace. I love you, darlin'," He added.

"I love you too my Creepy Stalker Crawdad-fan. Always have. Always will."

* * *

CALEB WALKED out of the bathroom and bumped into Jenny as she stood looking at pictures hanging on the wall. "Jenny?" He said, both surprised and overjoyed.

She turned around and tried to act surprised. "Caleb! What are you doing here?" She smiled and gave him a quick hug.

"Wow, I didn't expect to see you here!" He leaned in and gave her a big hug. "I wanted to surprise everyone. Is your mom okay?"

"Yeah, she's doing great. I had lunch with her earlier but wanted to stop by here and say hi. Laci demanded I stay and eat again," she faked a laugh. "It's great to see you. So, what changed? I didn't think you were going to come home for Thanksgiving."

"My boss took pity on me, guess I was whining about missing my family too much." He laughed.

"Well that's great. I'm sure everyone is thrilled to see you."

"Yeah, they were definitely surprised. It's nice being home, even better now that you are here. You look amazing." Caleb took her hand, but Jenny quickly pulled it away feeling quite awkward.

"I think it's time to eat. We should probably go get a seat, huh?"

"Yeah, you're probably right." He smiled.

When they walked into the dining room, Jenny took a seat next to Emma, purposely avoiding the empty seat next to Evan. He raised his eyebrow and wondered what she was doing, but figured it was best, given the circumstances.

Everyone else followed suit, and the table was overflowing with friends and loved ones. Mitch tapped the edge of his glass with his fork.

"Hey y'all," he paused waiting for the chatter to settle then took Laci's hand. "Before we eat, Laci and I want to say how grateful we are that y'all are here. We couldn't be more thrilled to have everyone home for Thanksgiving this year. Every year on this day especially, our tradition is to go around the table and share something you're thankful for, so Laci will start us off and I'll finish." He lifted her hand and kissed the top, as he did often.

"Well, I'm thankful for the love of my life who I couldn't imagine life without, my beautiful kids, my folks although they couldn't be here today, my amazing new helper, Jenny, thanks for all you've done for me these past few months," she winked at her, "and this bundle of joy that is about to greet the world in a few more weeks."

They each took turns sharing, then ended with Mitch.

"I have so much to be thankful for it would take me all day and then some if I started sharing," he chuckled.

"Well give us the Cliffs Notes, Dad. The turkey is getting cold!" Caleb said, giving everyone a good laugh.

"Yeah, yeah, yeah. I'll do my best, son. Speaking of my son Caleb, I want you to know how great it is to have you home. I've missed having you bud, but I'm proud of going after your dreams. I'm even more proud of the way you're handling the fact that Evan and Jenny dating now. It takes a real man to—"

"Mitch," Laci's eyes bulged out of her skull at his announcement, then she kicked him under the table for added emphasis. "He didn't know yet." She mumbled through her teeth.

Silence covered the room like a lead blanket, and it seemed an eternity before another word was uttered. "Well he does now." Mitch added.

Caleb cleared his throat. "Excuse me? What do you mean Evan and Jenny are dating?" Caleb asked loudly, then stood up and looked at Jenny with a scowl. "When you were going to tell me, Jenny? How long has this been going on?" Caleb's anger grew by the second.

"Calm down, son," Mitch interjected trying to defuse the situation. "Jenny, I'm so sorry, darlin'. I thought he knew." Mitch patted her on the shoulder, but she was already in tears. She jumped up and ran off to the living room.

Everyone else remained silent, simply looking at each other and wondering how this would all play out. Evan stood up and walked around to Caleb. "Dude, you need to calm down. We were going to tell you together after dinner today. We didn't expect you to be here!" Evan replied.

Without reply, Caleb drew his fist back and hurled it into Evan's jaw, knocking him backwards into Richard's lap.

"Jeez, Caleb! Chill!" Evan yelled. He shook his head trying to regain his balance, then rubbed his jaw as he stood.

"Caleb James Young!" Mitch shouted. "Both of you, take it outside. Now!"

They stomped off and made their way out to the porch.

Laci shook her head back and forth then dropped it in her hands. Instead of crying however, which was her normal reaction, she burst out in laughter. Slowly, the others did the same. "Happy Thanksgiving, everyone!" She added.

Emma was quite embarrassed by what had happened and figured Isaac would get up and leave. Instead, he leaned over and whispered in her ear. "Are your family holidays always this exciting?" He asked.

"Yep." She smiled.

"Cool. Mine are *so* boring." Isaac smiled in reply, then reached under the table and took her hand, giving it a squeeze.

Laci looked up and saw Maggie's face; solemn and confused. "You okay, Mama?"

"Are there fireworks later? I've always loved the fireworks at the park," she replied, slipping away again.

"Maggie, today is Thanksgiving. We're having all your favorites. Do you want some sweet potatoes?" Laci asked, worried at her state.

Maggie didn't respond. She stared at her plate, frozen in place.

Richard patted her on the shoulder. "Maggie, sweetheart. Did you hear Laci?"

No reply.

Laci stood up knowing something wasn't right. "Mama, did you hear me?" She shouted.

Maggie became almost catatonic. She wasn't even blinking.

"Richard, shake her!" Laci shouted. "Get her to come out of it! This can't happen today!"

* * *

EVAN PUSHED Caleb the minute they got outside, and with that, they broke into a full-blown fist fight, taking turns slugging each other and behaving like immature young men do when fighting over a girl. Mitch stood back and watched, and let them fight.

Caleb held his hand up to stop things, panting heavily. "You're a real jerk, Ev! Did you even wait until I left town before you asked her out? And how did you even know who she was?" Caleb wiped the blood from his mouth, still stinging from the last punch Evan gave him.

"Seriously, Caleb? You honestly think I would do something like that? What for? I didn't know who she was when I met her. She waited on me the night I drove into town. She told me her name was Rose, for crying out loud! I didn't know, I swear!"

Caleb laughed.

"What? Why is that funny?"

Mitch sat down on the porch, still quietly watching the scene unfold.

"I don't know. This whole thing is funny, I guess. I have no idea why I even got upset that you two were dating. It hurts, I'm not gonna lie. I really cared for her, but I suppose I always knew she wasn't the one. Besides, I kind of met someone at school." He smirked.

"You what! Seriously? You're going to punch me over a girl you don't even like when you have *another girl!* Dude, you're messed up." Evan cracked a smile.

"I know. Sorry, man. Knee-jerk reaction I suppose."

"It was a reaction all right." Evan dusted off his jeans.

"You two getting serious?"

"Yeah, I think we are. I mean, I told her I loved her. It wasn't really mushy or romantic the way it happened though," he laughed.

"That's great, Ev. Doesn't matter how it happened as long as you're open with each other." Caleb added, sincere in his words.

"Well, one thing is certain...we've caused quite a scene today. What now?"

"I don't know about you but I'm starving. Let's go eat, dude." Caleb chuckled, then shook Evan's hand, honorably, then they headed back to the dining room.

"You pack quite a punch, man." Evan mumbled, still rubbing his jaw.

Caleb laughed. "Sorry, dude."

They walked up the front porch steps to find Mitch standing at the top with his arms folded. "I see you two worked things out like gentlemen."

"I think we did." Caleb replied, no longer smiling.

"And I can count on this never happening again, correct?" His serious, deep southern voice inferred the weight of some heavy impending actions depending upon their answer.

"Yep. Yes, sir." Caleb and Evan replied simultaneously.

"Good. Let's eat then, shall we?" Mitch smiled, then gave them each a hearty slap on the back as they walked inside.

* * *

"MAMA! ANSWER ME!" Laci shouted.

The boys heard Laci shout then ran toward the dining room, not realizing what was going on. Mitch saw Richard shaking Maggie and lost it.

"Richard! Stop shaking my mother!" Mitch shouted, then walked over and shoved him away.

"Mitch, please. This happens from time to time. Give her a minute and she will come out of it." Richard said. "I'm sorry, I know it's not easy to watch, but shaking her seems to help her come back quicker."

"What if it doesn't, Rich? What then?"

"Then we deal with it, but you have to stay calm. I would never hurt her; you have to trust me." His voice was soft and kind, and it seemed to calm Mitch down a bit.

"You're right, I know you wouldn't. My apologies."

"Dad, what's going on?" Caleb asked, shocked at the situation at hand.

"Caleb, I'm so sorry, son. I haven't really had time to fill you in on what's going on around here, but your grandmother is having a spell, it's Alzheimer's bud. There's been a lot going on here lately." Mitch explained.

"Anything else I've missed out on over the last few months that y'all wanna tell me about?" Caleb asked to the group.

Isaac spoke up. "I like your sister, man. I'm not about to keep that a secret from this family," His face flushed. The entire table giggled, breaking the tension.

Emma's mouth dropped open. "You do?" She asked for clarification. Her cheeks turned bright pink, and even in the midst of the chaos, her heart raced, knowing how he felt.

"Why do you think I basically invited myself over today?"

"Good point." She giggled.

"Can everyone please be serious for a minute?" Mitch shouted out to the group.

"Mitchell Lee Young! Why on earth are you shouting? Will someone please pass me the sweet potatoes for crying out loud?" Maggie asked, as if nothing had ever happened.

Mitch sat down, exhausted. "And she's back." No one moved however, afraid of what would happen next. "Well, someone pass this woman some sweet potatoes." He added in his calm, southern tone, then almost in a flood of relief, the entire room erupted in laughter.

Mitch looked at Laci and took her hand, then leaned over to give her a quick kiss. "You okay, darlin'?"

"I am now." She smiled. "You?"

"I think so."

The rest of the day was less exciting, thankfully, and somewhat normal for the most part. It was a Young family Thanksgiving for the books. One they wouldn't soon forget. The holiday nearly over, Evan walked Jenny to her car so she could head home and check on her mom.

"I'm sorry I didn't trust you before, about the call from Caleb. I never want to make you feel that way again, because I do trust you and I love you with all my heart, Jeannette Rose!"

"Mercy, Jeep-man, you'd better stop this emotional outburst or I'm going to start crying."

"Cry all you want." He pulled her into his arms and held her tight, then bent his head down and kissed her gently. "See you tomorrow?" He asked.

"Absolutely," she replied. "Thanks for fighting for my honor today, and very sexy by the way."

"Oh really? Well I'll have to remember that for next time."

"Let's hope there isn't a next time. There are other ways you can be sexy ya know."

"I think I know a few." He winked.

"I love you, Evan. I don't want anyone else but you, ever." Jenny's heart leapt up to her throat.

"Then we should probably do something to seal the deal, don't you agree?" He asked.

Jenny's eyebrow raised. "What do you mean? I'm not quite ready for—" she stuttered.

"No, no! I would never ask that of you unless," he took a deep breath and looked up to the sky, asking the Lord for courage, "unless you were my wife."

Jenny's heart raced and her face turned beet red. "Your wife?" She smiled and her eyes widened. "Evan Kramer. What are you—"

"Marry me, Jen! I know we've only been together a few months, but I knew you were the one the minute you walked up to the counter that night in the coffee shop, something inside me lit up and you sparked it. I never want that feeling to go away and want you by my side the rest of my life! Will you marry me, Jeannette Rose?"

* * *

THE PHONE RANG.

"Hey big brother, what's up?" Brad asked.

"You got a minute to talk?" Mitch asked.

"For you? I've got a lot more than one. Shoot."

"Can you and Hannah get away for Christmas? Mom is getting bad, Brad. You need to see her again while she can still remember you. And, I have a sneaky suspicion our special package may arrive around then," Mitch's voice cracked. "I'm not gonna lie; I really need you, man."

Brad sighed.

"Aww Mitch, I wish we could, but this is our busiest season. I'm just not sure how we could pull that off, to be honest."

"Yeah, I get it. I had to ask, ya know?" Mitch's voice dropped as his heart sank.

"Look, I'll talk to Hannah and we'll look at the calendar and see what we can do. I need to see Mama, and I know you and Laci could use a break. Maybe we can figure it out, okay?"

"Thanks for trying, man. I understand if it's not possible, trust me." Mitch replied, some relief evident in his voice.

"Hey, that's what family does for each other. I'll always be there for my big brother, no matter what."

"No matter what." Mitch echoed. "Well call me once you know something. And if it turns out you can, let's keep it quiet. We can surprise Laci and Mama both, okay?"

Brad laughed out loud, knowing this trip had already been planned long ago, unbeknownst to Mitch. "You got it, dude."

* * *

JENNY'S EYES filled with tears and she threw her arms around Evan's neck, squealing and smiling from ear to ear. "Yes! Yes! Yes! My mom is going to think I'm crazy! Oh boy. She may not let me marry you. What do we do then?" Jenny's freak-out moment began.

"Okay, first, calm down. Second, you are saying 'yes'. You're *really* saying 'yes'? I heard you correctly, right?" Evan lit up.

Her hands cupped around his cheeks; she took a breath. "Absolutely, one hundred percent yes. I've never felt this way about anyone. Simply being around you and doing nothing makes me happy and I don't ever want to be without you. Ever." She leaned up on her tiptoes and kissed his lips softly.

"Don't worry about your mom, okay? We will tell her when the time is right and I'm sure she'll be fine."

"She is crazy about you, I'm not worried."

Evan smiled proudly. "Well, of course she is!" He winked. "Goodnight, babe. Drive safe." Their lips met for one last kiss, and she drove away.

"Goodnight, future Mrs. Kramer." He whispered to himself, still reeling from the moment. "Now to tell the fam." *Oh boy.* He thought.

CHAPTER 10

The week after Thanksgiving was filled with joy, starting with Richard and Maggie's wedding at the courthouse, which was small, incredibly short and one of the sweetest days they had enjoyed together in some time. Caleb went back to school, and the remainder of the week Mitch and the kids took it upon themselves to decorate the house for Christmas to make sure Laci didn't do it herself. Lights were strung from one side of the house to the other. A tall, live fir tree was placed in the family room, beautifully adorned with their traditional ornaments, and her favorite Christmas tree with the 'red dress', affectionately referred to as *Audrey,* stood in the corner of the dining room. Emma diligently worked on the tiny 'coffee' tree that sat on the snack bar filled with collectible Starbucks ornaments going back at least ten years or more. They even took the time to pull down the Christmas dishes and set them in their place. The house was beautiful, inside and out. The days that followed were dragging on and on for Laci. She continued to get bigger, felt more miserable, slept less and less, and became more anxious for the baby to arrive.

Winter was upon them, evidenced by short days that ended with pitch-black skies by five o'clock, and Christmas was fast approaching. The kids were all upstairs so Laci decided to take advantage of a quiet living room, knowing full well it wouldn't be that way for long. She curled up in her favorite chair wrapped in a soft, red fleece blanket and sipped her coffee from a big red mug that read *'Coffee Before Presents'*. The spirit of Christmas was all around though, and her heart overflowed. Even more so by the view of her belly poking out from under the blanket. She whispered quietly, "One more week 'til Christmas, little one. I can't wait to hold you in my arms. Geez, I've been waiting such a long time to see you!" She smiled and rubbed her tummy, filled with joyful anticipation.

Her gaze was drawn to the front porch window, adorned with garland and white lights that twinkled against the night sky. While admiring their glow, out of nowhere, Mitch jumped in front of the window making faces at her and blowing kisses.

"Ah!!" She screamed, nearly jumping out of her skin. "Mitch Young! What on earth are you doing?" She shouted through the window. "I'm nine months pregnant and nearly peed my pants!"

He and Evan had just returned from the winery, working late trying to get caught up before the baby arrived. He flew in the front door and walked over to Laci, still laughing and clearly amused by his own antics.

"Hey, darlin'! Sorry if I scared ya. You okay?" He knelt on the floor next to her.

Laci scoffed and rolled her eyes. "I guess, but not exactly the smartest thing to do to a pregnant woman at this stage of the game, though." She scolded him, trying her best not to crack a smile.

"Hey, I'm just doing my part to try and get him to come out, that's all." He leaned over and gave her a soft kiss. "I'm sorry. That better?" He asked in a deep, soft southern drawl, purposely dropping it an octave or two knowing how it made Laci weak in the knees.

Laci bit her lip. "Stop it, Mitchell Young. You know how that deep voice gets to me." She smiled. "And, your lips are cold."

"Guess you'd better warm them up then." A quirky grin on his face, he stole another kiss. "Seriously though, are you feeling okay? Little Mitch bouncing around and wreaking havoc in there?" He patted her belly.

"Yes love, we are both fine. I'm too tired to cook dinner though. Can we order in?"

Mitch laughed out loud. "Hmmm. You and cooking. Those two words don't really belong in the same sentence these days, do they?"

She slapped his arm playfully. "Not fair! You wanna carry this ten-pound, fidgety, squirmy, hiccup-prone baby around in your tummy for a while?"

"I'm sorry, darlin'. Of course, we can order in, but only if I have the strength to call. My lips might be too cold to talk. I might need extensive lip therapy." Mitch winked, then wiggled his way between her legs, her baby belly now wedged between them, until their lips met. As he sank deeper into her sweet kiss, Laci's fingers slid through his soft, thick hair and down the back of his neck, but suddenly her grip tightened like a noose.

"Ouch! I didn't think you liked it rough," Mitch joked, but reached up and touched his lip. A tiny spot of blood appeared on the tip of his finger. "What the heck, Lace?" He looked up at her and saw her cringe.

"Ahhhhhh!" She groaned, grabbing her stomach.

Mitch leaped up off the floor. "Holy cow, babe! Is he coming now?"

Laci looked up at him and scowled. "No Mitch, I thought I'd yell for no re-e-e-e-a-s-o-o-o-n! OOOUCH!"

"Got it. You stay here. I'll go get the truck and bring it

around. Breathe, babe. Hee-whoo-hee-whoo, just like we practiced." Mitch grabbed his keys and flew out the door.

The contraction passed, and Laci smiled, thinking about how many times she had been through this before—four to be exact, but quite a long while since the last one. For Mitch, it had been even longer—almost twenty years. The kids heard the commotion and came barreling downstairs.

"Mom? Are you okay? Is the baby coming?" Travis asked, his forehead wrinkled and worried.

Laci chuckled between contractions, her face half smiling and half grimacing. "I'm okay, buddy. He's not coming quite yet, but I think he will very soon. Mitch is going to take me to the hospital so the doctors can check on him, okay? Everything will be fine."

Emma took her mom's hand, concern all over on her face.

"I'm okay, sweetie. We'll call you as soon as we know something, okay? In the meantime, Evan is in charge." Laci told her.

"Mom. I can take care of myself!" Emma insisted in her best grown-up voice.

"What am I, chopped liver?" Todd asked.

"Todd. I know you are perfectly capable of taking care of things on your own too. You're both in charge. That better? And if this turns into us being gone several days, I'll call for backup."

"Evan always gets first dibs on the important jobs. I get the leftovers." Todd's shoulders dropped.

"Todd. I need you to be attentive to the kids. Evan doesn't do that near as well as you. He's more like a foreman on the job site to make sure the house doesn't burn down or something, but you're the one that has compassion and can care for them; you make them feel safe. I need you," she paused to breathe several times, then exhaled after the contraction passed. "Rich is down the street, so call him if you need anything. It will be fine." She added, breathing faster between each word.

"I got it covered, Mom. Don't worry." Todd hugged her neck and said goodbye.

Laci's contractions were hastening and becoming more painful. A few minutes later, Mitch ran back inside to walk her out to the truck.

"Bye mom! I love you!" Travis yelled before she left, then ran over and hugged her legs.

"I love you, buddy!"

"What is the baby's name going to be?" Emma asked.

"Well, what is the top girl and boy name from your list?" Laci breathed in hard as another contraction came on.

"Are you okay?" Emma looked worried, scared for her mom. "I'm sorry, Mom."

"It's a contraction, sweetie. All part of it and there is nothing to be sorry about. Now what were those names?"

Emma took Laci's hand and rubbed it as she walked toward the door. "I can't decide. I like Madison for a girl, but the boy's name is special. I think you should name him Michael, like the angel." Emma smiled her beautiful smile.

"OOOOOOhhhhhhh!" Laci squealed. "I love those names, Em. I think it's time for us to go now though, okay? I love you! Help your brothers for me." She smiled and kissed her goodbye.

Mitch escorted Laci out to the truck, and they were on their way.

Much to their disappointment however, they came right back several hours later.

They walked in the door to find Evan still awake. "Mom. Dad. What's going on? Everything, okay?" He asked, confused by their early return.

Mitch paused, surprised by the fact that Evan had just called him 'Dad' for the first time. "False alarm. The contractions stopped, and she wouldn't dilate." Mitch said, his voice tired and groggy. *Surely he was overly tired and misspoke,* he thought to himself.

"No snow. That's why." Laci mumbled in reply, then headed to bed.

Evan looked at Mitch, his eyebrow raised.

"Don't ask, dude." Mitch shook his head. "Night, Ev."

"Night. Dad. I hope that's cool with you…if I call you Dad, I mean."

"Very cool indeed. Thank you, son."

SCHOOL WAS out and Caleb returned for Christmas break, the kids were back together, and all were enjoying the holiday. Everyone except Laci, that is. Her mood grew lower with each passing day that she didn't go into labor.

Finally, Christmas Eve had arrived at the cabin but still no sign of their sweet baby. Laci woke, crawled out of bed, and immediately pulled back the curtain hoping to see even the smallest sign of snow in the clouds. *Nothing.* She mumbled to herself. Her frustration had reached its limit, however.

"Another NOT WHITE Christmas! I thought we were practically guaranteed a white Christmas down here?" She vented in a loud voice.

Mitch yawned. "Well, good morning to you too, grumpy butt." He laughed. "Come back to bed. It's too early to be up."

"Tomorrow is Christmas, Mitch. When is this baby going to arrive? Where is the snow?"

"Well, let me see. My ever-so-accurate meteorological abilities are a bit rusty, but I'll get right on that snow-cast as soon as I can," he sat up and patted the bed next to him. "Come over here, babe."

"I'm tired of sleeping."

"Fair enough, but will you at least stop worrying about the snow? Why is it so important?"

"It's rain, just frozen, and I need it, Mitch. I don't know why. I simply want a white Christmas. That will make everything better. Then the baby will come, and I won't have to worry anymore."

"Worry about what? What is it, Lace?" He asked, now concerned by her comment.

"Worried that something will happen at the last minute and we'll lose this baby. I'm scared, Mitch." Laci finally sat down on the edge of the bed.

Mitch moved over behind her and wrapped his arms around her belly, gently pulling her onto his chest and kissed her cheek. "Darlin', you've gotta let all that worry go. Do you really think God wants you hanging on to that? It's not healthy for you or the baby, and this is Christmas, Lace! You need to have faith that everything is going to be okay. The docs told us that you are healthy; the baby is healthy. Believe in that. Believe that God has this covered, okay? Because He does." He squeezed her tight.

She sighed and took a deep breath. "I'm sorry, babe. You're right. I just want to see his face. I asked God for a white Christmas as a sign that everything would be okay. Sounds stupid, I know."

"It's not at all. I get it. But you can't put God in a box like that. He's much bigger than that, ya know. Be still for a while today and listen to Him. We are going to see this baby any day. I know it." He kissed the top of her head then whispered softly, "I love you, darlin'."

"I love you, too. I'm sorry I'm such a whiny butt." She giggled.

"You can whine to me anytime."

"Well, right now I have a ton to do! Starting with coffee, then making the breakfast casserole for tomorrow."

"What about today?"

"What do you mean?"

"Ya know, breakfast… for today? Or are we taking a twelve-hour fast?" He teased.

"Ha ha, very funny." She pushed him over. "If you're so hungry, then you can come downstairs and make *today's* breakfast while I work on tomorrow's!" Laci stood up and turned around, trying to get him out of bed. Instead he grabbed her arm and gently tugged, pulling her back into bed and kissing her softly.

"Oooh, yuck! Your breath stinks, Mitch!" She squealed, laughing at him. "Get your 'BT' up or I'll go eat a bunch of garlic and come back up here and give you a long French kiss!"

"I will, I will. I'd still kiss you though. Garlic or no garlic, your kisses are still sweeter than the sugar rim on a lemon drop in the summer sun." His sweet southern charm still moved her beyond words.

She cracked up laughing. "Oh! The baby kicked! Feel it, Mitch! Right here." She put his hand on her belly, smiling at him. Her belly bounced again, the imprint of a tiny foot pushing out through her stomach. "Did you see that?" Laci's heart overflowed. Her face beaming, she leaned over and gave Mitch another kiss, lingering as their lips danced together in perfect harmony. "You're a nut, you know it? But I love it when you mess with me. Apparently, our baby does too. Merry almost Christmas, handsome." She caressed his stubbly cheek, drawing him in for one last kiss.

"Now that's much better." He replied.

* * *

THE DOWNSTAIRS WAS AN ICEBOX, especially the kitchen. Laci kicked up the heat, flipped on all the Christmas lights in the house, then turned on the Christmas music. She looked around and took in the beautiful scene, noticing the thin, white layer of frost that lined the edge of the windows; Mother Nature's special touch to complete the holiday feel. She spent a few minutes relaxing at the kitchen table enjoying her coffee, read a few pages of her favorite book, then made the casserole.

Eventually, Mitch came down and had no sooner put the casserole in the oven, when the doorbell rang.

"You expecting someone? It's a little early, for crying out loud." Mitch asked.

"Not unless it's Richard. I hope nothing is wrong." Laci immediately filled with worry.

They walked over and opened the door to find a porch full of people standing outside, shivering. Laci's parents were there, whom she hadn't seen in months. Maggie, Richard, and hiding in the back, Brad, Hannah and even Chloe popped out from around the back! They had *all* come to surprise Laci and Mitch. The gift of family had arrived.

Laci was overwhelmed to the point of tears, bawling and hugging everyone as they entered the house. "How did this happen? Who—?" Laci stuttered, still amazed by their arrival.

"Maggie." Rich stated.

"What? How?"

Maggie smiled, fully coherent with all her wits. "I started planning this back in October before things got bad. I had Richard help me buy their tickets and arrange everything in case I wasn't—well, you know." She looked down.

Laci ran to Maggie and wrapped her arms around her neck, hugging her tight. "Maggie, I don't know what to say. I'm so grateful for you and this precious gift, our families finally all together. I don't even know how to thank you." Laci cried, and continued to hold her close.

"You already did, my dear. You love my son, and God blessed

me with yet another beautiful daughter—you. And soon a beautiful grandbaby! Thank you for everything you've done for me, even when I didn't deserve it," she smiled. "Trust me, I know I was quite the *pill*, far too long." She laughed.

It wasn't too long until the kids finally woke and rolled downstairs to see everyone sitting around the kitchen table drinking coffee and playing cards. Travis screamed with joy at the surprise guests, especially happy to see his Uncle Brad and their grandparents.

Evan stumbled in and yawned, then his eyes popped open. "What the heck is going on? Grandma?" He said, shocked to see Laci's mom and dad sitting amongst the group.

"Hi, baby doll! Merry Christmas! Come over here at give Grandma a hug!"

They piled in the kitchen and started to fill their bellies with breakfast, cereal, fried eggs, bacon, and oatmeal. Every kid fixed something different, but Laci didn't care.

Travis, however, walked over and climbed up onto Laci's lap. He looked up with his sweet smile, growing wider by the second.

"What's up, buddy?" She asked.

"This is a *happy* family." He replied and a little yawn escaped his mouth.

Laci squeezed him tight. "Yes, it is, Trav. Yes, it is." Laci's heart nearly burst with joy as she looked around. Her house had come to life and overflowed with laughter, tears and joy. Unending joy.

LATER THAT DAY, Mitch walked in the dimly-lit living room to find Laci curled up in her chair.

"You okay, darlin'?" Mitch asked.

"Trying to be still, per your orders, remember?" She giggled.

"As much as I can be anyway. I'm beyond ready to see this baby, Mitch. I so wanted to see snow the day he was born."

"I know. He will come, the time isn't right yet. Faith, remember? Have faith."

"Faith that snow might fall?"

"Faith that the snow *will* fall at just the right moment."

"Well, Christmas *is* the right moment and it hasn't happened." Laci squeezed his hand, then stood up and walked over to the window, staring out into the woods. Mitch sensed she needed some space, so he left her alone and returned to their guests.

The arrival of the Christmas visitors had set Laci's emotions on overload, so while everyone was busy visiting and catching up, she threw on her coat and snuck out the front door to catch her breath and take in the brisk, cold air.

She walked around, voicing her thoughts out loud into the cold air, tiny white puffs of breath from her mouth as she spoke. *I love my life, my kids, and Mitch is the absolute love of my life. I want for nothing and I know it's silly to want this snow, but I do. The most important thing though is for this baby to be healthy. I feel closer to you when I'm outside, that's all.*

The clouds above made everything look gloomy, but it was a perfect fit for Christmas Eve; far better than sunshine, or even the rain she loved so much. She walked around to the back of the house. When she got to the deck, she stopped and peered through the oversized bay window that looked into the kitchen. Behind the glass were the smiling faces of all those she loved more than life itself, and although muffled, she heard the sound of their laughter and it filled her heart with joy and all that Christmas brings.

At that moment, a tiny snowflake slowly drifted down and landed on her nose. At first, she thought she was just seeing things. Another appeared, and then another. Laci looked up and smiled, then closed her eyes and tilted her head back so she could catch them in her mouth as they fell. She felt like a little kid and wanted to spin around but knew her body wasn't really up for that. The flakes grew larger, falling faster and faster and her face was now wet from the melted snow. When she opened her eyes however, the few soft snowflakes had turned into flurries, a veritable snowstorm in a few short minutes. She gasped with delight. "Let it snow!" She yelled with joy, holding out her hands and walking around in circles. It reminded her of a day, not long ago, when she had danced in the rain and asked God to heal her cancer.

"It's snowing!" Travis yelled, running to the window. "Can I go outside with mom?" He asked.

Mitch raised his eyebrow. "What are you talking abou—?" Mitch turned to the window and saw Laci standing in the snow. "What in the world is that woman doing?"

Immediately, he tore out the back door.

"Laci Jean!" He shouted as he ran down the deck stairs toward her.

"It's snowing, Mitch! It's really snowing!" She shouted with excitement and turned toward him, but as she did her foot slipped on the snow-covered grass. Her legs gave way.

"LACI!"

The ground was too slick for him to get traction which prevented him from catching her before she hit the ground. It was like they were both moving in slow motion. Mitch only managed to get close enough to slide one arm under her shoulder. She groaned as she collided with the snow-covered grass.

Motionless.

"Lace! Are you okay, darlin'? Laci, look at me!"

He brushed the snow off her cold face, listening to her labored breathing.

"Ooops," she said, then began to giggle.

* * *

THE ENTIRE FAMILY turned toward the window and watched.

White knuckled, Travis gripped the windowsill. A few short moments later, he screamed, "Mom fell down!"

Evan flew out the door as fast as he could. Brad and Caleb followed right behind him.

"Mom! Mitch!" Evan shouted as he ran towards them.

"It's fine, Ev! She just slipped. She's okay!" Mitch replied from across the yard, breathless and still a bit worked up from her fall. "One of you bring her a blanket!" He yelled.

Caleb heard his request and turned back around to go get it.

Brad and Evan approached. "Should we lift her?" Evan asked the group.

"I don't think we should." Brad added.

"Well, we certainly can't leave her laying here on the ground, it's too cold!" Mitch replied.

"Anyone gonna ask me what I want?" Laci mumbled, shivering and her teeth chattering.

"Laci, darlin'! I'm so sorry. Does anything hurt? Are you okay to stand?" Mitch asked.

"I think soooo-ooo!" She groaned, grabbing her stomach.

"Was that a contraction?"

"No, Mitch. I won the lotto. Yes, it's a contraction!"

"I think she's feeling better." Brad jested in his typical sarcastic fashion.

Mitch's brow furrowed. "Brad, not now."

"Okay, okay."

"Ahhhhhhhhhhhh!" Laci groaned, then began to breathe faster.

"What's wrong, Mom?" Evan was beyond freaked out at this point.

"My water broke," she said softly, her face still grimacing.

"Oh geez. That means that baby is coming, huh?" He asked in a squeaky voice.

Mitch laughed. "Nothing gets past you, does it, slick?"

Evan rolled his eyes. "Give me a break. This is my first experience with childbirth."

Laci turned her head and looked at Mitch, still laying on the ground next to her. "Mitch, the whole family is here, it's a beautiful night and it's snowing! It's finally time!" Tears flowed from her eyes.

"You're absolutely right, darlin'. The timing is perfect." He smiled and kissed her forehead. "Maybe next time you ask someone to go outside with you and not scare us all to death though, okay?"

"I don't look for there to be a next time, but you've got a deal." She replied.

"Well, I'd say we'd better get you up and off to the hospital so we can have us a baby." His smile was as big as Texas.

"Coming through!" Caleb shouted as he came running toward them with the blanket.

"Ahhhh!" Laci's head lurched forward during another contraction. "Thanks, Caleb. Can you get me up now, guys? I'm fine, really." Laci added, anxious to get off the cold, snow-covered ground.

"Evan, go get the truck and drive it around –and turn up the heat." Mitch said, then he and Brad got around Laci and positioned themselves to lift her up. "Slow and steady, Brad."

"Aww, man! I thought I'd do my old one-two launch move like I did on the high school football team. Really get her up with some gusto so this baby will pop out even faster." Brad laughed his belly laugh. "Geez, brother, I'm not that stupid. Give me *some* credit, will ya?" He joked.

Evan pulled up with the truck and Mitch and Brad lifted her

up inside, tucking the blanket around her. "Keep breathing, Lace. We're on our way." Mitch said, and kissed her cheek.

Evan rolled his eyes at their display of affection. "Really, you two? This isn't the time! Get out of here."

"This is exactly the time, slick. You'll figure that out someday though, trust me." Mitch said with a chuckle. "Get everyone to the hospital little brother. Think you can handle that?"

"Yes, go! Let's go, Ev."

Brad and Evan took off to the house to share the news, and Mitch and Laci drove off.

Mitch took her hand as Laci pushed through another contraction on the drive, snow still coming down in huge white flakes. "You got your Christmas wish, Lace. A Christmas baby and a blanket of beautiful snow."

"I did." She smiled in reply. "Now we just have to have faith that everything is okay after me falling tonight and being silly." Laci took a deep breath and let it out, a bit worried and feeling guilty for her antics earlier. *Please let this baby be okay, Lord. I need him to be okay.*

"Faith through falling snow," Mitch replied.

The *White Christmas* song immediately began to play softly on the radio and Laci's eyes popped open the minute she heard it. Her smile widened and, in that moment, her heart was happy and filled with joy.

CHAPTER 11

"Ahhhhhh!" Laci screamed. Several hours had passed, but finally the contractions were closer and closer together and although he was being a bit stubborn, baby Young was about to make his way into the world.

"Push, Laci! Push through it, babe!" Mitch squeezed her hand as if it helped in some way, but he knew there was nothing that could ease her pain until that baby was out.

She gasped for air as the contraction subsided, then smiled up at Mitch. "He's being stubborn, like his momma." Laci said, her speech a bit slurred from sheer exhaustion. "We're never gonna have this baby, Mitch."

"Why on earth would you say that?" He asked.

"Because the contractions are too far apart." Her eyes drifted closed and opened wide again.

Mitch chuckled softly. "Laci, they are less than thirty seconds apart."

Laci didn't even realize that she was falling asleep between contractions. "They are—oooooh! Here it com—ugh!" She groaned from the deepest recesses of her body, feeling every ounce of pain as it flowed in waves from the top of her abdomen all the way down.

"I see the crown, Laci. You're doing great, Mom!" The nurse's voice was filled with excitement and on some level that gave Laci a sense of calmness to get through it, knowing what was ahead.

The doctor walked in and sat down at the end of her bed. "Alright you two, let's have a baby," he said with a smile.

"You ready to push again, babe?" Mitch squeezed her hand and brushed the hair back from her sweaty forehead.

"So ready," Laci replied. Tears flowed down her red cheeks.

"Alright Laci dear, on the next contraction I need you to give me a big push okay?"

"Okay, Doc," she paused between her quick breaths. "Here it comes!"

"Push, babe!" Mitch urged.

Her groans of pain began softly then turned to deep growls. They grew louder as she pushed through the contraction. One final, exasperated yell signified the end. Pain subsided.

"One more good push, Laci, so get ready, okay? He's almost out!"

And that quick, the contraction was there, piercing her abdomen like tiny little knives. *Please let this be the last one! I want to see this baby!* She thought as she pushed. It was over. The pain was gone as quick as it had come.

No cry.

No baby coos.

What was taking so long? Is he okay?

Laci was groggy and unable to articulate her words from sheer exhaustion.

"Doc, what's wrong?" Mitch's voice rumbled. "Why isn't he crying?"

Then a tiny little squeal pierced the silence in the room. It was music to Laci's soul in every way.

"Thank God!" Laci cried out, bawling and crying a gut-wrenching cry of relief.

"Here she comes, Mom." The doctor reached over and laid a tiny, naked baby right on top of her chest. She was still a little messy and covered in gooey, sticky fluid, but Laci didn't care, and she wrapped her arms around the tiny body and kissed her forehead.

"Hello there, beautiful," she whispered, still sobbing.

"Wait, Doc. Did you say *she*?" Mitch asked, still a little dazed from the stress.

The doctor and the nurses all laughed. "Yes, Mitch. You have a beautiful little girl there." He replied.

Mitch looked at Laci and their beautiful baby. "Hannah's dream was a little off. We have a daughter, darlin'," he said in a whimper, completely overwhelmed with love for both of his girls. He leaned down and kissed Laci softly. "I love you, Laci. So much. You have no idea how beautiful you look right now." He added.

"I think you're just high on baby love, babe." Laci giggled. "But thank you. I love you too. I can't believe she's finally here!"

The nurse came around to the other side of Laci's bed. "Hey there, you two, mind if I take her for a little bit? I need to wash both of you, and then I'll get her all bundled up and ready to come see you in a few minutes after you're settled in your room, okay?" When she looked down to pick her up however, she immediately noticed her purplish skin color. "Amy, can you get me some suction, please?" She yanked up the baby quickly and laid her in her little clear bed.

The device turned on and sounded like somewhat like the suction tube at the dentist office.

No baby cries. No coos again.

"What's wrong?" Laci's heart sank. "What is it?" She asked in a panic.

"It's okay, guys. She still has a lot of amniotic fluid in her lungs and we need to clear her airway. We'll get it out, don't worry. This is completely normal," she replied. Quickly the other nurse unhooked the suction device and pushed their baby out of the room.

"Where are you taking her? What's going on?"

The doctor came back inside their room. "Everything is okay, guys. We have a bigger suction machine in the nursery area, so they've taken her there to make sure they get it all. She's going to be fine, trust me. They'll give her a bath, and you'll be holding her again in no time. Until then, you must be exhausted so the nurses will get you cleaned up, in a fresh bed with warm blankets, and you should probably take a nap because this may be your last chance to sleep for a while." He smiled.

Laci and Mitch were still concerned, but a little more at ease now. "Okay, Doc. I think I could use a nap too," Mitch chuckled.

The doctor patted Mitch on the back. "Yes, both of you have earned a rest. Congratulations. She's beautiful by the way. Do you have a name picked out yet?"

They looked at each other and smiled, knowing exactly which one they wanted.

Faith.

* * *

It had been hours since Faith had been born. Laci and Mitch both slept right after they got back to her room, but she'd been up awhile now and wondered when they would bring her back.

The nurse walked in to check Laci's vitals.

"You're bringing her back in soon, right? Is she doing okay?" Laci asked impatiently.

"Don't you worry, Miss Laci. They are taking good care of her. She aspirated a little after they brought her back so it's hospital policy to keep her under constant watch for several hours after an episode like that." The nurse replied, never looking Laci in the eye, simply continued to do her job in somewhat of a hurry.

"Aspirated?" Laci needed clarification.

"She choked a bit on all of the fluid still in her lungs. It happens now and again with newborns, Miss. They'll be bringing her in soon I'm sure." She added, then gently patted Laci's hand and forced a little smile.

The nurse left the room and Laci looked over at Mitch sitting in his recliner, still napping.

"Mitch!" Laci shouted across the room.

Startled, he sat straight up in his chair. "What? What's wrong, darlin'?" He got up and walked to her bed.

"Something is wrong. I can feel it. They're not telling us something, Mitch. The nurse just told me Faith *aspirated* or choked or something. Can you go find out what's wrong? Please? I need to see our baby."

"Yes, yes I'll go see what I can find out. I'm sorry I slept so long, Lace. You should have woken me sooner."

"It's okay, babe. I know you're tired. It's been a long day. I need to hold her. Now."

"I'll be back."

MITCH LEFT the room to get some answers, leaving Laci alone with her thoughts. She laid her head back and closed her eyes, trying not to worry. Her mind raced. *What is wrong, Lord? What's going on with her? I know something is wrong I can feel it in my bones. Please, please let her be okay! I NEED her to be okay!*

Maggie and Rich tiptoed into the room. "Hello, Laci my dear." Maggie said softly.

Laci immediately opened her eyes and smiled. "Maggie!" She reached her arms out for her mother-in-law and hugged her tight, and the tears poured.

"Sweetie, what's wrong? Where is Mitch and the baby?"

"Mitch went to check on her. Oh, Maggie! I'm so worried something is wrong with Faith."

"Faith. What a beautiful name, my dear. And I'm sure everything is fine so try not to worry. You're experiencing a lot of emotions right now, you just had a baby!" Maggie tried to reassure her.

Laci pulled out of her arms and looked at her. "You look wonderful, Maggie. I'm so happy to see both of you. How are you, Rich?" She asked, wiping the tears from her eyes.

"I'm good, Laci. Quite good. It's a good day today." He winked, and Laci knew it was to reassure her of Maggie's state of mind for the moment.

"Rich, why don't you go see if you can find Mitch and check on things. Us girls need to visit a minute." Maggie urged him with her sweet southern voice.

Laci remembered the first time she ever heard Maggie's sweet voice on the weekend Mitch took her home to meet his family. She was so nervous and worried they wouldn't like her, and just as she'd feared, Maggie didn't quite approve of her. What a long way they had come since then though, and today they finally had a true friendship as mother and daughter-in-law. Too little too late unfortunately. It was only a matter of time before Maggie didn't recognize any of them. She had progressively gotten worse since Thanksgiving, so each day she was alert and living in the present was a gift from God.

"The nurse told us that Faith choked or something after they took her away so now they have to keep her under observation. I think there's something more going on. I'm worried, Mom."

"My darling girl, I know you are. It's so scary until you can hold them in your arms and protect them yourself, isn't it? I remember when I had Mitch. He was too big for me to deliver on my own, so they had to use forceps to pull him out. They squeezed his head so hard with those clamps that his little head was pointed for weeks after he was born. I called him my little conehead baby," she smiled at the thought. "It was so scary, and I worried he'd be deformed for the rest of his life." She shared, squeezing Laci's hand for comfort.

"I never knew that. I'm sure that was scary. And that explains why he still has a big head, in other ways." Laci giggled, referring to Mitch's sometimes big ego. She and Maggie laughed together in the moment.

There was a bustle at the door, then from behind Maggie appeared a baby cart being pushed by Mitch, grinning from ear to ear.

"Faith!" Laci squealed. "My baby girl! Give her to me, Mitch." She reached out her arms like a child herself, anxiously waiting.

"I'm working on it, darlin'. Give me a sec." He turned the cart around and wheeled it closer, then lifted baby Faith out and gently handed her to Laci.

"She's simply beautiful, Laci." Maggie stated, tears rolling down her face.

They all gathered around Laci's bed, watching and listening to every movement and sound little Faith made. Laci laughed out loud. "She's finally here." Tears pouring again from her eyes as she held her baby close.

"What did they tell you, Mitch? Anything else?" Laci asked.

Mitch looked at her with a look of concern.

"Mitch. What's going on?" Laci prodded, and then the doctor entered the room before he could reply.

"Good evening, everyone. How is our little Faith doing?" She asked. "Do you mind if I squeeze in here and check her real quick?"

Maggie and Rich stepped to the back of the room to let her in. She took little Faith from Laci's arms and moved her over to the little bed to do a quick check. "She looks simply beautiful, Laci. Have you had a chance to feed her yet? Are you going to try and breastfeed?" The doctor asked.

"No, she just got here, Dr. Greene. This is the first time we've seen her since she was born. They told me she aspirated. What does that mean? Is there something wrong?"

The doctor moved closer to Laci's bedside. "She's just fine, don't worry. Basically, it means she was choking and couldn't breathe due to the fluid in her lungs, so they had to suction it out to help her breathe. When they did, the nurse discovered that Faith has a cleft in her soft palate. Do you know what that is?"

Laci sat up, fearful of the next words that would come. "No. Is it serious? Is she going to be okay, Dr. Greene? Please tell me she's okay," Laci asked, crying. Anxiousness had set in and her stomach churned.

Mitch took her hand. "What does all that mean, Doc?" he asked.

"It's a type of birth defect that caused the back section of the roof of her mouth to not fully formed, so the soft tissue is missing, there is a hole there. This will make it more very difficult for her to eat and explains why she choked after she was born. The amniotic fluid went up through the hole and into her lungs; basically drowning her. We're going to have you try and breastfeed, but she may not take to it. Her mouth muscles are going to be quite weak at first."

"What? She has a birth defect? That means something went wrong during the pregnancy, doesn't it? I did something wrong, didn't I?" Laci was overwhelmed with guilt; fearful she had done something to cause Faith's condition.

"Not at all, Laci. There was nothing you did that would have caused this. Sometimes it's genetic, family history, or something unique that occurs in the womb. You have a beautiful girl! There is nothing to worry about. We'll get you some help with nursing and as soon as she is eating and her vitals are good, you can all go home in a day or so." The doctor's voice was reassuring, and for the first time Laci breathed a sigh of relief.

"What happens if she can't latch on or take the bottle? What does that mean? Will she be able to eat solid food ever?" Laci's thoughts were spinning out of control as she spouted off questions in rapid fire.

"Let's try and focus on getting you comfortable with feeding first. Yes, she'll be able to eat normally one day, but the hole will need to be repaired with surgery at some point. We're also going to bring you a special bottle to help supplement her feedings with formula. It's called a Haberman bottle."

"Okay, but what if she quits breathing again?" Mitch asked.

"Don't worry about that for now. She's doing great, so take it slow and keep her head tilted upright as best you can when she's eating okay? She is healthy in every other way; we just need to make sure and pay attention to things and make sure she gets all the nutrition she needs."

Faith gurgled and cooed as the doctor held her.

"Can I have her back now, Dr. Greene?" Laci asked, and everyone in the room chuckled at her eager words.

The doctor laid Faith back in Laci's arms, wrapped so tight in her little blanket that it was hard to imagine how she could breathe. Laci kissed her tiny pink cheeks, pulling her close to her chest and breathed in her clean, fresh baby scent of lavender and vanilla that still lingered from her recent bath; no sweeter scent on earth.

A little while later, Laci's mom and dad snuck into the room with all the kids.

"Mom! Dad! Merry Christmas!" Laci shouted in joy. It meant so much to her that they could be there and share in the excitement and she was overwhelmed. She hugged her mom's neck as the tears fell like rain. "I love you both so much!"

"Aww, we love you too, baby girl. I'm so happy for you and Mitch. Your dad and I wouldn't have missed this for the world. Quite the special gift we all received today!" Her mom replied.

Emma and Travis ran up to Laci and hugged her tight. Todd stood back and played it cool, a bit anxious to get close to Faith.

"Come here and hold your little sister, Todd. I'll help you," she said softly, hoping to help ease his nerves.

Todd walked closer and took the baby in his arms, smiling from ear to ear.

"Can I hold her too, Mom?" Travis asked.

"It's my turn next, Travis." Emma stated emphatically.

"Hey guys, let's calm down. Everyone will get a turn, okay?" Mitch chimed in, smiling at the group gathered in the room. All the people he loved on the earth in one place, enjoying this new little life that had come into the world.

Evan and Jenny had also stopped by and after a few minutes, he decided to share their big news.

"Hey, since you're all here. Jen and I have something we want to tell you." He cleared his throat. He took Jenny's hand and paused to catch his breath.

"Well spit it out, son." Mitch grinned and winked at Evan, knowing he was a bundle of nerves.

"I asked Jenny to marry me, and she said yes." He said quickly.

The words came out so fast in his nervousness that they

barely heard him, but the message was clear, and the room erupted in applause and laughter. Hugs for the newly-engaged couple went around the room and life at that moment was seemingly perfect – a Christmas to remember without a doubt. It lasted but a few seconds, but that was enough and exactly what they needed.

"Brad, can you go see if your daddy is home yet?" Maggie blurted out, then wandered toward the window. "Dinner is going to get cold if he doesn't hurry up."

Silence fell over the room. Rich stood up from his chair and took Maggie by the hand. "Let's go home, Maggie darling." He said softly. "Sorry everyone, but I think it's time we get back. Congratulations you two. I'll call you later, Mitch." Rich added.

"I'll walk you out, Rich."

"Bye, Mom." Laci said quietly, saying goodbye to her seemed harder that day. It was only a matter of time before she would be gone for good. Laci's heart was heavy at the thought, but light at the same time as she stared into Faith's sweet face. *Oh, Lord how grateful I am to you for this little girl you gave us to help fill the loss that is sadly closer than I care to admit. Please don't let Maggie suffer. Mitch won't be able to handle seeing her like that for long.*

Laci's mom and dad snuggled the baby for a while and visited with Laci. After Mitch returned to the room, he could see that Laci was exhausted.

"I think it's time to call it a day, everyone. Momma is looking pretty tired over there." He said to the group.

"No, I want to hold Faith one more time! Please, Mitch?" Emma asked, hugging Mitch's waist.

"One more time." He laughed in reply.

"You're such a pushover, Mitch Young." Laci winked at him.

"You women. You always do that to me; I can't help it."

. . .

SOON THE ROOM WAS QUIET. Baby Faith slept quietly in her bed and Mitch was quietly reading a book in his chair.

"You doing okay, babe?" Laci asked him.

He looked over at her and smiled, closed his book, and walked to her side.

"The love of my life just gave birth to my daughter, and *you* are asking *me* if I'm okay? I don't know how I got so lucky to have you in my life, Laci Jean Young. You are the most unselfish, kind, caring woman I have ever known, you know it?"

"Keep going, keep going." Laci winked, goading him.

He laughed. "I mean it, Lace. I have never been so happy in my life than I am at this moment. Even with my mom getting worse by the day, I still get to wake up next to you every day and love you for the rest of my life. I don't think I could get through this without you right now. And now we have a beautiful baby girl to love and care for. I couldn't have ever imagined my life being this good if you'd asked me on the plane that day. You truly changed my life for the better, darlin'. I love you so much, Laci." He leaned over and kissed her soft lips, pulling her into his arms.

"I feel the same, love. I'm so sorry your mom is going through this. I know it's hard to watch, but we are all here for you, and I think this little girl will be a breath of life for us in the days ahead. I love you too, babe."

"Let's get some sleep." He hugged her goodnight.

CHAPTER 12

Winter had arrived, and that week saw the coldest weather that part of North Carolina had seen in years. Laci loved the rain, but she hated the cold unless it was helping create little white snowflakes to fall on the ground.

"Turn up the heat, Mitch. It's freezing in here." She pulled the fuzzy, red blanket up over her and the baby.

"I did, darlin'. Give it time." He laughed.

"I don't want her getting worse."

Faith was already three weeks old and, for the first time since coming home, had taken ill as many newborns do. She had an ear infection and a cold; nothing extreme but enough to cause Laci even more concern due to all the challenges around her birth and her cleft palate.

"The doctors said she'll be fine once the medicine has time to kick in. Don't worry, babe."

"Wish that was possible." She leaned down and kissed Faith's head poking out from their blanket. "You headed to the barn?"

"Yeah, Evan and I need to get the rest of those bottles labeled and packed up for an order. You okay? Need anything before I head out?"

"Nah, little Miss and I are happy as clams." She smiled looking down at her, overwhelmed with that 'new mom' love.

"I could disappear, and you'd never remember me, would you?" He chuckled, realizing he'd dropped in status since Faith was born, and rightly so. He leaned down and cupped his hand around her cheek, then pulled her lips to his.

Laci lingered in his kiss, feeling that familiar chill run up and down her spine and soaking in the sweetness of the moment. "Mitch Young. There is no place in my world where you don't exist or reside in every part of my mind, body and soul. I never want to live a day without you. You're my Creepy Stalker Crawdad-fan, babe," she paused, then whispered, "You're my one."

"I love you, Laci Young."

"And I you." She winked and he went on his way.

Laci cherished the next hour cuddling Faith and napping on the couch, but it was almost time for Faith's bottle. Laci slid Faith off her chest and laid her onto the couch so she could prep the bottle and get the medicine ready. About halfway into Faith's feeding, Laci burped her then stopped to give Faith her medicine.

She popped the syringe in her little mouth and pushed out the medicine, waiting for her to swallow it. Nothing dripped out, but suddenly Laci noticed that Faith's face was getting red and her little eyes were big and round, almost as if she was scared. The red face began to turn a shade darker—purple almost—and it was then that Laci realized Faith wasn't breathing. She was choking.

"Faith! Breathe, baby girl!" She screamed, then tried to sweep her little mouth thinking she could remove whatever was in her airway, but nothing was there. In a panic, she picked Faith up and threw her over her shoulder and patted her back over and over, trying to get her to breathe.

Nothing. Her hands shaking, she picked up the phone and dialed 9-1-1. Her sobbing made it hard to tell them what was going on, but she finally got it out. "Please hurry!" She begged, then threw down the phone.

Faith's little face was grayish blue—lifeless—and her eyes now closed.

"Come on, sweetie! Please breathe for Momma!" Laci shouted, tears streaming down her face.

Seconds had turned to minutes and she still wasn't breathing. Faith still in her arms, she ran out the front door into the yard. "Mitch! Help!" She screamed as loud as she physically could, but he was too far away to hear. Snow was coming down in huge flakes and she could see the breath in front of her face. She fell to the ground, Faith held tight inside her arms. "Please, God! Please! Don't take her! Don't take another baby from me, please!" She yelled up into the air as the snow fell on her tear-stained face and suddenly time seemed to stand still. The silent air felt heavy, and then she heard his voice speak softly to her heart...

Faith. Not your daughter, but in Me. Have Faith in Me as you have hope in my rain; as you see the grace after my storms. Have Faith in Me, through my falling snow. Faith, Laci. Have Faith that I have Faith in my capable hands.

* * *

MITCH AND EVAN put away their last crate of bottles and decided to take a break, then suddenly Mitch was overwhelmed with a sense of worry so strong that his chest tightened. He stopped moving, thinking it would go away, but it never left. His heart told him something, somewhere, was wrong. *Go now.*

Mitch had learned from a previous experience to trust his gut when he felt these nudges, of what he could only believe was a nudge from God himself.

"Evan. We gotta go. Now." Mitch yelled out.

"What's wrong, Dad?"

"Honestly, I'm not sure. Maybe nothing, but it's time to take a break anyway. Let's head back to the house, okay?"

"Yeah, sure thing."

"I've only felt this one other time in my life, Ev. It was the day your sister called me and told me your mom had collapsed in the front yard. That day changed my life forever. For the better honestly. But something isn't right, that's all I know."

"I remember that day. Let's get out of here."

They immediately got in the truck and headed home.

* * *

LACI TOOK a deep breath and quickly stood up, then ran back in the house and slammed Faith on top of the kitchen counter. She knew what she had to do.

"AHHHHH!" She screamed out. "Please baby, breathe! Breath, Faith!" She could have sworn Faith blinked, and it almost seemed like her color was coming back but still there was no movement. She was about to start CPR when the EMTs busted through the door and yelled as they entered the house. "We're in the kitchen!" Laci screamed, falling to the floor on her knees and holding her stomach.

One EMT lifted Laci up off the floor and moved her to a chair, while the other one immediately started working on Faith. The young EMT with Laci made every effort to keep her talking and help divert her attention from Faith. Laci's mind was a fog and everything around her seemed to move in slow motion. In her humanness though, despite God's silent words she had felt just moments ago, she still feared for her baby girl's life.

"I—I need to call my husband," she stuttered.

The EMT helped Laci get Mitch on the phone so they could explain the situation. Laci was in shock.

"She's back!" The EMT shouted.

"Faith!" Laci screamed. "Is she okay? Let me see her!"

Thank you for giving her breath again, Lord! Why am I still so scared, though? This isn't over is it? She thought.

"We need to get her to the ER right now, ma'am. Do you know how long she's been unconscious?"

Laci stared out into space, lost for words, searching for the answer. It had felt like such a long time. She recalled the events and time best she could, then they helped her up into the ambulance behind Faith. Laci looked down at Faith on the gurney and continued to cry, softly stroking her little arm where the IV had been inserted. "Will she be okay?"

"They're going to do several tests on Faith, ma'am. She'll have to have a spinal tap and it won't be easy to watch, but it's necessary given the length of time she may have been without air." The EMT explained, careful not to disclose too much information that would scare Laci.

"Will she have brain damage?" Laci asked, begging for an answer. She was smart enough to know that when someone goes without air, it can affect brain function.

"We won't know that ma'am until they do some more tests. Let's not jump to any conclusions yet, okay?" He took Laci's hand to help calm and comfort her the best he could.

"What's your name, sir?" She asked.

"Dylan, ma'am." He replied.

"Thank you, Dylan. Thank you for saving my baby's life today." Laci leaned against his chest and cried softly but cried so hard her stomach muscles physically ached.

Mitch finally arrived at the hospital and the doctor came in to talk to them. A tall, gray-haired man around sixty years old or so, wearing the normal white-coat doctor attire. The oddity to his wardrobe were the orange Crocs that stuck out from under his blue scrub pants. Laci saw them and of all things at that moment, they made her smile. *Quirky choice.* She thought to herself. *Good.* In some strange way, it made her see him more like an average person, not just a doctor. That, along with his smooth, kind voice, helped Laci feel at ease.

"You had quite a scare today, Mrs. Young. Your daughter is beautiful and breathing fine on her own right now. We don't really know how long she was without air though, so we need to run a few tests to see if there was any brain damage. I know that sounds scary, but we need to know. It's not an easy test to perform and it's very painful to watch, so I would encourage you not to be in the room when they do it. Why don't you both take a walk and grab some fresh air, cup of coffee or something. It doesn't take long to do the test, so give us about ten minutes and we'll be done." The doctor laid his hand on Laci's shoulder. "It's going to be okay, Mom." His smile reassured her in some small way.

Mitch shook the doctor's hand and they left the room to get some air. Outside, a light snow had begun to fall and already the ground was covered in a thin white blanket. The stunning silence and beauty of that moment was exactly what Laci needed. She looked up and closed her eyes, put her hands out and felt the snow falling softly on her face.

Lord, I don't even know how to keep breathing right now. I've lost a baby before, but somehow this is worse. She's breathing again and I know you did that, but we could still lose her. Watching her suffer is the worst pain and if you must take someone, please take me. She doesn't deserve this! Why can't I feel the faith I'm supposed to feel!

"Faith is going to be okay, Lace. She is breathing. That's the main thing. We'll take the rest minute by minute." Mitch pulled her into his chest and held her tight, wishing he could shield her from all the pain and hurt she was feeling in that moment.

Laci's body shook inside his arms and she buried her face in his chest. Her tears released the tension and frustration from the events of the day, one she would not forget as long as she lived.

The nurse stepped outside. "They're all done with the test, Mr. & Mrs. Young," She stated.

They walked back inside and directly to Faith. The sound of her soft whimpers broke Laci's heart and she wanted so badly to pick her up and hold her tight, but she couldn't. Instead, she hovered as close as possible and held her tiny hand between her fingers, rubbing her baby soft cheeks; anything to make sure Faith could sense her mom was there next to her.

She whispered softly in Faith's ear, *"We're right here, baby girl. Daddy and Mommy are right here, and we love you so much."*

A couple of hours passed, and after what seemed like a hundred tests, the doctor finally came in with the news.

"We need to transfer Faith to a children's hospital that is better equipped to handle her situation. She's breathing, and the spinal tap was clear, which is what we needed to know. Given her resuscitation at birth and her cleft palate however, we don't want her to suffer any more episodes, and there may be more going on than we realize."

Laci tilted her head, her brow furrowed. "What do you mean, '*her resuscitation at birth*'?"

"Her aspiration and the fact they had to administer CPR to revive her after she stopped breathing. It was in her records." He shared, as if they already knew.

"Wait. We were told she choked or aspirated or whatever you call it, but they never told us she stopped breathing!" Laci's voice screeched in her discontent.

"Lace. Honey, calm down." Mitch said, putting his arm around her to settle her.

"No! We never knew this. Why weren't we told this! That explains why it was over twelve hours before we even got to see her after she was born. If we had known..." Laci rambled on.

"It wouldn't have changed anything if you had known, Mrs. Young. You had just given birth, were exhausted, and I'm sure they didn't want to alarm you, given that she was revived and stable at that point." The doctor added.

Laci took a deep breath. "I suppose you're right. I'm sorry, I'm so scared right now. What happens next, then?" Laci squeezed Mitch's hand and looked at him with an apologetic smile.

"We put her in an ambulance with one of you and you head over to Asheville Children's Medical Center. They're the best. They'll know exactly how to treat her and get her the help she needs. Trust me. It's the best place for her."

"Okay, then. When do we leave?" Mitch asked.

"Now. The sooner she gets there, the sooner you'll get the answers you need." The doctor replied. He stood up to leave, shook their hands, and even gave Laci a side-hug. Unlike many doctors, he was compassionate and had taken his time to be a person while still being a good doctor to their daughter.

"Thank you, Doc. You've been great." Mitch replied.

Laci made calls to Evan and the kids, to Richard and Maggie, and even though they had just recently been there, Brad and Hannah would once again be on the next flight back to North Carolina to stay with the kids.

"Faith. The answer is in her name, Lace. We have to believe it's going to be okay."

"I know, I keep hearing that," she chuckled to herself.

"What's that mean?" Mitch asked, a little confused by her comment.

"Remember when I told you about me playing in the rain that day, I was about to give up on myself after my breast cancer treatment? I was dancing around in that cold November rain and before I collapsed, I felt something. Something special. Like God was talking out loud to me."

"How could I forget it. He spoke to me that day too, remember?"

"Well, it happened again today when I was outside in the snow yelling for you. I had Faith in my arms and right after that, I took her back inside and it wasn't long before she was breathing again. I know it was God. But why am I having trouble believing it?" She explained.

"Lace, I heard Him today too. Before Evan and I got in the truck, my chest tightened, and I knew something was wrong. Not with me physically, but with you."

Laci's mouth fell open a bit at their coinciding experiences. "What? How does this keep happening to us, Mitch? It's impossible, right?" She shook her head in wonder.

Mitch wrapped his strong arms around her and pulled her close. "With God, all things are possible. Isn't that how that verse goes?"

Laci smiled for what seemed the first time all day. "It is indeed. Apparently, we *both* needed Him today." She added, then closed her eyes and soaked in the love and strength she felt while inside his arms.

"Why don't I call Evan and give him an update?"

"I think that's a wonderful idea." Laci kissed him quickly and he dialed Evan's number.

* * *

EVAN FINISHED COOKING a small spaghetti dinner for everyone, but they sat staring at their food and twirling the noodles around on their plates with their forks. Travis was on the couch, he had cried himself to sleep after he heard the news about the baby.

Eating was the last thing they wanted to do, fearing the worst about their new baby sister.

"Guys look, we have to eat. Baby Faith is going to be okay; I know it. We need to have *faith*. Isn't that what mom and Mitch would say to us? We have to believe it's true." Evan's pep talk wasn't exactly working, judging by the somber looks on their faces.

Emma's eyes filled with tears as she thought about the worst possible scenario. "I just got a new sister and now I might lose her. Why would this happen to an innocent baby?" She yelled, then ran off to her room.

"Em!" Evan shouted, trying to get her to stop.

"Dude, let her go. She needs time." Todd replied. "I'll go check on her in a minute." Todd and Emma had become close since Evan left, and he felt exactly what she was feeling. Sadness. Pain. Fear. And everything in the middle. They were all worried.

Evan's phone rang and he quickly answered, seeing it was Mitch.

"Hey, Dad. How is she? She okay?"

"Hey bud. Yes, Faith is breathing on her own and she's better, but they have a lot more tests to run to make sure there wasn't any damage to her body while she was without oxygen. We won't know much until after we get to Asheville Children's. We're headed there soon. Are you all good?"

"Wow. Asheville huh? Well, that's the best place for her. I'm sure everything will be okay. Is my mom around?" Evan tried to hide the fear in his voice as best he could.

"Of course, son. Here she is. Love you, Ev."

Laci took the phone. "Hey sweetie! How is everyone? You

okay?" Laci asked, fighting back the tears. She missed her kids so much already.

"Hey mom. Yeah, we're doing great, don't you worry. I've got things covered here. We just ate and the kids are tired, but we're fine. Emma's kind of having a rough time of it, but I'm trying to help them stay positive." The quiver in his voice more than obvious.

"Ev. You don't have to pretend, son. I know you're worried I can hear it in your voice. We all are, trust me. Little Faith is going to be fine, though. I know it. She will be coming home soon, okay?"

Evan broke down and wept, no longer able to hide his fear. "I'm so sorry, mom. I didn't want to cry on the phone, but I'm so worried."

"I know, baby. I know. But she's breathing and she's pink as a peach. I've gotta get back in there with her, but I'll call you as soon as we get to the children's hospital. She's going to be okay, Ev. Give the kids a kiss for me." She said softly, cutting through the tears. "I love you, Evan."

"I love you, Mom."

"Who was that?" Todd asked, coming back into the kitchen.

"That was Mom. Faith is better but they're taking her to Asheville Children's to do more tests. Might be more problems since she wasn't breathing for so long." He recounted the update.

"Wow. Well, she's breathing. That's what we hold on to. That's the good we need right now. Why don't you hit the shower and I'll do the dishes?" Todd urged, giving Evan a brotherly pat on the back.

"Thanks, Todd. Thanks for talking to Emma, too. She okay?"

"She will be. Why don't you tell her the good news before you shower?" Todd smiled.

Evan smiled in reply, glad to have the chance to cheer up his little sister. He walked up to Emma's door and tapped softly.

"Hey Em, can I come in?"

"I guess so."

He walked in and saw her face down in a pillow, whimpering softly. "Mom called."

Emma popped straight up out of bed and turned to look at Evan. "Is she—oh, Evan is she?" She sobbed louder.

"No, no! Emma, she's fine!" He walked to her bedside and pulled her into a big bear hug, squeezing her tight. "Faith is breathing and she's doing fine!"

Her eyes brightened and she began to smile from ear to ear. "Really? They're on their way home?" She asked, hoping to see her new baby sister soon.

"Not yet. They are going to run a few more tests to make sure she is super good, but then she'll be home, okay?" He explained, trying to ease her worries.

"Oh, Evan. I'm so happy! Thank you! I'm sorry I was upset earlier. I promise I'll eat some of your spaghetti." She laughed and for the next several minutes they giggled and horsed around as only brothers and sisters can do, enjoying the moment.

"So, tell me more about this Isaac character. You like him? Did he freak out after Thanksgiving?"

Emma laughed. "He thought we were cool; can you believe it? I think he likes me too." Her cheeks turned a light shade of pink as she talked about him.

That night, all was well.

* * *

THE FIRST NIGHT at the hospital was just a matter of getting Faith settled into a room. Her tiny little body was swallowed up in her big bed, so Laci built a horseshoe out of blankets and put them in the bed to keep her from rolling around, then the nurses swaddled her tight and laid her down in the horseshoe. The wires and tubes connected to nearly every inch of her body looked like something from a sci-fi movie, making it hard to touch her or hold her. All Laci could do was stand over her bed and softly stroke the baby-fine hair on her head.

"You need to get some rest, darlin'. We've got a long night ahead I'm sure and an early morning once the doc comes in. I'll take the first watch, okay?"

"Not sure I can sleep, Mitch. I'm so scared. I know something is wrong." Laci rubbed her forehead, fighting off a headache.

"Sleep will help you and her. You can't be strong for her unless you take care of yourself and she needs you to be at your best right now. We'll take things minute by minute, Lace. Get some sleep." Mitch kissed her forehead and led her to the cold, vinyl-covered hospital couch. "Better not dress in that sexy t-shirt or I might cause a ruckus." He winked at her, trying to get her to smile.

"Really, Mitch? You pick now to be a tease? Where were you last night?" She laughed softly.

"Touché." He lifted her chin and kissed her softly. "See you in your dreams."

"I love you. Please wake me if she needs me." She smiled and laid down.

AN HOUR LATER, nurses came in to help feed Faith, but shortly after a few sips, Faith began to choke and once again stopped breathing. Laci awoke to alarms and buzzers, nurses bustling and calling out codes like something from the set of a crazy medical TV show. Laci stood up and flew to Faith's bedside to try and see her.

Blue skin.

Eyes closed.

Quiet. Lifeless tiny body.

"Shake her! Do something!" Laci screamed at the team working on her baby girl.

Another alarm sounded. The nurse pounded on Faith's back while she hung upside down between the nurse's hands, her little head dangling.

Finally, Faith coughed and cried out a little raspy cry that got louder and louder, announcing to everyone in the room that she was not only breathing, but she wasn't happy at all.

THE DOCTOR APPROACHED Faith's bed. "Let's get a heart monitor on her and prep the lab for a barium swallow. We need to know if her epiglottis is working properly. After that's done, we'll know if she needs a feeding tube or not." The doctor's orders were relayed in a calm, confident manner, then he turned to Laci and Mitch. "Mr. and Mrs. Young. Can we visit outside for a minute?"

Laci was still shaken from the scene that had just taken place. She looked down at Faith, hesitant to leave the room.

The doctor put his hand on Laci's shoulder. "Mrs. Young, your daughter is stable now. It's okay, and we won't be long, I promise."

Mitch took Laci's hand and they followed the doctor in the hall.

"Let's walk down here a bit. That room on the right is a little less noisy." The doctor led them into a small refreshment-type room with pale yellow walls and pictures of encouraging words, appropriately selected to help loved ones stay calm, most likely.

The smell of coffee still lingered in the air from a recent one-cup brew. "Please, sit down. I'm Dr. Haugland and I'll be overseeing the care for Faith while she's here," he said.

Laci walked past him to find a chair, noticing he smelled of both antiseptic and cologne which she found odd, yet nice. "Nice to meet you, doctor. Why does she continue to stop breathing when we feed her? What's going on?" Laci's voice was scratchy, and her eyes were bloodshot and burning from the excessive number of tears she had shed throughout the day.

"I'm not sure yet until I see the test results, but it appears Faith may have life-threatening reflux. We'll need to do a barium swallow test on her in a few minutes and see how that goes. This test will check the function of the flap in her throat that covers her airway when she eats. I'm almost positive, given her soft cleft palate, that she is basically drowning every time she eats. Or could potentially. Did you and Faith's pediatrician make a plan for the cleft palate repair?"

Mitch looked at Laci and knew she was unable to respond. "Umm, no. Not yet. It's only been three weeks and we haven't even had a chance to get used to her being around let alone anything else."

"I understand, I'm sorry. I know this has been an exhausting day for both of you. I'm going to call in a gastro specialist to have her evaluate Faith. Her name is Dr. Holland and she's the best in the country. I trust her implicitly on cases like this, and I know she'll be able to advise us on the next steps. Go back and relax if you can, and as soon as the results are in, we'll make a plan. Do you have any questions for me right now?" He asked.

"If she has the reflux, what's the plan to fix it?" Laci asked.

"There are a few different options we could take, one being surgery of course, but we'll talk through them once we know more. Is that okay?" Laci inhaled a sharp breath as she processed that word, 'surgery'. *Oh, Lord. What has this little girl done to deserve this? Nothing! Please take this. Please keep her safe. I can't lose her, Lord. I won't lose her!* She thought, staring off into space.

Mitch took Laci's hand, knowing she wasn't handling the news well. "I think we're ready to get back to our baby, Doc. Thank you for your help," he said.

"I understand, Mr. Young. I am a father to three girls and there is nothing worse than watching them hurt or suffer when you are powerless to fix it or make it better. My team and I will do everything we can to get her home soon, okay?" His kind, confident tone seemed to reassure him.

"Thank you."

BACK INSIDE FAITH'S ROOM, Laci picked her little one up, careful not to pull a wire or mess up her IV. Mitch pulled up a recliner closer to the monitor so Laci could sit down and hold her.

"I'm not putting her down until I have to, Mitch. I need her next to me." Laci pulled Faith to her bosom and tears dripped down on top of Faith's tiny head.

"It's okay. I understand. She needs to be in your arms too, trust me." He wrapped his arms around them and kissed Faith's head. "It's going to be okay, sweet girl," he whispered.

Laci looked up at the love of her life, and as scared as she was for their little girl, she couldn't ignore the overwhelming sense of peace at that moment. Mitch was her rock, her everything, and she knew Faith would be okay despite the tough road ahead. "I love you, Mitch. So much. I don't know what I'd do without you in my life, I truly don't." Laci smiled, and a single tear rolled down her cheek.

He smiled and kissed her forehead. "I love you, darlin'. You'll always have me. You both will."

It was going on eleven o'clock when the nurse came in to

take Faith down for her test. Laci held Faith tight as they were chauffeured by wheelchair to the lab, grateful for every second she had to hold her baby girl. The nurse took Faith and sat her in a baby car seat in an upright position, then placed it up on a tall, metal exam table. To the side was a long camera lens connected to what looked like an x-ray machine. Once Faith was somewhat still, they positioned the camera next to her chin, turned it on and proceeded to feed her a bottle containing a thick orange liquid.

"What is that?" Laci asked the nurses.

"It's a special liquid glows so we can see it through the x-ray. It allows us to see how she swallows and how all the parts are working when she eats or drinks."

The monitor next to us turned on and we could even see the liquid flowing down her throat. Laci couldn't help but think that it was rather fascinating to watch and marvel at how amazing these tests were to figure out things like how a baby swallows.

After a few drinks, Faith stopped drinking.

"Come on, Faith, keep drinking, sweetie," the nurse said in a sweet voice.

Nothing. Faith started to turn red and suddenly the nurse yanked her out of the seat. "She's aspirating!" She yelled. "Get me some suction, please." She laid her down on the table.

"What's wrong? Faith!" Laci screamed, and Mitch grabbed her hand. "Hold on, Lace. Let them do their job." He squeezed tight, doing his best to keep her calm.

Another nurse grabbed a long tube and shoved it down Faith's little throat. The suction sound was loud, sucking out the orange fluid and clearing her airway. A few seconds later, Faith coughed and cried out a loud cry.

"Thank, God!" Laci exclaimed. "Please let me hold her!" Laci tried to pull away from Mitch.

"Hold on, Lace. Hold on, okay?" Mitch pulled her into his chest and wrapped his arms around her and Laci broke down, burying her head in his chest. "She's okay, babe."

BACK IN THEIR ROOM, with Faith sound asleep after her recent ordeal, the doctors arrived to make a plan. Dr. Haugland walked and introduced his specialist. "Laci, Mitch, this is Dr. Rosson. She is our leading expert on the Craniofacial team here at Asheville Children's."

"Hi, Dr. Rosson. Nice to meet you." Laci said, barely able to speak she was so exhausted.

"Nice to meet you both. I'd like to examine Faith, if I may. I know she's sleeping, but I'll do my best to try and not disturb her."

They walked over to Faith's bed. "Of course, whatever you need to do." Mitch replied.

The doctor began to examine Faith's tiny head, bending down to look at her face from eye-level from both sides of the bed. She gently pressed her fingertips on Faith's chin, down her neck, then back up again. "This is a classic case of micrognathia."

"Do you want to share in layman's terms, doc?" Mitch asked.

"Absolutely. Faith has something called *Pierre Robin Syndrome*. It's a rare type of birth defect and caused by a sequence of events. Her lower jaw is too small and sits back farther than it should be. Basically, the chin didn't grow out fully when she was in the womb, which caused the tongue to press upward, which caused the soft cleft palate, which causes the tongue to be somewhat displaced, so it falls backward when she lays flat and obstructs her airway. Then, when she tries to nurse or drink from a bottle, she doesn't have the strength in her chin to suck and get enough milk out. I'm guessing you couldn't get her to latch on while breastfeeding, and her bottle feedings were taking a while, is that right?" She asked.

Laci's eyes widened. *Finally, an answer!* "Yes! I couldn't understand why it was taking her so long. I would no sooner finish one feeding and she would be hungry again." Laci had felt like such a failure when she couldn't breastfeed like she'd wanted, thinking she had been doing it wrong. An odd sense of relief came over her knowing it wasn't her fault.

"Her muscles are too weak. I believe the flap in the back of her throat isn't working as well as it should either, is that correct Dr. Haugland?"

"That's correct. She failed her barium swallow test earlier. The flap doesn't close all the way." Dr. Haugland replied quietly, confirming her assessment. "Why don't we step down the hall to the family area so we can talk normally and finish our conversation. Faith needs her sleep; she's had a long day," he added with a kind smile.

They all walked to the empty conference room and took a seat around a small, round table covered with images of tiny butterflies. Laci nervously traced the outline of one with her fingertip, not wanting to think about things for a few seconds.

"Okay, here's what we have," Dr. Rosson began.

Laci looked up and took a deep breath.

"With *Pierre Robin,* there are two major challenges. Faith's chin is receded back more than any that I've seen in a long time. Given her rapid weight loss since birth, we can't rely on mouth feedings anymore so we need to surgically insert a G-tube so she can get the nutrition she needs through a feeding tube. Second, she still has a severe case of reflux and trouble breathing. I would recommend we do a laparoscopic Nissen fundoplication."

"You're going to explain that one, right doc?" Mitch asked.

Laci and Mitch looked at each other, scared for their baby girl and the uncertainty ahead.

"Of course. Basically, we will twist the top of Faith's stomach closed so that fluid, or air, can't escape up from her esophagus – she won't be able to choke, gag, throw up, or even burp like other babies would. It's a common surgery, although lengthy – usually two to three hours. I will also do it laparoscopically, so it's less invasive with only three small incisions. As tiny as her body is, it's the best course of action without a doubt."

Laci began to cry softly. Listening to her describe the procedure and imagining Faith living off a feeding tube made her nauseous. "How will she pass gas? She'll have to do it some way?" She asked.

"We will show you how to do that after the G-tube goes in. An empty syringe is inserted in the tube and the bubbles and gas in her stomach will escape up through the tube and into the syringe. I know this sounds strange and scary," Dr. Rosson leaned forward and took Laci's hands, "but Faith needs this surgery in order to eat and not drown. Trust me, I'm a mother too and I know how hard this is, but I promise you it's lower-risk, and recovery time is minimal. I need to stress that Faith could potentially drown during a feeding if we don't do this surgery, Mr. & Mrs. Young. At this stage, we need to act sooner rather than later."

Mitch put his arm around Laci and pulled her into his side, kissing her head as she laid it on his shoulder. Large tears rolled down her cheeks. "We have to do it. We can't let her continue to suffer like this." Laci said quietly.

"I know, darlin', I know." Mitch agreed, then nodded to the doctors. "How soon can we get it done?" He asked.

"I can schedule it first thing in the morning. She'll go tonight without food, but by nine o'clock tomorrow she'll be hooked up to her formula and getting what she needs without risk of choking. You'll most likely be here for two more weeks to make sure she's gaining weight, and everything is progressing as it should, so you may need to make arrangements."

"Thank you, both. Yes, please schedule it. The sooner we get her well, the sooner we can all go home. Our kids miss their new baby sister." Mitch's face was stone sober, but inside his stomach was churning.

"We'll take good care of her. You have my word." Dr. Haugland replied.

"Agreed. Faith is in good hands." Dr. Rosson added.

The doctors said their goodbyes, then left Laci and Mitch alone to process the news. They simply held one another for a few minutes without a word. Nothing needed to be said. Flowery words wouldn't make it go away, but their silent prayers, uttered in the quietness of their hearts, gave them all the comfort they needed.

"He's got our little girl in the palm of His hand, Lace. I know it. We have to believe." Mitch whispered.

"We have to have... faith." She smiled up at him.

CHAPTER 13

Evan, Jenny and all the kids were hanging out at the house, anxiously waiting for an update on little Faith. It was late, but no one could even think about sleeping.

"So, you two are really getting married?" Emma asked, blushing a bit at her own question.

"That's right. What's it to ya, sis?" Evan joked, then hooked his arm around Emma's neck and rubbing the top of her head with his other hand to mess up her hair.

"Stop it, dork!" She punched his leg in retaliation.

"Evan! Leave the poor girl alone already," Jenny said, laughing at their antics.

"When is the wedding?" Emma probed, secretly hoping they would make her a bridesmaid.

"Well, we haven't really had time to think about it. It will be a while, Em. There's no rush." Jenny said, then noticed the look of confusion on Evan's face. "Right? Or do you have a different plan, Mr. Kramer?"

"Maybe. I mean, we don't have to get hitched next week or

anything, but how long were you thinking?" Evan's curiosity was up.

"I don't know, like a year or so. That's not that bad, is it? Ev, your mom just had a baby. Your Grams isn't doing well. We have plenty of time, Jeep-man," she added.

"Hmm. Ok."

"That's it? Just *'hmmm'?*" Jenny kicked his foot, taunting him.

"I don't know. A year seems so far away." He pulled her into his arms. "I want you to be my wife, Jeannette Rose. Is that so bad?" Evan's cheeks pinked up instantly.

"Why, Evan Kramer, I would have never guessed you for such a romantic." She winked at him, then he tackled her to the floor and hovered over her head, kissing her playfully.

"Gross! Take it to your room. Gag!" Travis shouted.

Evan hopped up and grabbed Travis by the waist, throwing him over his shoulder. "What did you say, little man?" He tickled Travis making him cackle, which made all of them laugh and for a minute, they took a break from their worries about baby Faith… until Evan's phone rang.

He stopped and set Travis on the floor, then answered the phone. None of them uttered another word.

"Hey, Dad. How is—how is she?" Evan asked, then listened intently to Mitch's update, his face not showing any emotion. "Wow. Okay. I'll let everyone know. Tell Mom we love her, okay?" He hung up then looked down at the floor for a minute, gathering his thoughts.

"Well?" Todd asked. "Spill it, bro."

"She's okay. She has a birth defect that's causing her trouble. She can't eat with a bottle and that's why she's been losing weight. It's also the reason she quit breathing." He took a breath.

"And?" Emma prodded. "Is she going to be okay, Ev?"

"She's having surgery in the morning. They're going to put a feeding tube in her stomach so she can eat. It's going to be how she eats for a long time."

The room was quiet for a minute. Travis clung to Todd's waist, squeezing him tight.

"Look, the main thing is, Faith is doing fine right now and they're going to help her so she can eat and come home soon. They've figured out how to help her. We have to believe she's going to be okay, guys." Jenny added, wrapping her arm around Emma's shoulder. "We will all drive over to Asheville to see her tomorrow, okay?"

"Really? Oh, thank you!" Emma began to cry and hugged Jenny's waist. "I'm so worried about her. I want my sister back, Jenny."

"I know, sweetie. She's going to come home, don't worry." Jenny hugged her tight.

"Let's get to bed, guys. We need to get up early and get to the hospital. Jenny, you can sleep here if you want." Evan needed her there more than ever.

"Of course! Let me call my mom and check in. I don't want to be anywhere else but here with all of you." She smiled and took his hand.

"Can you sleep in my room, Jenny?" Emma asked.

"I'd like that a lot, Emma. Thank you," Jenny winked at her, then walked away to call her mom.

Emma and Travis went up to their rooms, but Todd lingered behind. "Hey man, is there something you're not telling us?" Todd sensed something more serious.

"She could die if they don't do this surgery, Todd. It's serious. They have to go in and twist her stomach, it's not just a feeding tube going in." Evan took a deep breath. "I'm worried, not gonna lie. Mom isn't doing good and I'm even more worried about her. I hate this!" Evan smacked his fist against the nearest wall.

"We need to be there for the surgery. I don't want her there without us." Todd replied. "They both need us there for them."

"We will be there. Night, Todd."

"Night, Ev. Love ya, man," Todd reached over and hugged Evan's neck. "And I'm really happy for you and Jenny. She's super cool. I wouldn't wait a year either." Todd smiled, then headed to bed.

Jenny walked back in the room. "I'm good to stay. My mom said to tell you hi."

"By the way, we still haven't told your mom with everything that's happened."

"We will. Soon, Ev, I promise. We have more important things going on right now. That can wait, okay?"

"She needs to know, Jen, and I don't want to wait a year. I want to marry you, and the sooner the better. Can we shoot for six months? Like June maybe?" He pulled her into his arms.

"Once Faith is through this and okay, we'll tell her I promise. Besides, what's the rush? You know I'm going to marry you. I don't want to live my life with anyone else but you." She hugged his waist and smiled up at him, her heart pounding.

"Is it so bad that I want to be your husband as soon as I possibly can? I've lost a dad, almost lost my sister today, and will probably lose my step-Grams sooner, rather than later. Life is short, Jen. I don't want to waste any more of it. You're the yin to my yang, Miss Jeannette Rose. Will you marry me this coming June, please?" He stuck out his bottom lip and batted his eyes, smiling playfully.

Jenny rolled her eyes and laughed at his antics, and her heart overflowed. She couldn't deny his request, and admittedly didn't really want to wait either. She smiled, "Looks like June it is." She squeezed his cheeks between her hands and pulled his sweet face in to hers. "I love you, Evan Kramer," she whispered.

"I love you, Sassy-pants." Evan kissed her soft lips, pulling her close. If there was a way he could have made that kiss last forever, he would have.

"Come on, Jenny!" Emma yelled from her room.

Jenny pulled away with a sigh. "Bedtime buddy is calling."

"Think of it this way, you're already loved by my whole family. It doesn't get much better than that." Evan added another quick peck on her cheek, and they headed to bed.

* * *

BRAD AND HANNAH arrived at the house and as he started to knock on the door, Evan opened the door and nearly bumped into Brad as he headed out to start the car.

"Brad?" Evan shouted, giving him a big bear hug.

"Hey, slick. Where on earth are you going this early?"

"To the hospital, man. Mom didn't even tell me you were coming! Geez, I'm glad to see you guys. But we gotta go!" He laughed, then peeked around at Hannah standing behind him. "Hey, Hannah." Evan walked over and gave her a hug.

"Hi, sweetie." She replied.

"Let's get the kids and get out of here then. Mitch sent me an update; her surgery is at eight."

ONCE THEY ARRIVED, they made their way to Faith's room. Despite a few faint whimpers from other babies in the distance and some quiet chatter among the staff, the hospital was rather quiet, given the early hour.

Evan knocked on the door to make sure it was okay to enter.

A groggy Laci looked over at Mitch, asleep on the couch. She smiled and got up to answer the door.

"Hey, Mom," Evan said softly, smiling.

Laci's mouth flew open and she wrapped her arms around

his neck. "Evan! Honey, what on earth?! I'm so happy to see you!" She didn't notice the other kids at first, but once she did, the quietness of the morning was no more. She let a squeal of joy as she hugged the kids.

Mitch heard the reunion at the door and walked over to pull them all inside. "Hey, ya'll, you might want to move the party inside the room," he grinned. "Good to see you, guys" he whispered. They all moved inside and continued with the hugs and hellos.

"Jenny. I'm so glad you could come up with them. It's so good to see you, my dear!" Laci hugged her future daughter-in-law tight and kissed her cheek.

"What am I, chopped liver?" Todd added in his loving, sarcastic tone. Laci loved how he could always make her smile even in the worst of moments.

"Get over here, you big dork." She laughed, hugging Todd's neck and tickling his ribs in reply.

"Mom, can I hold her?" Emma asked quietly.

Laci took Emma by the hand and walked her to Faith's bed. "She's still sleeping, but you can go up and see her," she whispered. Laci's smile spread from one side of her face to the other, having her kids all together.

Mitch and the boys stood at the end of Faith's bed. "I have no idea how you didn't wake her up with your squeals, but I guess babies are pretty used to sleeping in noisy bellies, especially yours." Mitch joked.

Laci gave him 'the look', and stuck out her tongue, smiling.

Everything felt normal in that moment. They smiled, laughed, poked fun and were reveling in every minute of their family moment, but it was short-lived.

The door opened, and Dr. Haugland and his team poured into the room. "Good morning, everyone. Mercy, we have quite the crowd today. Brothers and sisters, I presume?"

"Morning, Doc. Yes, they just walked in. Our oldest drove them all up this morning to see their sister and be with us." Mitch smiled cordially, suddenly anxious.

"Well, we are here to take little Faith up to prep for her surgery, but we can spare a few more minutes," he smiled. "I'll be back in ten minutes so you can all hold her and give her some love before we go up, okay? Only mom and dad will be able to go into the prep area, however. After we move to surgery, we'll walk you back to the surgery waiting room so you can all be together. Any questions for me?"

They nodded a 'no', and he left the room.

"Can I pick her up now, Mom?" Emma asked.

"Let me pick her up and I'll hand her to you. She has lots of wires and tubes connected to her, so you need to sit down to hold her." Laci walked over to Faith's bed and looked down at her peaceful, precious little face, hating that she had to disturb her, but it was time to say their goodbyes. She picked her up slowly and Faith stirred, yawning at first then opening her eyes to look around. She turned and laid her into Emma's arms, then propped a pillow under her arm for support.

Baby Faith looked up at Emma and a huge smile appeared on her face.

"Mom, look!" Emma squealed. "She's smiling at me!"

Mitch took Laci's hand and they smiled at each other. "She's a happy girl." Laci said. "She loves her big sister, too."

"Okay, come on, sis. Someone else's turn." Laci picked Faith up and they all took turns holding her for a minute, kissing all over her tiny cheeks until she began to get a bit fussy from all the corralling.

"Better get your hugs in, Dad." Laci moved over beside Mitch and they held Faith together, leaning over her and kissing her head, whispering 'I love you's' in her ear.

A tear rolled down Mitch's cheek. "Mommy and Daddy are

right here with you, Faith. We will see you real soon, okay?" He kissed her one last time.

The doctors came in a few minutes later and walked them through the procedure, then took Faith and laid her in another baby cart to wheel her out.

Mitch pulled Laci close and looked in her bloodshot eyes, both of their now faces soaked from tears. "She's going to be fine, Lace. I know it." He hugged her tight, laying his head atop hers, and they stood still, crying softly in each other's arms.

"It's time to go, Mom, Mitch." Evan said, laying his hand on Laci's shoulder.

AFTER FAITH WAS PREPPED for surgery and they said their good-byes, then Laci and Mitch walked to the waiting room, glad to see they were the only family in there for now. Quietly, Mitch led them in prayer and the waiting began.

ONE HOUR.

TWO.

TWO AND A HALF.

"WHY HAVEN'T we heard something by now?" Laci stood up and paced the room. It was the fourth time in the last hour she had walked rings around the room, unable to calm her mind. *Lord, I can't take much more. I know she's in your hands, but dang it I need to know what's going on! Is that too much to ask? I know, I know.*

Trust you. Have faith. Well my faith is FAILING! Please let her live, Lord. I need that little girl to LIVE! She battled with God in her head, not winning of course. "I'm going out to get some air." She pushed the door open with a bit of force, letting her frustration show.

Seeing a window down the hall, she walked toward it. Once there, she looked out and saw it. Snow. It fell slowly, but thick and heavy like a sheet of white rain. *Faith... through my falling snow.* She recalled the words God had spoken to her heart the night that Faith had stopped breathing. *I'm so sorry, Lord, for not believing you. For not trusting you. Thank you for this beautiful white, frozen rain. My rain.* Laci closed her eyes and prayed. Knowing how much she could handle, God sent her to a window to show her His glory, and the promise that he'd made to keep Faith in His hands.

Laci smiled through the alligator tears that rolled down the curve of her cheek, then looked up and mouthed a silent 'Thank you' into the air. She walked back to the waiting room with a peace in her heart for the news that would soon come.

THREE.

"YOU'RE AWFULLY CALM, DARLIN'." Mitch noticed a difference in her once she returned from her walk. "Chat with the big guy, did ya?" He grinned, knowing full well she'd had a moment of clarity.

"As a matter of fact, yes. And our little girl is going to come through this. I know it." She smiled and took his hand, squeezing it tight.

"I knew that. I was waiting for you to catch up," he chuckled and gave her a quick kiss on the cheek.

"You're so ornery, Mitch Young. You know it? I don't know why I put up with you!" Laci teased quietly.

"You know *exactly* why. Don't you play with me, woman." He poked her ribs.

Their playful banter went back and forth a bit, smiling and messing around with each other like two teenagers. Both at peace for the first time since Faith's journey began.

Evan looked at Jen and rolled his eyes, watching the display by his mom and Mitch, then laughed. "Hey, you two, calm down over there. You're going to get us kicked out of here."

"Yeah, Mom," Emma chimed in, a smile on her face.

IT WAS the break in tension that they all needed, and before long they were all laughing together and being silly. The time passed faster now, and the fourth hour had come and gone without anyone noticing for once.

The door to the surgery wing suddenly swung open and Dr. Rosson walked into the waiting room. She slid his head covering off and folded it in his hand, then looked at the family and smiled a shallow smile.

Everyone became quiet and still, but Mitch quickly stood and took Laci's hand, pulling her close. "How is she, Doc?" He asked.

"She did great," Dr. Rosson replied, and the smile on her face stretched farther. "The Nissen procedure went extremely well, and the G-tube went in easily. It took longer than we thought because Faith also had a sliding hiatal hernia, so we repaired that as well. But that was small in comparison. She is going to be covered with bandages and wires, and you'll have to be very careful with her G-tube. It will be attached the entire time she's here, but we'll teach you how to use it, clean it, and how to do the feedings. We'll also need to keep her on a heart monitor longer than we originally anticipated. Her heart is very strong, but we picked up a heart murmur during surgery so we need to make sure it doesn't cause further complications. Then sometime around October we'll schedule her for a cleft palate repair, and I suspect she'll need ear tubes shortly if the ear infections continue. *Pierre Robin* patients often have hearing challenges as well. I know it's a lot, but we'll take it day by day. She is in recovery now. Give us a few minutes to get her cleaned up and stable, then I'll call you all back to see her, okay?"

"Praise the Lord! That's wonderful, Doctor!" Laci exclaimed, hugging Mitch's neck in joy. She turned back around with tears in her eyes. "How was the heart murmur missed before, though? This is the first we've heard of it. Has it always been there?" Laci asked, still relieved but overwhelmed by the news at the same time.

"As she grows, so does her heart; and it beats louder. Sometimes the murmurs are so faint at first, it's harder to pick up when they are first born. I would suspect that's why it wasn't caught sooner. It's nothing to worry about. Most newborns have heart murmurs and it should repair itself with time. She has much bigger challenges right now, trust me, but nothing that she can't overcome. She's a little fighter, that's for sure."

Mitch smiled, "She gets that from her dad," He chuckled, and the kids all laughed at his comment. He turned to them. "Hey now, no comments from the peanut gallery back there. She is her daddy's girl, no doubt."

The laughter in the room was a healing rain over Laci's soul.

"Well, let's go see our girl!" She shouted.

* * *

FAITH WAS DOING GOOD, and the kids headed back home. It had been a long, exhausting day of learning how to feed Laci with her new feeding tube and the machine, learning how to 'vent' the gas from her tummy through the tube connected to her belly, learning how to clean her wounds from surgery, and more. They were both beyond exhausted and Laci had already fallen asleep in the recliner, Faith sleeping on top of her chest. She wasn't about to let go of her any time soon.

Mitch smiled as he watched them sleep. *Thank you for them, Lord. That woman is the love of my life... and that little girl. Well, she's perfect. I don't even deserve this life.* He thought to himself.

Mitch made his bed on the oh-so-comfortable hospital couch and laid down, but before his head hit the pillow, his phone buzzed. He looked down to see who it was.

Richard.

Please. Not Mama. Not now.

CHAPTER 14

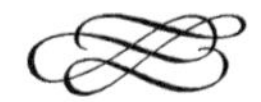

Richard and Maggie left the café and headed back to the house, a short distance away. It was their favorite part of the morning and they needed a distraction while they waited on news about Faith's surgery. If she was able, Rich took her every day despite the weather. A mere month ago, they were walking to and from the café, hand-in-hand, but in the last few weeks, Maggie had become too frail and weak; now bound to a wheelchair to prevent falls. Thus, their visits to the café were fewer and farther between. Maggie's condition had become increasingly worse even in the last couple of weeks; her lucid moments fewer and fewer. She was even combative at times, and often refused to eat which was causing rapid weight loss. While in the house, she had increasingly more accidents and it was all Richard could do some days to take care of her most basic needs. She would even push him away when he tried to bathe her, screaming and yelling hateful words at him. Then there were the days when she could barely speak at all; the worst of all.

That day however, Maggie woke up smiling and exceptionally sharp—back to her old self, remembering things she hadn't recalled in months. Rich knew it would be short-lived, but he was grateful to have her back, even for a few precious hours or minutes.

"I think you ate enough ice cream for both of us, and then some." Maggie teased. Her arm shook as she lifted it up and opened her hand. Rich stopped pushing her wheelchair, then took her hand and walked around in front of her, bending down and squeezing her hand gently in his. Slowly, he brought her soft hand up to his lips and kissed it softly. Suddenly, Richard had an overwhelming feeling that he needed to talk to his Maggie and share some things with her while she was in a positive, 'present' state of mind; before she left him again.

"You are the light of my life, Maggie Young. I still can't believe I get to wake up next to you and love you every day. I give you this promise... to love you forever. Your friendship has meant so much to me these last several years, and I thought you'd never marry me!" Richard laughed.

"That was a fun day, wasn't it? I think I even caught the judge tearing up at one point." Maggie smiled as she reminisced. Their wedding day was the Monday after Thanksgiving—the two of them, Laci, Mitch, the kids, and their best friends all gathered together at the courthouse. She even recalled the color of the flowers in her small bouquet.

"It was truly the perfect day, until today."

"Why today?"

"Because today is even more perfect than yesterday, and the day before that. You're more beautiful today than yesterday and I am so thankful I get to call you my wife. Seeing you smile makes me so happy, Mags." Richard stood up and put his hands around her cheeks, kissing her softly.

"I love you too, Rich Westmore and I always will, even when I'm not here. You are the prince I never thought I'd ever find, but I guess you found me, didn't you? You saved me, and I will always be grateful." She paused, then smiled at him with a smile that was so bright it could have pierced the darkness. "Make sure they know, Rich."

"Know what, sweetheart?"

"I need them all to know how much I love them." Maggie replied softly.

Richard raised his brow at her comment but brushed it off and simply kissed her again. "They know, my love. They know. It's getting colder out here, though. We'd better hurry home." He started pushing her again; so happy in the moment that he hummed a tune as he walked. Out of nowhere, a brisk wind suddenly swirled around them and the temperature dropped even more. "Oooh, I'd better hurry! Looks like snow might be coming and that wind is crazy! Are you warm enough, Mags?" Richard asked, rubbing her shoulder with a free hand.

Maggie was silent.

"Maggie? You okay, sweetheart?" He stopped her wheelchair and walked around again to check on her. She stared into the distance as if she couldn't hear him, so he bent down and turned her face toward him. "Maggie!" He shouted.

Her eyes were glazed over, looking past him - hollow and empty.

"Mags! Honey? Talk to me, sweetheart. Look at me!" Richard yelled louder, firmly shaking her shoulders to try and bring her back.

Maggie suddenly threw her arms out and screamed. "Get away! Who are you? I don't even know you! Someone, please help me! This man is trying to hurt me!" Maggie's arms flew around like she was swatting at flies and she continued to scream and yell for a few more seconds, then stopped. Her eyes closed and she was silent. Slowly, her head drifted down, then her whole body began to slide down in her chair turning limp and unable to hold herself up. Like a rag doll, she fell forward onto Richard and he sat there holding her in his arms.

Snow began to fall, and within seconds it was coming down all around them. He was helpless, and simply looked to the sky and yelled out for help.

"Maggie!" He shouted. "No, Maggie. Not yet, please!" He cried out for help and two bystanders not far from where he stood came rushing over to help and called 9-1-1.

Once again, his Maggie had disappeared.

They arrived at the hospital and she was still unresponsive. Rich knew her body had already begun to shut down. After hours of running tests, the results were all the same, and so far, no one had given him any hope. Finally, Dr. Edwards arrived.

"Rich, I'm so sorry. I was on my way back in town when I got the call and came straight away." He replied in his proper British accent.

"Hey, Doc. Thank you for coming." Rich took a deep breath. "I knew it would happen fast, but I didn't expect it this soon, honestly. Will she come out of it this time? Ever?"

"Her body is giving up, Richard. I suspected she wouldn't last much longer after our last visit, but it has progressed much faster than even I thought. Everyone is different. Some are not able to handle the physical toll it takes on the body, or the mind. I can tell she's not been eating with her body so frail and thin. When did the incontinence begin?" Dr. Edwards inquired.

"A couple weeks ago. She couldn't keep food down and we can't get out as often due to all her accidents. It's all I can do to get her to the bathroom in time." Richard lowered his head, feeling defeated, failing to care for her like she needed.

"This is *not* your fault, Richard. This is a horrible, ugly disease that steals the life from our loved ones one day at a time. One memory at a time, and hers even more so with the rapid dementia. People who haven't experienced a loved one go through this will never understand how it can deteriorate the body as well as the mind."

"And the soul. Her soul is in there, but it's hidden. I just want her to find her way home in peace, Doc."

"I think it's time you called her sons, Rich. They need to come say goodbye. I don't expect her to leave here. I'm so sorry."

Rich looked at the floor, gathering his thoughts. "I understand. I'm afraid that's not going to be easy. They are all in Asheville. Mitch's baby had surgery this morning. How much time exactly?"

"Hours at best. I'm sorry, Richard. Don't wait too long, though." The doctor placed a comforting hand on Richard's shoulder. "I'll step out so you can make your calls. Please let me know if you need anything. We'll make her as comfortable as we can." He added.

"Thank you, sir."

Richard pulled out his phone and dialed Mitch's number. It was after midnight, but it couldn't wait any longer. He took a deep breath and dialed.

* * *

MITCH WALKED out of the room and into the hall so as not to wake Laci and the baby.

"Hey Rich, how's it going? Everything alright?" Mitch asked.

Richard didn't reply right away, and his silence was reply enough for Mitch to know. "It's Mom, isn't it? Is she—?" He held his breath and waited for an answer he wasn't yet prepared to hear.

"No." Rich cleared his throat to push away the tears. "Not

yet. Soon, I'm afraid, son. She went unconscious on our walk back home from the café this morning. It was such a lovely morning, too," he paused to gain his composure. "She was so sharp today, Mitch. It doesn't even seem possible. One minute she's laughing and remembering everything like the Maggie we've always known. The next minute, she didn't recognize me and was yelling and screaming. Then she disappeared. I fear for good this time."

Mitch inhaled, trying to comprehend the news. His mom was dying. She could be gone before he got back home. The lump in his throat overcame him and tears began to fall from his eyes.

"I think somehow she knew it was the end."

"What makes you say that?" Mitch asked.

"Something she said right before she lost consciousness. She said, *'I need them all to know how much I love them'*." Rich broke down and cried softly.

"We know, Rich. We all know. And it's okay. Brad is at the house. I'll call him and send him to the hospital to be with you and Mom. I'll leave as soon as I tell Laci. You did everything you could, and it's okay. We need to let her go." Mitch replied.

"I'm so sorry to have to give you this news with everything going on. Is Faith okay?" Rich asked, kicking himself that he hadn't asked sooner.

"She's great, Rich. The surgery went well. She's a little fighter, they said. I tried calling earlier to tell you, but it went to voicemail. I guess I know why."

"I'm so glad, that's a blessing, Mitch. I'll let you go, and see you soon, son." Rich replied, his voice heavy with sadness.

Mitch hung up, then cried softly at the realization that his beautiful mother would soon be gone from his life. It didn't seem possible. In one day, his little girl was given a second chance at life, and his mother would lose hers. He slammed his fist against the wall, releasing the hurt building inside his heart. After a few minutes, he took a long, deep breath and went back in the room to tell Laci.

They were sleeping so peacefully. He had no choice. She had to know.

He put his hand on Laci's shoulder and whispered, "Lace. Laci wake up, darlin'." He shook her gently.

Laci stirred and looked up at Mitch, smiling at her sweet husband. "Hey babe," she replied in a whisper. "What's up?" As Laci blinked and became more alert, she saw the sadness in Mitch's face and knew. She scooted up in the chair, careful not to wake up Faith. "Mitch? What's wrong, babe? Is it—"

"It's about Mama, Lace. She collapsed earlier today, and she's been in the hospital all day, unresponsive. Rich waited as long as he could to call me because of Faith, but we just got off the phone. The doctor doesn't think she'll come out of it, Lace. She may only have a few hours left." Mitch knelt on one knee beside Laci and rested his head on her leg, weeping softly at first, then sobbed uncontrollably.

Laci's eyes filled with tears, rubbing her hand softly on his head. "I'm so sorry, babe. I can't believe this is happening."

Mitch stood up, then he helped Laci out of the chair so she could lay Faith in her bed. She pulled him into her arms to comfort him as best she could, and together they wept, holding each other tight.

Laci took a breath between sobs. "You need to go, Mitch. Go to her, now. Faith is doing great, and we will be fine, don't worry. Go say goodbye, and even if she can't open her eyes to look at you, just know she hears you," Laci added, then leaned up to kiss him goodbye. "I love you, Mitch. Go."

"Are you sure you're okay with me leaving?"

"Mitchell Young, I am fallible in many ways, but I am pretty strong when I need to be," she kissed his lips. "I've got this, and we have doctors all around us. I will call you if anything changes okay? Please tell her how much I love her." She said, crying harder.

"I know you are, and she knows, darlin. She's always known, and she loved you from the very day she met you, ya know," he paused to collect his words. "I think she knew her time was almost over. Rich said she gave him a message before she lost consciousness."

"What? What message?"

"She said, '*I need them all to know how much I love them.*' Maybe she is ready, Lace. Is that weird?" He wiped the tears from his cheek.

"She's always been a very wise woman, and I couldn't agree more. Her giving him that message was what she needed to have peace of mind. She's ready to be home with your dad. That's what she's always wanted."

He sniffed, wiped the tears from his eyes, then gave her one last kiss goodbye. "Go back to sleep. You need to rest; it's been a long day."

"Drive carefully, Mitch. Please text me when you get there. I worry, ya know." Laci squeezed his hand and he left the room.

Once out of sight, she fell backwards into the chair and sobbed quietly, praying for Mitch and Brad and the difficult hours ahead. *I won't understand this for a while, Lord. I need him HERE. Why did you have to take Maggie now, of all times! We were finally on such good terms and I had so many things for us to do. She wanted so badly to see her granddaughter come home. Why now? This isn't fair. Not one bit! I know I'm being selfish, but I'm pretty damn mad right now, in case you're wondering. My little girl had the fight of her life today and now you go and do this. Not cool!* She continued to sob as her thoughts raced, but slowly calmed and eventually felt a sense peace as she continued to talk to God. *Get Mitch there safely, Lord. Please tell Maggie hi for me when you see her, okay? She'll most likely be wearing a bright orange pantsuit and matching accessories as she strolls through the pearly gates.* Laci giggled at the thought, and that's exactly what Maggie would have wanted.

* * *

THE DRIVE back to Crystal Creek was long and hard on Mitch, seeing mental images of his mom flash through his mind during his life. She was his rock. The one who always 'got him'. She was his best friend, and as much as he loved his dad, he'd died so early in Mitch's life that he never had the closeness to him like he did his mother. Maggie and all her fancy outfits and her fancy jewelry. Her matching shoes and handbags for every occasion. He remembered how intimidated Laci was of his mom when they first met, and it made him chuckle out loud. *Mama, please wait for me. I need to see you one more time.*

Finally, he arrived at the hospital and made his way to his mom's room and found Brad standing by his mom's bed, and Rich sitting on the other side holding her hand, his head laying on the edge of her bed. Quietly waiting. Mitch opened the sliding door, stirring them both to look up and greet him.

"Mitch," Rich stood up and turned to hug his neck. "I'm so sorry, son. I did everything I could to get her to wake up. She's shutting down I'm afraid." He added.

"Don't you dare apologize, Richard. You were the best thing that happened to my mom during all this and I'll forever be grateful for your friendship to her over the years, and for taking such good care of her. She sure loved you. I always knew you two were meant to be together, it just took me a minute to get used to the idea," Mitch chuckled softly.

"I've loved her for many years. After she lost your dad, we

bonded over our grief. It had only been a few months before that I had lost my wife as well. I knew then that God had given me a friend for life, and I always hoped for more. She was worth the wait." Rich smiled. "I'm going to step out so you boys can have some time alone, okay? She can hear you. I know it in my heart."

"I'm going to step out to get some coffee. It's your turn," Brad added.

Mitch stood staring at his mom, laying there silent, peaceful. He couldn't help but admire her beauty despite her frailty. He walked closer to her bed and sat down.

"Hey, Mama. It's Mitch," he paused to take her hand, then attempted to inhale a deep breath despite the pounding in his chest, fighting back tears. "I'm sorry it took me so long to get here. I was hoping you might wake up for me, give me an earful or something. Baby Faith is doing great, and she has a feeding tube now, but she's going to be okay. We're in for a long road ahead, but she'll get through it. She's got a lot of your fight and spunk in her. I sure wish you could open your eyes and come home so you can see her again. Her hair is getting redder by the day, like yours. I'm glad you got to see her and hold her. There are some who don't ever get that gift, but I'm not real happy with God right now, Mama. I know you wouldn't approve of that, but I needed that off my chest. I don't understand why He has to take you away from us so soon. It's not fair." His voice elevated, but he took a deep breath to clear his mind.

He lowered his head onto her arm, clenching her hand. "I had all these things I wanted to say to you, but now that I'm here, I want to tell you how much I love you, how much I have loved being your son. You are the most amazing mother I could have ever asked for. You know that, right?" He chuckled softly to himself. "Of course, you do. You brought *life* into our life growing up, all the time. Maybe that's why I fell so hard for

Laci. She brought me back to life after I lost Karen. I never thought I'd love again, but between you and me, I don't know if I ever loved Karen this much. I know that probably sounds bad, but on some level, what I feel for Laci is stronger and deeper, like we were always meant for each other. That sounds silly." He chortled. "I know you are ready to go and be with dad, and that's okay. Brad and I are going to be okay. And we'll take care of Rich, too."

Only the monotonous beeping of her monitor replied.

"Faith won't remember you on her own, but we'll make sure she knows who you were, I promise." He laid his head down again, crying softly for several minutes.

Brad returned and laid his hand on Mitch's back. "You doing okay, big brother?"

Mitch stood up and hugged Brad so tight he nearly cut off Brad's air. Mitch broke down, sobbing into Brad's shoulder. Brad patted Mitch's back, consoling him as best he could. "It's okay, bud. We're going to be okay. She raised us right, ya know."

Barely audible, Mitch replied through his tears. "I know, man. I'm gonna miss her. All her feisty, fussy ways of meddling in everything, trying to run our lives all the time, always so proper and, well, ya know."

"How well I know." Brad laughed quietly.

Suddenly one of Maggie's monitor alarms sounded, and Mitch turned to see her eyes open, her arms flailing about in the air trying to take out her IV line. "Mama!" He and Brad ran to her, one on each side of her bed.

"Hey there, Mama. Calm down, okay sweetie? Brad and I are here with you. Can you hear me?" He asked in a louder voice, then noticed how yellowed her eyes were.

"No. No help," Maggie said, her weak voice was nothing but a scratchy whisper.

"We will help you, Mama. Whatever you need. What is it?" Brad added, patting Maggie's arm to help calm her.

"NO!" She yelled as best she could. "NO tube. NO help."

Brad looked over at Mitch. "She wants these tubes out. No help." Brad interpreted. "Mama, you want the IV tubes out?" He asked her.

Maggie immediately calmed down and turned her head toward Brad, nodding yes. "My baby boy." She said in a scratchy voice, barely able to talk. She knew him. She knew everyone there.

Richard ran in the room, the nurse following behind to check on Maggie.

"She's awake, Rich," Mitch said with a smile, and moved aside so he could see her.

Richard walked up to her bed and leaned down to kiss her on the cheek. "Hey beautiful! How's my girl?" he smiled.

"It's okay," she said softly, then tried to lift her hand up to his cheek, but it started to fall. Rich caught it and held tight as the boys shared what Maggie had said minutes before he walked in the room. They asked the nurse for direction.

"It's up to you. I'll send the doctor in as soon as he arrives, and we will honor her wishes, if that's what you want," the nurse said, then explained the process of what would happen once the tubes came out. They all agreed, and the nurse left to make the necessary preparations and contact the doctor.

Brad leaned down to his mom's ear. "I'm here, Mama. Hannah is too. I love you so much. It's okay now. We're all going to be okay."

"I love you, son. You be good. Hannah is your forever girl." She smiled, then coughed and took a deep breath. She turned her head to Mitch.

"Hey, Mama. He stepped a bit closer and Rich gave him her

hand. "You are my best friend, and I'll always love you." He wept.

"I know, sweet boy. I love you. And don't ever stop loving your sweet wife. Laci saved you with her love, and your life is full of *life* because of her." Maggie smiled, looking around at all those she loved in her life. "Please tell them all I love them." She said. A single tear rolled down her cheek and her eyes closed for the last time. Her head slowly fell to one side and they all saw it; a tiny smile on her face. Her last moments were exactly as she would have wanted, surrounded by her boys and the man she loved.

"They know, Mama. They know." Brad leaned down and kissed her forehead. "I love you." He whispered, wiping the tears from his eyes. Hannah walked up behind Brad and took his hand in hers, then quietly walked out of the room.

"I see that smile on your face, Margaret Young. You did it again, didn't you? You got your boys all together and became the center of attention. Always the drama queen. Tell Daddy I said hello, okay? I love you so much. I'm sure gonna miss your spunk." Mitch whispered, tears rolling down his face. "Bye, Mama." He forced a smile through the pain in his chest, then kissed his mother on the forehead for the last time.

Before Mitch walked out though, he turned to Rich and hugged him tight. "She loved you more than you know, Rich. Thank you for taking such good care of her," Mitch said softly, then joined Hannah and Brad in the hall.

Together, they mourned quietly in that raw moment of loss and love.

No words were spoken.

No words were needed.

Maggie was home at last.

* * *

THE NEXT SEVERAL months weren't easy by any means, but over time, the sadness felt by Maggie's loss was replaced by immeasurable joy as they watched little Faith grow and overcome insurmountable odds. They continued to lean on God and one another, holding strong to their faith.

Faith...even through falling snow.

FULL CIRCLE

Life for the Young family continued to move on, as life does. They'd suffered loss, but also received the tremendous gift of new life; baby Faith. The road to her recovery was paved with challenges—two more surgeries, ear tubes, mild hearing loss, horrible stomach aches after each tube feeding, and more. Laci and Mitch spent many sleepless nights keeping watch to make sure she was still breathing even though almost every night she slept on Laci's chest. Every tube feeding was followed by a 'venting' process, removing the gas from her tummy. Some were so bad that Laci thought Faith would pass out from the pain. Those especially left Laci in tears and both exhausted. Those moments were hard to endure, but thankfully long gone. Her cleft palate was repaired, the ear tubes were helping, her lungs were strong, the heart murmur was gone, and she was finally able to sleep in her own bed, although she still slept on Laci's chest now and then, more for Laci's comfort than Faith's.

As Faith grew, she reminded them more and more of

Maggie; a gentle reminder that she would always be with them. Not only did she get Maggie's red hair, but Faith was also a spitfire; tiny, fierce and full of life. Despite the challenges from the *Pierre Robin Syndrome*, Faith was thriving. Her smile could light up a room; happy, healthy and growing stronger every single day. She would soon celebrate her first birthday, then after that, her feeding tube would be removed once and for all. Cheeseburgers were now her all-time favorite and she could drink on her own from a sippy cup—a cup she loved so much, it rarely left her mouth. Even when she wasn't drinking, it dangled between her teeth like a pacifier as she waddled from one end of the house to the other like she owned the place.

Mitch and Laci's family grew closer through it all. Shortly after Maggie passed, Brad and Hannah even moved back home to Crystal Creek to help with the kids. It was hard for Hannah, but she loved Brad and his family more than anything, so they left her B&B under the care of a new manager and made the leap. A leap of *faith*. Their adopted daughter, Chloe, moved with them too and was already working at the winery. What no one expected was Chloe and Caleb falling for each other over spring break. They talked and dated whenever they could over the next several months while he was still in college, and when summer rolled around, he popped the question and she said yes.

Evan and Jenny didn't quite make their June wedding with all the family challenges, but it worked out for the best. Laci had wanted to plan it all along, and she got her wish. Of course, instead of planning one wedding, she was now waist-deep in planning *two*. A double Christmas wedding to be exact, to be held at home in the Three Vines wedding barn. Where else, right? Amid everything else, Laci and Mitch celebrated their three-year wedding anniversary and decided it was time to take a short vacation, a time to reconnect and recover from the past year's events that had taken such a toll on their family.

* * *

LACI STOPPED PACKING for a minute to get Faith out of the laundry basket, laughing and tossing clean clothes around the room for fun.

"Mom! Don't forget your swimsuit!" Emma yelled from down the hall. She ran into her mom's room and jumped up on the bed. "What is going on in here? Faith, you're a mess!"

"She's definitely making a mess, that's for sure." Laci kissed Faith's cheek, set her on the floor, then watched her take off running again. "Don't run, Faith!"

"She's not listening, Mom."

"I can see that, Emma. Thank you for the news bulletin."

Emma popped a bubble with her gum, kicking her legs around in the air. "You'll be swimming in some beautiful blue lagoon this time tomorrow. Are you excited?" She asked, watching her mom pack.

"I am! It's been a long year and Mitch and I really need this break before the boys' wedding. You going to be okay without me for ten *whole* days?" Laci plopped on the bed next to Emma, both staring up at the ceiling.

"Mom, I'm almost seventeen. I'll be fine. Kind of crazy, isn't it? Brad and Hannah move back, and Caleb falls in love with Chloe, their foster daughter, who is kind of our cousin in a weird way. So now Chloe will be my... step-sister-in-law?" Emma laughed.

"It's a little unorthodox I suppose, but Chloe isn't a cousin in the normal, blood relative way. Okay, *yes*. It's kind of weird, but isn't it also neat how God works?" Laci smiled.

"Yeah, it's cool. I like her a lot too. Isaac said it was fate; that sometimes God's plan isn't what we want, but it's usually what we need to make our life better."

"My, my. Isaac sounds like a very smart young man." Laci's heart overflowed, knowing her daughter's boyfriend was already making God part of their dating life. "How is he doing, anyway?"

Emma rolled her eyes. "He's fine," she blushed. "He asked me to Sweetheart, ya know."

"What?" Laci squealed. "When were you going to tell me this, after I boarded the plane?"

"You've been so busy, and I wanted to tell you in private, without Mitch around. Not being mean, but just you and me, ya know?"

Laci kissed Emma on the forehead and smiled. "I know, sweetie. I get it, and I'm so excited for you! Are you nervous, happy, excited?"

"All of those, I guess. He's really great, mom. You should hear him speak at our youth service on Sundays. He's really got a heart for God. I think it makes him cuter somehow," she giggled.

"Men that express their faith do tend to be more attractive for some reason. I suppose it's because their heart is in the right place. Most of the time anyway." Laci winked. "Make sure his hands stay in the right place at that dance." They both laughed.

"Oh, Mom! Whatever!" Emma grabbed a pillow and smacked her mom with it in fun. Then Laci returned a pillow blow and the fight was on as they laughed and giggled so loud half the house could hear them.

"What is going on in here?" Mitch walked in, laughing at their antics. "You two are a mess, and Mom isn't getting any packing done." He stood next to the bed looking down at them, laughing. "Do I need to get in the middle of this fight?"

"No! Girls pillow fight only, dude." Emma replied, but decided to throw a pillow at him for fun.

"Hey, little lady! You'll wish you had never thrown that

pillow punch." He grabbed his own and before long, the whole family was in their room throwing pillows all over and smacking one another, laughing and cackling.

"Okay, okay. Uncle!" Laci shouted. "I can't take anymore! I have to finish packing so we can get out of here. You all have your chores and assignments for the week, right?"

"You're a party pooper, Mom!" Travis said, hopping off the bed.

"Sorry, bud. Mitch and I have to get out of here or we're going to miss our flight."

"Evan, Todd, if you two need anything call Rich or Brad. They'll be here in a flash."

"Man, it's so nice that Brad and Hannah back home. I've been looking forward to Hannah's cooking all week!" Evan said.

"Are you saying that my cooking isn't as good as Hannah's?" Laci's eye raised, poking Evan in the ribs. "Huh? Huh?" She tickled his ribs, pushing him out the door. "Just for that, go do the dishes. Be gone with you!" Laci laughed. "Any son of mine who disses his momma's cooking doesn't get a free pass, dude."

Mitch closed the door behind Evan. "Finally. Alone at last." He turned around and took Laci in his arms.

"Oh no you don't, Mitch Young. Not right now. We have thirty minutes before we need to leave. Scram!"

He leaned down and lifted her chin to his lips, kissing her softly. "Just a kiss. I promise. I'll save the rest for later."

"One kiss." She smiled at him, then wrapped her arms around his waist and enjoyed the warmth of his lips against hers.

* * *

THE ANNOUNCEMENT SOUNDED over the loudspeaker. *'Gate 3C*

now boarding for Flight 765 to LaGuardia, then on to Rio de Janeiro, Brazil.'

"That's us, darlin'."

Laci and Mitch made their way onto the plane and found their seats. Once settled and buckled in, Laci rested her head back against the seat, then looked up and took a long, deep breath. As she read the random signs above her seat, her eye caught the letters for the corresponding seats.

D, E, F.

She looked at her boarding pass again, still in her hand; 16E

Wait. That means he's... 16D. What on earth? She thought.

Her mouth hanging open, she turned to Mitch. "Mitchell Lee Young!"

He winked at her. "What?"

"How did you—" She stopped, unable to hold back the tears.

"Aww, darlin'. What's wrong?" Knowing full well she had figured it out.

"Our seats." She paused and took a breath, "this airline. It's all the same from the first time we ever met! How on earth did you do this?"

Mitch took her hand. "Lace, the day I sat down in that seat next to you was the day my life changed forever, and I could have never imagined this amazing life we have if you'd asked me before that day. I think back on how I almost lost you to cancer, then we lost our first baby, then my Mama, who loved you so much, by the way." He smiled, then lifted Laci's hand to his lips, as he often did since they first met. "We've gained a sister-in-law, and an adopted niece, and even though we almost lost her too, we held on to our faith and now we have our own beautiful baby girl, *our* Faith. If that isn't enough, we're about to have two daughters-in-law when we get back home. Saying it out loud doesn't even do it all justice, honestly. Darlin', you put life back in my life at a point when I didn't even want to keep living. You saved me, Lace. I can't imagine my life without you and for as long as I live, I'll love you with every breath I have in me."

Mitch reached down into his carry-on bag and pulled out a long, thin velvet box and handed it to her. "Happy Anniversary, darlin'." He said in his deep, rich southern voice.

Pools in her eyes, she blinked and released a cascade of tears flowing down her cheeks. "I didn't get you anything." She mumbled through the tears and opened the box to find her very own beautiful, silver bracelet that Mitch had given her right after he proposed. Her original charm was still in place, but two more were there where it once held only one.

HER FIRST. The bright sapphire raindrop - to remember ***Hope... in the rain*** **she loved.**

A NEW SPARKLING diamond lightning bolt - to always look for ***Grace... after the storm.***

AND A GLISTENING PEARL snowflake - to keep the ***Faith... through falling snow.***

LACI'S LIPS CURVED UPWARD, her smile lines catching the tears that still trickled down. Words weren't enough to express what she felt for him at that moment. Mitch was a gift from God. Her one. The man who captured her heart, who helped her see the world differently and become the best version of herself. The man in whom she was completely and hopelessly in love with since the very moment she laid eyes on him.

She reached up and cupped her hand around his scruffy, bearded cheek, pulled his lips to hers and kissed him softly.

In a whisper, she said, “I’ll love you forever, Mitchell Young; my Creepy Stalker Crawdad-fan.”

“I know, darlin’. As I will you.” His deep, rich, sweet southern voice left Laci breathless once again.

AUTHOR'S NOTES

This book was written in honor of my friends and family who have either been touched by Alzheimer's personally, have a loved one who is currently suffering, or who lost a loved one to this horrible disease. A few of you shared your personal stories with me, which inspired many of the events in this book, and for that I am truly grateful. May their beautiful memory live on in you and your family for years to come.

Alzheimer's is the 6th leading cause of death in the United States and 5.8 million Americans are living with Alzheimer's. By 2050, this number is projected to rise to nearly 14 million. One in three (1 in 3) seniors die with Alzheimer's or another dementia, and it kills more than breast cancer and prostate cancer.[1]

This book was also inspired by real life events and written in honor of my son Ethan, who was diagnosed as a newborn with a rare birth defect known as Pierre Robin Sequence/Syndrome.

Pierre Robin Syndrome is a congenital condition recently linked to genetic anomalies at chromosomes 2, 11 or 17, often called ***Pierre Robin Sequence,*** the disease is a chain of developmental malformations, each leading to the next. The sequence includes a small lower jaw, a tongue which tends to ball up at the back of the mouth and fall back towards the throat, breathing problems, and a horseshoe-shaped soft cleft palate may or may not be present. [2]

Ethan was born in 2004 with a cleft soft palate and had to eat with a special bottle at birth. At three weeks old however, he choked and stopped breathing. After resuscitation, spinal taps, test after test, and an ambulance ride to Vanderbilt Children's Hospital in Nashville, TN, he was soon diagnosed with Pierre Robin Sequence/Syndrome. *He also had a sliding hiatal hernia, life-threatening reflux and had to have immediate surgery to twist his stomach and correct it so he wouldn't drown when eating. They inserted a feeding tube (G-tube) and he lived on that his first year of life. He couldn't burp or pass gas unless it was through his tube. He would stop breathing in the middle of the night, so for his first year of life, he slept on top of my chest sitting up in bed almost every night. His dad and I lived in fear of him dying for at least the first six months, and I rarely slept that year, something I wouldn't wish on any parent. He was a strong little guy though, and although tiny in size due to his eating, he began to grow and get stronger and stronger. Ethan made a full recovery. His palate was repaired, and he began eating and drinking normally at the end of his first year. Many cases are far worse than Ethan's, so we were grateful that he was able to make a full recovery. Ethan is our miracle, and his dad and I are grateful to God every day for his gift of life. If you have a child with* Pierre Robin, *you're in our prayers. Never give up hope!*

Ethan will turn 15 this year and is happy and healthy, and his dad and I are truly grateful to all our friends and family who walked this road with us during that time...Sheryl & Todd Williams, Kasha & Mark Vindiola, Jennifer Chapman, Carmen & Zuly, and the countless caregivers who took such excellent care of Ethan while he was at Vanderbilt and at Ft. Lewis/Mc-Chord Medical Center. Thank you!

[1] Visit alz.org/alzheimers-dementia for more information about Alzheimer's and how you can help. Please support your family and friends who are living with this disease.

[2] Visit Faces-cranio.org/Disord/PierreRobin.htm for more information about *Pierre Robin Sequence.*

(L) Ethan, at age 4 - 2008. Taken just after his second of three set of ear tubes. (R) Ethan, at age 14- 2015. Graduated eighth grade happy and healthy!